SARAH

SARAH

A BENJO LANE CASE

J. Michael Roper

4 Augustine Entertainment

1

The driver of the late-model Cadillac sedan slowed down to a crawl and eased the car over onto the grassy shoulder of the road. The road was a narrow two-lane strip of asphalt that wound its way through the countryside several miles away from the city limits, so there wasn't much of a shoulder, but the driver didn't want to stop in the center of a lane of traffic. The driver, David Whiteside, the much older of the two men in the vehicle, was always a careful driver, and he didn't want to take a chance on someone rounding the curve he'd just passed and smashing into the rear of his nice car. David, a tall, gangly man with a pleasant, scholarly face, a beak of a nose, gray hair, and shrewd eyes, was a lawyer and had been one for going on forty years. His chosen career had made him overly cautious sometimes, but being cautious and observant were traits that had made him a damned good lawyer with a fearsome reputation. That observant and cautious side was also what made him extra careful, even when doing mundane things like driving.

Once he felt that he was far enough off the road, David pointed to the narrow entrance of what appeared to be a driveway on the opposite side of the road. The driveway was hard-packed gravel and it disappeared through the trees on that side of the road. A black metal mailbox on a wooden post with the number 1380 on the side of it in stick-on reflective white numbers stood beside the driveway like a lonely sentry. "This has to be it," David said. "Billy said it was thirteen eighty and that it was in the middle of nowhere."

The young man in the passenger seat, a fair-skinned young man with red hair and a smattering of freckles and round-framed glasses named Chase Fleming, glanced up from the screen of the cell phone he held in his hand. "GPS on my phone says this is the place," he said.

"Well, if the almighty cell phone says this is the place, it must be the place," David retorted. "There's only one way to find out if this is our guy and if he's interested in helping us."

Chase just shook his head and grimaced as David drove back onto the road and then turned into the driveway. The old lawyer still wasn't a fan of modern technology and its effects on society. It was one of the quirks that Chase loved about him. Chase's mother had been David's legal assistant for more than twenty years, having started working with David when Chase was still a newborn. The old lawyer, forty years Chase's senior, had been more of a kindly, older uncle than his mom's boss, buying Chase and his sister cool Christmas gifts and even letting them go on vacations with him and his family. Chase had worked part-time at David's law firm filing papers and running errands during his teenage summers. Those summers working in the law office and his love and respect for David were the reasons that Chase, a twenty-two-old recent college graduate, wanted to be a lawyer. He had already been accepted into law school. At the moment, Chase was working with David's firm, Whiteside and Bowman, full time until he started law school in the fall.

Chase knew that David looked at him as the son he'd never had. That love and respect for Chase, his sister, Sarah, and their late mother was why David was helping him. This trip was the first step in what Chase prayed was the journey to finding answers about what had happened with his sister, Sarah. Now, as David maneuvered the vehicle up the driveway, Chase glanced over at the older man. "No matter if this guy helps us or not, I appreciate everything you've done to help me," Chase said. He started to get choked up but he fought it off. "You didn't have to be involved in this whole, tragic mess."

David turned and looked at him. He looked faintly offended. "Look, kid, what happened to Sarah has me lying awake at night staring at the ceiling too. I want to know what happened for all our sakes, including your mom's. Your mom, Reena, was a wonderful person who was with me for years. She helped me make it. Literally, in the early years there were times her paycheck was late and more than a couple where it bounced, but she stuck with me. I owe it to her to find out what happened."

Chase wanted to say something else, but he was afraid that if opened his mouth he must burst out bawling like a baby. He managed to simply nod. Thankfully, before the moment got too awkward, the driveway ahead of them emerged from the thick trees on each side into a large, cleared area that looked like it had once been a forest meadow overlooking a small lake. A two-story log cabin with a green metal roof sat at the crest of a small hill with a wide front porch overlooking the lake, and a small area of neatly trimmed grass around the lake and what would be considered the front yard of the cabin. The driveway ended at a paved area at the side of the house with a two-bay garage built of the same logs as the main cabin. A black pickup truck, a Ford Raptor, was parked off to one side of the paved area.

"Nice place," Chase said.

"It is," David agreed. "Billy told me this fellow likes his privacy. He looked around through the car's windows. With the exception of the clearing where the house sat, everything else was thick trees and rolling hills. "It's definitely private."

David continued slowly forward until the driveway ended at the paved area and the side of the house. One of the garage's bay doors was up. The inside of the building was brightly lit with fluorescent lights. Inside the bay, the two men could see what appeared to be a very well-equipped home gym complete with a heavy bag hanging from the rafters. The heavy bag looked old and was heavily-taped. It was still swaying as David parked the car and killed the engine. A single figure emerged from the open bay just as David and Chase opened their doors and climbed out of their vehicle. The figure, a man, walked over to meet David.

Chase walked around the front of the SUV and got his first good look at the man who'd come out of the garage and was approaching them. His first impression was shock. When David had told him that they were going to go meet a private investigator, Chase had pictured someone similar to the private investigators he normally dealt with at David's firm: older, retired cops who were either bored with retirement or who needed to supplement their pensions or wannabe cops who just couldn't seem to get hired by a law enforcement agency. Every single one of them was out of shape, with beer bellies or the soft appearance of men who spent way too much time sitting in front of a computer screen or slinking around trying to see in motel room windows. Most of them, especially the wannabe cop ones, tried to act like they were tough guys, but, in reality, they were about as intimidating as a box of kittens. The man walking over to David was anything but one of those guys. The man approaching them was about six feet tall and what Chase's college buddies would have described as "jacked" in awed voices. The guy was built like a brick wall with the lean, hard muscles of a mixed martial arts fighter or boxer. He wore only tennis shoes and running shorts and his bare chest and arms were completely covered with intricate, colorful tattoos. He looked to be in his mid-to late-thirties. He had short black hair that was slicked back with sweat, a mustache, and a goatee that dropped to about six inches below his chin. His face was all angles, with a wide mouth and a nose that looked like it had been broken before. Women probably would have described him more as striking than handsome. At the moment, he had a serious who-the-hell-are-you expression on his face. His eyes were hazel and filled with calm intelligence. Just looking at him told Chase that the guy probably didn't miss much. The intelligence in his eyes compared with the muscles and tattoos was a striking dichotomy. In a shirt and tie, he would have fit in in a corporate boardroom. Shirtless or in blue jeans and a tee shirt, he looked like he could win a bar brawl on the bad side of town.

The guy approached them and stopped a few feet away. He had a towel draped over his shoulders that he was holding by the ends with both hands and he was pouring sweat. Obviously, they had interrupted his workout. "Can I help you?" the guy asked. His voice was surprisingly ordinary for such an unusual- looking man.

"Ben Joe Lane?" David asked. He offered his hand. "My name is David Whiteside. I'm an attorney. This young man with me is named Chase Fleming. We're sorry to bother you, but we would like to talk to you for a few minutes."

The man looked down at David's proffered hand. He released the end of the towel and held out one hand to show that his knuckles were taped up. The tape was stained with blood; the guy must have really been laying it to the heavy bag right before they arrived. "I don't think you want to shake my hand right now, Mr. Whiteside. And my name is one word, not two. It's Benjo. Kind of like Benji with an o instead of an I at the end. No middle name, just first name Benjo and last name Lane."

David withdrew his hand awkwardly. "My apologies, sir," he said calmly. "Mr. Lane, a colleague of mine, Billy Cleveland, told me that you are the man I need to talk to. I need a private investigator to help Chase and I find some answers."

The man's expression softened and a lopsided grin found its way to his face. Chase was startled by the transformation; Lane was one of those people with a very expressive face who could light up a room with a smile or clear it out with a glare. "Billy Cleveland," Benjo said. "He's my personal attorney and a good friend as well. He sent you to me?"

"Yes," David said. "I need a private investigator to look into a sensitive matter involving this young man here's family. Billy said you are a licensed private investigator. He also told me you were an investigator for the sheriff's department for over fifteen years. I tried to look you up online to get a telephone number or office address, but I couldn't find you. Billy gave this address and told me to ride out and take a chance."

"I don't have an office or a website, Mr. Whiteside," Benjo replied as he took the towel and wiped the sweat off his face and chest. "Full disclosure, I only got my PI license a few weeks ago at the suggestion of a psychologist I'm seeing. He thought I needed something to do to get me out of the house more. He thought that being a PI would be a good fit for me, given my background. My wife passed away a while back and..."

"I'm very sorry to hear that," David quickly interjected. "Billy told me a little about your situation. My sincere condolences."

A pained look flitted across Benjo's face. It was there for the briefest of seconds and then it was gone. "She was a firm believer in life insurance and she had a lot of it," Benjo replied evenly. "I'm a simple man, so based on what I have in the bank right now, I could go without working probably until I die of old age. That gives me the luxury of picking and choosing what I will work on. I didn't get my private investigator's license so I could chase after unfaithful spouses or try to catch auto accident victims faking injuries.

"What kind of cases will you take, Mr. Lane?" Chase asked as he stepped forward.

Benjo cut him an appraising look. "I take it personally if bad people get away with bad things, Chase," he said. "Justice is important to me. It matters, so I want the cases I investigate to be about more than someone trying to line their pockets or making their ex look bad in court so they can get the house."

"How many cases have you investigated, Benjo?" David asked.

Benjo grinned. "If I take your case, you will be my first one," he said. "It seems that the cases I have no interest in doing make up about ninety-nine percent of what private investigators do, so I'm unemployable."

Chase couldn't decide if he liked the man named Benjo or not. At the moment, he couldn't tell if the guy was just obnoxious or if the guy was serious about how he picked what he worked on. For all Chase knew, this guy could be the type to milk David's firm for a big payday and then claim he didn't find out anything or he could be the type to give him and David the answers they needed. Either way, Benjo's demeanor was rankling Chase. "My older sister-my only sister- was murdered, Mr. Lane," Chase said fiercely. "The cops know who murdered her; they've already investigated it, and the prosecutor's office has already ruled it justifiable, effectively closing the case and letting the person who shot her get away with it. Is that interesting enough for you?"

Benjo shifted his gaze over to Chase. "I must confess you have my attention, Chase," he said. "Also, going forward, both of you please call me Benjo." He glanced at both men. "Give me the short version, the who, when, and what."

"My twenty-five-year-old sister, Sarah Anne Fleming, went to a church just outside the city on a Tuesday morning seven weeks ago," Chase answered. "She went into the building and to the office of the church pastor's wife, a woman named Monica Cole. She's like the assistant pastor. In the office, my sister allegedly became aggressive and attacked Monica Cole with a letter opener the woman had on her desk. Mrs. Cole pulled a pistol she had in her desk and shot my sister twice in the chest, killing her."

"That would be the Monica Cole for Hope Springs Church?" Benjo asked as he slipped the towel back across his shoulders. "The big mega-church that opened in that vacant superstore building on Highway Forty? The church with all of the billboards and television commercials on the local channels?"

"Yes," David answered for Chase. "I suppose I should ask if you attend there before we proceed. I think about half the county does on Sunday. They claim they have over a thousand people every Sunday. If you do attend there, I don't imagine you would take the case. Do you go there, Benjo?"

"No," Benjo answered with a lopsided grin. "If I find God, I don't suspect it will be at the same place I used to go for a good deal on a television."

"That Monica Cole," Chase said. "They claim Sarah was harassing and stalking her, calling her several times. They claim Sarah even went to the church and assaulted the woman prior to the shooting. The sheriff's department investigated, then sent everything to local prosecutor's office. They came back and ruled it justifiable because Monica Cole was supposedly defending herself from a crazed stalker."

"I remember hearing a something about the case a while back when I was channel surfing and came across the local news," Benjo said. "I'm not trying to be harsh, but it sounded pretty open and shut."

Chase took a deep breath and fought to keep his composure. "I've read all of the news stories. I've seen everything people write on social media. They've made Monica Cole some kind of hero for killing my sister." His eyes started to tear up, but he fought it. "That's not my sister, Benjo. My sister was a registered nurse and the sanest, sweetest person I ever knew. She had no mental health issues and didn't even really go to church anywhere. She wasn't stalking Monica Cole. I have no idea why she was there and what happened that made Monica Cole shoot her. Something is not right about this! My sister was murdered. I want to know why."

Benjo nodded placidly, then turned his attention to David. "What's your role in this, David?" he asked. "Are you wanting to sue the Coles for the death?"

"No," David said. "Chase and Sarah's mother came to work for me when they were toddlers. She worked nearly twenty-two years for me before she passed away from cancer four months ago." He looked at Chase fondly. "Chase, Sarah, and Reena, their mother, are family to me. I've known Sarah since she was three. Her mother used to bring her to work and I had a spare office in my practice set up as a playroom. I also want to know what happened. To the people who really knew Sarah, what the police and the Coles claim happened is outlandish. I need to know what happened that resulted in a pastor's wife having to shoot that sweet, hard-working, kind girl I loved like another daughter."

"Chase, were you and Sarah close enough for you to be able to know if she was having any mental health issues?" Benjo asked. "Someone can be struggling with mental health issues and those around them not recognize it. As someone who's struggled with grief, depression, and other issues over the last year since my wife died, I've gained a whole new perspective on mental health issues."

Chase was about to answer the question, but before he could a huge creature emerged from the open garage door and started walking toward where the three men stood, causing him to completely lose his train of thought. At first Chase thought it was a large, oddly colored dog, but a second look told him that it wasn't a dog at all. It was the biggest cat Chase had ever seen. The thing was huge, measuring at least four feet from the tip of its nose to the end of its tail. Its fur was long and a mottled mix of yellows, browns, and grays. The fur on its head and face were short, causing the long fur on its neck and body to make it look like the cat had a mane. Its eyes were a piercing blue. It had to weigh at least thirty pounds. The monstrous cat slinked over to stand beside Benjo. It was so tall that its back reached slightly above Benjo's knee. That astounded Chase because Benjo was probably slightly over six feet. "What the hell is that?" Chase blurted.

Benjo reached down and scratched the massive cat's back affectionately. It was a surprisingly tender gesture from a man who looked so tough and intimidating. "This is Harley," Benjo said nonchalantly. "She's my cat." The cat sat down and stretched its head up for even more scratches. Sitting flat, the cat's head was about mid-thigh on Benjo.

"That's the biggest cat I've ever seen in my life," David said. "She looks like she ought to be in a zoo."

"She's a Maine Coon cat," Benjo said as he stroked the cat's head. "They are the biggest domesticated cat breed in the world. Harley is big, even by Maine Coon standards. We didn't know she was that breed when my wife and I found her as a stray on a motorcycle road trip three years ago. She was so little at the time that we had to bottle feed her. We brought her home in my wife's motorcycle saddlebag, hence the name, Harley." He looked down at the cat. "She's a big baby unless she thinks I'm being threatened. Then, she's better than any watch dog." He looked back at Chase. "You were saying?"

Chase tore his eyes away from the massive cat to look back at Benjo. "Sarah was a registered nurse at the county hospital," he said fiercely. "She was a trauma nurse in the emergency room. I spoke to her on the telephone at least three times a week and saw her in person at least twice a week. She was always the same Sarah I've always known. The only time I saw her demeanor change was after our mom died from cancer. She took care of our mom while she was in hospice. After mom passed, Sarah seemed preoccupied and a little distant sometimes, but I assumed it was grief and sorting out our mom's affairs."

Benjo stopped scratching the cat's head and looked at David and Chase. "Do you have any of the paperwork from the police investigation? Copies of reports or anything?"

"I've got copies of the police reports and statements from the Coles," David said. "I also have a thumb drive of security footage from the church the day Sarah was killed. The church had security cameras on the exterior doors, the main entrance lobby, and the parking lot. It just shows her going into the building. I don't have everything the police have, but I think I have enough to give you a fair picture of what happened. Everything is in a file I have here in my car."

"If you give me the file, I'll take a look at it," Benjo said.

"So, you'll take the case?" Chase asked hopefully.

"I'll take a look at what you've got and what I can find online," Benjo replied. "If I think there's something there worth looking at, I'll take the case. If I think it's a waste of time and resources, I'll tell you that. I'll call you in a couple of hours to let you know what I've decided."

"That's reasonable," David replied. "I respect your judgment. Let me get the file for you."

"There's one thing you both need to know," Benjo said as David started to turn and fetch the file from his car. "Once I take a case, I solve it," Benjo said. "It's a personal thing with me. I don't do half measures and I don't quit until I find the truth."

"That's what we want," Chase said eagerly.

"Everyone says that until the truth turns out to be something they didn't want to hear," Benjo said. He stopped scratching the cat's head as he spoke, causing the cat to look at him disdainfully and stroll away. "One thing I've learned is that people constantly surprise you, and most of the time it's something bad. They do something you never thought they would. Also, everyone has secrets and a dark side." He locked eyes with Chase. "Essentially, I'm asking you both if you can handle the truth."

Chase and David looked at each other for a few seconds. "We can," David answered.

Benjo nodded. "Give me the file," he said.

David hurried to the Cadillac and retrieved an accordion file. "Everything I have is in there, including the thumb drive and the coroner's report," he said as he handed the file to Benjo. "There's also a card with my personal cell phone number on it and a note with Chase's cell phone as well."

"You should be hearing from me later this afternoon," Benjo said. "I'll call you once I've made a decision. If I decide to not take the case, I'll drop the file at your office tomorrow."

"What's your fee?" David asked.

"If I take the case, you'll cover my expenses," Benjo said. "We'll decide what you owe me when I'm done. I do promise you that my fee will be fair and reasonable, even by lawyer standards."

"Billy told me you would say that," David said. "He also told me that I can trust you, so I will. Just bear in mind that this is coming out of my pocket personally and not some insurance company or corporation."

"I won't gouge you, sir," Benjo replied. "Have a safe trip back to town. It was nice meeting you both."

With that, Benjo turned and walked back into the garage with the file in his hands. Chase and David looked at each other, shrugged, got back into the car, and left.

Once they were back out onto the main highway, Chase broke the silence. "That was different," he said. "That's a strange dude." He shook his head. "And that cat looks like it ought to be in a zoo."

"I agree on both counts," David replied as he accelerated down the highway. "He's a little odd, but I guess I would be a little odd too if I had gone through what he has."

"What do you mean?" Chase asked. "What's this guy's deal?"

"Billy Cleveland told me a little bit about it," David explained. "He knows a lot because he was Benjo's attorney during everything. Does the name Jacob Clement ring a bell?"

Chase thought for a moment. "It seems like it should," he said. "It sounds kind of familiar." Suddenly, it dawned on the younger man. "He was the guy they think was running a drug ring or something like that, right?"

David nodded. "Jacob Clement was the younger son of the Clement family, the family that owns a few car dealerships in this state. Jacob was the black sheep who owned a towing service and a garage. He was a pretty good businessman on his own, apparently, because he was supposedly pretty successful. He allegedly had a dark side, too, because his name kept coming up around some pretty shady deals involving drugs and stolen vehicles.

"Benjo was a detective with the sheriff's department here," David continued. "I don't know what put Clement on Benjo's radar, but Benjo ended up focused on him relating to some missing persons who were linked to him. The missing persons led to a drug and stolen car ring. It was all supposed to be secret, but, allegedly, someone in the sheriff's department tipped Clement off about Benjo's growing investigation. The question at the sheriff's department has always been was it intentional or did loose lips sink ships? No matter what it was, Clement realized Benjo was closing in on him, so Clement started doing whatever he felt was necessary to cover his tracks. One of his businesses had a fire break out that gutted the whole building. A couple of shady characters Clement associated with also went missing, possibly bringing his victim count to at least six people."

"Wow," Chase said. "I don't remember reading anything about this in the local news."

"It was kept pretty quiet," David replied without taking his eyes off the road. "The investigation was supposed to be a secret and Clement was doing everything possible to hide evidence while simultaneously coming across as Mr. Small Business Owner and Upstanding Citizen. Apparently, Benjo was building a pretty solid case because Clement got desperate enough to try to take Benjo out of the picture."

"I remember this now," Chase said. "It was all over the news. We even talked about it in class."

David nodded. "Slightly over a year ago, Benjo and his wife, Presley, an elementary school teacher, were leaving a social function put on by the school Presley worked at when two masked men confronted them in the school parking lot. The two men just walked up and opened fire," David said somberly. "Presley was hit three times and died instantly. Benjo was able to draw his own weapon and return fire, killing both attackers. Turns out they were hired hitmen and Benjo was the target. Both men were gang members from Florida with long rap sheets. One of them had a picture of Benjo in his pocket. Presley Lane was in the wrong place at the wrong time."

"That sucks," Chase said softly. "I imagine he blames himself a little."

"The state police stepped in and handled the investigation because Benjo was a police officer and he had shot two men," David continued. "It took the state police about ten minutes to zero in on Jacob Clement as the man who hired the dead hitmen. One of the dead would-be assassins actually had a piece of paper in his shoe with the letters J. C. and a cell phone number on it. When the state police went to question Clement three days after Presley Lane's death, they found him in his kitchen floor at home. He'd been shot four times, two in the chest and two in the head."

"Someone wanted him dead," Chase said.

"And one of the main suspects was Benjo Lane," David said. "He was unaccounted for in the time frame in which Clement was shot. Also, the state police determined that there might have been a couple of instances where Benjo could have figured out who their main suspect was. There was also security camera footage from a neighbor's house that showed a brief glimpse of Clement's killer leaving the house through a back door. The killer was masked and in dark clothing, but the height and build could be Benjo. He was questioned, but denied his involvement in anything. There wasn't enough other evidence, plus given Clement's alleged criminal ties, the list of possible suspects was rather lengthy. The investigation of Clement's death is still open. A couple of weeks after his wife's death, Benjo resigned from the sheriff's department."

"Was he mad because he was a suspect in Clement's death?" Chase asked.

"I think he was furious because the person or persons that he felt tipped off Clement were either never identified or nothing was done to them," David said. "Also, the sheriff was going to put him on uniformed patrol because of the questions about his possible involvement in Clement's murder."

Chase sat there for a few moments absorbing what he'd just heard. The interior of the car was silent, save for the hum of the tires on the pavement. "Do you really think this is the guy who can find out what happened with Sarah?" he finally asked.

"I don't know," David replied. "I do know that this case is something I don't trust to any of the other private investigator I know locally. They are all retired cops, and the problem is that retired cops don't think other cops can do any wrong, so they would probably not dig into Sarah's death the way they should. Also, I know what Billy told me about him."

"And what was that?" Chase asked.

"I've known Billy for well over twenty-five years," David replied. "We've worked together and we've been opponents in court. One thing I can tell you about Billy is that he's not one to exaggerate or overstate anything. Billy calls it like he sees it and he's also an excellent judge of people. When he recommended Benjo, he told me, "If I committed a crime and I knew he was investigating me, I would just walk into the police station and confess because I was going to end up in jail anyway. I might as well save myself all of the time looking over my shoulder and worrying.""

"Wow," Chase said.

"Yep," David said. "I really think he's the man to tell us what happened with Sarah. My gut tells me he will get to the truth. I just hope the truth is something we can handle."

"Sarah was murdered," Chase said defiantly. "I don't care what the police or the prosecutor says."

"I think so too, Chase," David replied. "I just hope Benjo sees it our way and takes the case."

2

Back at the cabin, Benjo emerged from the shower, toweled himself dry, and dressed in jeans and a tee shirt. His muscles were sore from the morning workout, but that was okay. The physical pain and pleasant tiredness were a distraction from the mental and emotional pain that always seemed to linger just at the edge of his mind. Once he was dressed, he walked out of the bathroom, through his bedroom, and into the kitchen. He grabbed a bottle of water from the refrigerator, sat down at the kitchen table, and grabbed the file he'd tossed there before taking a shower. He opened the bottle of water, took a sip, and untied the string that kept the accordion file closed. He removed the sheaf of papers from the file, sat back, and flipped through the contents. The papers consisted of the official police report from the incident in which Sarah Fleming was shot, a few of the investigating detectives' supplemental reports, Monica and August Cole's statements, and the pathologist's report from Sarah's autopsy. A single computer thumb drive slid out with the sheaf of papers. Benjo put the thumb drive aside, settled back in his chair, and began to read the official reports.

The police report painted a pretty simple picture of what had occurred the day Monica Cole shot Sarah Fleming twice. On a rainy Tuesday morning seven weeks earlier, at approximately nine fifteen AM, Sarah Ann Fleming, a twenty-five-year-old white female, arrived at the Hope Springs Church building. Sarah entered the building through an unlocked side door and made her way to an office belonging to Monica Cole, the assistant pastor of Hope Springs Church and the wife of head pastor August Cole. Monica Cole, a forty-two -year-old white female, was sitting in her office when Sarah, a woman she had seen recently in the crowd at church services, entered her office. According to Monica, Sarah began cursing and abusing her, claiming that Monica was responsible for issues she was having in her personal life. Monica claimed that she attempted to reason with Sarah by telling her that she did not know Sarah personally. This agitated Sarah to the point that she physically attacked Monica with her fists. Monica fought back by shoving Sarah away and attempting to keep her desk between the two of them. Sarah became even more enraged and grabbed a metal letter opener from the surface of Monica's desk. She tried to stab Monica but Monica managed to get away and get to her top desk drawer. Monica kept a nine-millimeter pistol there she'd bought for self- defense. Cole claimed she tried to force Sarah to leave her office at gunpoint, but Sarah lunged at her with the letter opener again, prompting her to fire twice. Sarah was struck once in the chest and once in the upper right abdomen. Sarah collapsed to the floor, mortally wounded. Seconds later, August Cole, Monica's husband and the church's founding pastor, came into Monica's office from a second door that joined his personal office to Monica's. He was attempting first aid when the church's secretary, a woman named Marsha West, also entered the office after returning from an appointment and discovered what had happened. Marsha called the police and an ambulance.

Benjo took a sip of water and moved on to the next paper in the stack. It was a supplemental report from the lead investigator at the scene, Detective Dale Marsh. At the sight of Marsh's name, Benjo felt his stomach tighten and the anger start to build. Benjo and Marsh had worked together for several years at the sheriff's department. They had once been friendly- not friends, just friendly- and even partners on several cases. Benjo had very quickly figured out that Marsh wasn't a very good detective, or even a very good cop in general for that matter. Actually, Marsh had a job at the sheriff's office only because his father, a local businessman whose successful auto body repair shops had given him deep pockets, was one of Sheriff John Crowe's biggest donors. Marsh's job at the sheriff's department was political payback, plain and simple. Luckily for Benjo, he and Marsh didn't cross paths enough for it to vex Benjo. Benjo had simply worked his cases and picked up Marsh's slack if he was unlucky enough to have to work a case with him. Benjo really didn't care who office politics put where, as long as it didn't affect him. Unfortunately, it had ultimately affected Benjo in a terrible way. Now, just the sight of or mention of the Marsh's name awakened cold fury in Benjo.

Benjo hated Marsh because Benjo knew that Marsh was the one who tipped off Jacob Clement that he was the focus of Benjo's investigation. When Benjo's investigation of Clement first started, no one in the sheriff's department had known at the time that the Marsh family's auto body repair empire had a business relationship with Jacob Clement's towing company. Marsh hadn't volunteered that information either. That relationship had come to light following Clement's death. The state police had uncovered it during their investigation into Clement's murder. The state police investigators had not only found paperwork linking the businesses, but also a couple of pictures of Marsh and Clement partying together in social settings. Common sense dictated that Marsh was the one who tipped off Clement, a family friend and drinking buddy. The only question was whether it was intentional or unintentional. Whichever one it was, there was no way Marsh could have known that Clement would try to have Benjo murdered, killing his wife in the process, but that didn't excuse that fact that a police officer might have tipped off a criminal with inside information.

Since learning that Marsh was very probably the leak, simply being around Marsh infuriated Benjo to the point he worried about his self-control. Following Clement's demise and the resulting investigation that pointed to Marsh as the leak, Benjo had expected that Marsh would be fired and face criminal charges. Unfortunately, there wasn't enough evidence that Marsh had actually told Clement anything to file criminal charges. With no criminal charges or solid proof of wrongdoing, Sheriff Crowe had let Marsh off the hook without even a demotion. That was too much for Benjo to take, so he had resigned from the sheriff's department

Benjo wrestled the anger back and continued to read Marsh's supplemental reports that detailed his steps during the investigation. Marsh had pulled Sarah's cell phone records. There were three telephone calls from Sarah's cell phone to Monica Cole's office prior to the deadly confrontation. Three telephone calls over several days hardly constituted telephone harassment, but that's how Marsh had written it up. The first was for about seven minutes. The second call, two days later, was for just a few seconds, most likely indicating a hang-up. The third call, placed the day after the second call, had lasted almost twenty minutes. There was also an incident where Sarah had come to the church during a Sunday service, approached Monica Cole, and physically assaulted her by grabbing at her shoulder. Paul Tucker, the man in charge of the church's security, was also interviewed. He claimed that they had seen Sarah on the property numerous times in the days leading up to the shooting.

Another full hour passed as Benjo continued to read over everything in the file, including the Coles' statements and the autopsy report. Benjo stopped long enough to make himself a sandwich and a glass of iced tea before he sat back down and continued reading. Once he had read over everything, he grabbed a legal pad and pen and started making a few notes. Once his notes were complete, he grabbed his laptop, inserted the thumb drive from the file, and started watching video footage. The footage was from the church's security camera system. The cameras were on the outside of the building. In the footage, Sarah Fleming could be seen parking her car in the church's parking lot on the eastern side of the building. Sarah emerged from her car and walked to the side of the building carrying some papers in her hand. She went straight to the side door, turned the handle, and walked in casually. There was no footage of her once she entered that door.

There was a second video clip below the one showing Sarah entering the building. The date and time on the second video clip were three weeks prior to the day Sarah was killed. The clip was from a camera that showed the lobby of the church and the main entrance. The clip showed Monica and August Cole standing in the lobby speaking to members of their congregation as they were leaving. The Coles were standing in the lobby near the sanctuary doors leading into the worship area and speaking with or shaking hands with members of their church as they were leaving. Apparently, this was something the two of them did after every service. In the short video clip, Sarah Fleming approached Monica Cole's side and reached out to touch her shoulder. Monica suddenly turned and looked at Sarah as if startled. Sarah pulled her hand away and moved on as other people flocked around them. According to Marsh's supplemental report in the file, this incident was when Sarah assaulted Monica Cole, although calling that brief contact an assault was a real stretch. The church's security director, Paul Tucker, had provided this clip after the incident with Sarah.

Benjo was just finishing watching the footage when there was a loud beep from living room area that adjoined the kitchen. The beep was from the automatic pet door he had installed for Harley, the cat, in the cabin's side door. The cat wore a collar with a small radio transmitter that opened the door automatically when she approached it and closed automatically once she had passed through it. The pet door was designed for large dogs, but the huge cat was as big as, if not bigger, than some dog breeds. A few moments later, Harley slinked into the kitchen and rubbed up against Benjo's leg. He absentmindedly reached down and petted her. The cat began to purr loudly. The big cat's purring was louder than the refrigerator's humming motor in the quiet kitchen. "What's up, girl?" he asked the cat. The cat looked up at him, meowed loudly, and strolled away. "I'll take that as a 'nothing much'" Benjo said as he watched the cat head for the living room where, if she followed her usual routine, he would find her dozing on the rug in front of the cabin's fireplace.

Benjo removed the thumb drive and used the laptop to pull up the world wide web. He typed the names of the Coles into one of the major search engines and waited. In just a couple of seconds, he had several pages of information on August and Monica Cole and several pictures of them. August Cole was a handsome, dark-haired man with piercing blue eyes and a smile perfect for toothpaste commercials. Monica was a pretty blonde with long hair, high cheekbones, and dimples when she smiled. Both of them could have come out of a Hollywood casting agency to play the role of 'Perfect Couple'. The search engine also pulled up links to a couple of sermons Pastor Cole and Hope Springs Church had posted online on various platforms. Benjo watched a couple of the sermons and a couple of songs the couple performed as a duet before one of their services. Benjo had to give the Coles credit; they were interesting to watch and listen to. August was a charismatic and powerful speaker who kept your attention. Monica had a powerful singing voice and could play a piano extremely well. One thing Benjo noticed immediately was that August was the main character and Monica was the adoring sidekick. During the song numbers, it was obvious that Monica was making sure she wasn't overshadowing her husband. Benjo wondered if that was an act or if that dynamic continued when they were in private.

Now that he knew what they looked and sounded like, Benjo turned his attention to the other information. Most of it was biographical fluff pieces put out by their church. According to the published biographies, both of them had grown up in the area and were childhood sweethearts who dated all through middle and high school. August's father was the pastor of a local Baptist church and well-known for his fire and brimstone sermons. The elder Pastor Cole had even drawn national attention for his fierce stance against sex education in local schools in the mid-1980s. Perhaps because of the stress of being a typical "preacher's kid", beginning around the age of seventeen, August had experienced a period where he was a self-described "child of the devil." He'd become addicted to drugs, alcohol, and partying, all behaviors which had led to his strict father disowning him and throwing him out of the house. His life had spiraled out of control to the point that he'd been arrested and even done a couple of years in prison for drug offenses. In prison, he'd rediscovered his love of Jesus Christ and gotten saved. After getting released from prison, he'd married Monica, who'd stuck by him, and dedicated his life to "spreading the Gospel and ministering to others", according to his biography. When no church would hire him, he became a traveling preacher. He became so popular that he soon rented a space in a strip mall and started Hope Springs Church. The church had grown by leaps and bounds. It was now housed in a state-of-the-art building with a child care center, classrooms, and a studio where the Coles did a show for a local cable channel and social media. The church now held three services on Sunday with an average attendance at each service of two thousand people. They also did numerous community outreach programs, but their biggest one was a program that ministered to prison inmates and drug addicts in rehab facilities.

Benjo spent nearly an hour reading up on the Coles and their church. At first glance, they seemed an unlikely pair to draw a stalker, especially a young, seemingly sane woman with no history of such behavior. However, hard experience as an investigator had taught him that few things were ever what they seemed. Sarah could have suffered from some undiagnosed mental illness that had led her to start stalking Monica Cole and then attempt to murder her. Or, there might be some personal issue there that no one knew about, such as an extramarital affair. August Cole was forty-two years old, according to his biographical information, still relatively young, and a tall, handsome man in a position of power and authority. Women found such men attractive. It was easy to see how a young woman could become infatuated with him.

Benjo stood up from the kitchen table and walked into the living room. The living room had huge windows that overlooked the lake and the forest beyond it. Harley lay sprawled on her side on the rug in front of the fireplace. She opened her eyes and looked at him as walked by her. Benjo stood at the window and looked out across the lake. It was a sunny day without a single cloud in the sky. A single hawk flew majestic circles over the forest. "Maybe Sarah was having an affair with one of the Coles," Benjo said aloud. "What do you think, cat?" Harley's reply was a look that was somewhere between acknowledgement and disgust that he could come up with something so asinine. "Yep, me too," Benjo replied.

Benjo remained there for several minutes, staring out the window and thinking about the case. While reviewing the case file, he had noticed a few things that struck him as odd, things that would have made him ask questions if he had been the detective assigned the case. He could take the case, dig around, and just see what turned up. The easier thing to do, however, would be to not get involved. He could tell David Whiteside and Chase Fleming that he didn't see anything that would lead him to believe that the case was anything but what it looked like on the surface: a troubled young woman who'd forced a confrontation for some reason only she knew and who died as a result. If he didn't take the case, he could continue to stay at home and do whatever he pleased. He liked the freedom of not having to answer to anyone, but the staying at home part didn't appeal to him anymore. Ever since Presley's murder, he had kept to himself in order to deal with his grief and loneliness. Unfortunately, the grief and loneliness were still the problem. No amount of working out, reading, watching television, or other hobbies could keep all of his tangled emotions at bay. He'd been battling depression on and off over the last year. That depression was what had sent him to the psychologist who'd suggested getting his private investigator's license. He was okay now, but the dark cloud of depression was always hovering on the edge of his mind. He knew that it wouldn't take much to send him to a very dark place that he might not find his way out of.

He looked back at Harley. The cat was sitting up and watching him intently. "Should I take the case, Harley?" he asked aloud. "I could take the case and find out if this young lady was murdered or I can stay here at home and continue to talk to my- way- oversized house cat. Which one should I go with?" Harley cocked her head at him and yawned. "Presley would want me to help," Benjo added.

At the mention of his wife's name, the big cat turned its head and looked up at the mantel over the fireplace. A framed picture of Benjo and Presley taken on their wedding day fifteen years earlier stood there. Beside it stood the silver urn that contained her ashes. She had always wanted to have her ashes scattered in the Black Hills of South Dakota, the place where her family was originally from and the place they had honeymooned. Benjo planned to go there and fulfill her wishes, but the thought of doing it was too much for him to bear at the moment. The cat gazed at the picture for several seconds, then turned and stared back at Benjo. The cat's piercing blue eyes never blinked.

Benjo looked at the urn. "I miss her too," he said to Harley. For a few weeks after her death, he'd continued to talk to her as if she was still there. That had passed, but he'd started talking to the cat instead. He didn't know which of those two things was weirder; that he spoke with his deceased wife as if she was still there or that he held entire conversations with his pet. Neither could be considered a sign of good mental health. "If I take the case, I can help her brother," Benjo said to the cat as she cocked her head at him in a curiously human way. "It might give them some closure and maybe even a small measure of vengeance. Plus, Marsh was the lead investigator. If I can prove he got it wrong, it will some payback for him getting Presley killed."

The thought of humiliating Marsh clinched it for him. Unlike Sheriff Crowe and the state police, who claimed they couldn't prove that Marsh was the one who'd tipped off Jacob Clement that he was under investigation, Benjo was one hundred percent sure that Dale Marsh was the leak. Benjo believed in simple, logical facts and the facts were simple: Dale Marsh could have learned about his investigation into Jacob Clement and Marsh had a friendly relationship with Clement. Based on those facts, Marsh was the only one who could have or would have tipped off Clement. That certainty of Marsh's guilt had left him with such a bitter hatred for the man that he'd briefly considered killing him. Luckily for Marsh, Benjo's cooler, rational side had prevailed in that argument. However, a chance to humiliate and embarrass the man was too tempting to pass up.

His mind made up, Benjo tore his eyes away from the mantel and walked back into the kitchen. He found David Whiteside's card in the file. He used his cell phone to call the number. The lawyer answered on the first ring. "Mr. Whiteside, I saw some things in the reports and on the video that left me with some questions that I think need answers. I will take the case," Benjo said.

"When will you start?" Whiteside asked through the phone.

"I already have," Benjo replied. "Going forward, you are my attorney if any legal issues arise around this case and my investigation of it. Also, I'll need to meet with Chase to get more info on his sister. I would also like to check out where she lived. According to the police report, she had an apartment as her home address. The sooner I can speak with Chase and visit the apartment, the better."

"Hold on, Mr. Lane," David said. Benjo waited as David turned to speak with someone else. Benjo recognized the voice as Chase Fleming's. "Chase will meet you at his sister's apartment tomorrow morning at nine AM," David said when he came back on the phone. "Sarah paid her rent in advance, so Chase has until the end of this month to move Sarah's stuff out. "

"I'll be there," Benjo said.

"I just want to add that I appreciate your involvement," David added. "She was a special young woman and she meant a lot to me, even though I'm not blood kin."

"You might regret my involvement, sir," Benjo said honestly. "I think we might kick a hornet's nest on this one. The sheriff's office might not take kindly to being second guessed, especially by me."

"Then they should have done their jobs better," David replied gravely.

"I think we're going to get along very well, David," Benjo said. "I'll be in touch."

With that, Benjo ended the call. He left his cell phone on the table and walked into the living room. Harley the cat looked up as he walked from the kitchen, "And so it begins, old friend," Benjo said as he walked by.

Harley yawned, settled her massive head back on the rug, and closed her eyes.

CHAPTER 4

<h1 style="text-align:center">3</h1>

Sarah Fleming's apartment was on the second floor of a two-story apartment building that was part of a large apartment complex named Winterhaven Apartments on the city's east side. All of the buildings in the complex looked almost exactly the same, save for occasional differences in the vinyl siding that made up part of the exterior of each building and a letter of the alphabet that differentiated each building from the other. The buildings, though similar, were nice and the grounds and pool appeared to be well-maintained as Benjo drove through looking for Building H. He also noted that most of the vehicles in the parking lot outside each building were nicer, late model vehicles, indicating that the complex catered to young professionals or well-off older retirees. The apartment complex was just a few blocks away from the hospital where Sarah and her then roommate had both worked as nurses. The number of parking stickers for the local hospital system he observed also told him that a fair number of the complex's residents were in the medical profession as well.

Benjo found Building H and saw that Chase Fleming was already there waiting for him. The young man was leaning against the front fender of a Toyota Camry that Benjo assumed was his and sipping from a travel mug. Chase was clad in a suit and tie. Benjo wore jeans, hiking boots, and a short- sleeved, button- up shirt with an open collar. Benjo parked in an empty spot beside Chase's Camry and got out of his truck. Chase looked at him apprehensively as he got out of his truck. "Good morning," Chase said nervously.

"Good morning, Chase," Benjo said. "You look nervous."

Chase set his mug down on the hood of the car. "Not really," he said. "This is going to be tough for me," he added as he held up what Benjo assumed was a key for his sister's apartment. "I've only been here twice since she was killed. One was the day she was killed to get some stuff the funeral home needed. The second was the day after when her roommate, Darcy, called me to tell me that the apartment had been broken into and that some of Sarah's stuff was missing."

That news stopped Benjo in his tracks. "Someone broke into your sister's apartment?" he asked.

Chase nodded. "Literally, the day she was killed," he said. "Darcy, Sarah's roommate and best friend from nursing school, came home from staying at a friend's house the night after Sarah died to find that someone had broken in and tore up their apartment. Whoever it was took some cash Darcy had left lying on her dresser and Sarah's laptop, which was sitting on the kitchen table. They left the television and some other stuff you would have thought they would take. They also ransacked Sarah's room."

"How'd they get in?" Benjo asked.

"They picked the locks on the front door, even the deadbolt, and walked right in," Chase said bitterly. "The maintenance men for the complex wear khaki work pants and red shirts with the complex name on it embroidered on the front. About eight PM that night, after Darcy left, one of the neighbors saw a man wearing khakis and a red shirt working on the lock with tools. The man, a white guy in his twenties, according to the witness, had a ball cap pulled down low. The neighbor didn't recognize him as one of the regular maintenance men, but he assumed the guy was a new employee fixing the lock. The neighbor didn't realize anything was fishy until he saw the police here the next morning after Darcy found the door unlocked and the place ransacked when she returned the next morning." He shook his head. "The maintenance manager here had no idea who the guy was. It seems that he was someone who figured out what the staff here wore and came up with a similar outfit so he could blend in and do what he needed. The police said it was probably someone who read about Sarah's death online and decided to see what they could get. Whoever he was, I hope he rots in hell."

"Did he take anything from Sarah's room?" Benjo asked.

"Just her laptop computer," Chase replied. "There was nothing else to take. Sarah's purse was in her car in the church parking lot when she was killed. It had her wallet, checkbook, cell phone, and other valuable stuff in there. Sarah was never a jewelry fan, so she didn't have much of that stuff. The coroner's office gave me her jewelry after, you know." He looked away and cleared his throat. "Whoever the piece of trash was, all he did was take her computer, tear up her bedroom, and go through her desk and stuff. If he took anything else, we couldn't tell."

"Interesting," Benjo said. The timing of the burglary so close to Sarah's death could be a coincidence, but in Benjo's mind, coincidence ranked right up there with the tooth fairy: such a thing was possible, but highly unlikely. He made a note to check with the city police. The apartment complex was in the city limits. "Let's go have a look."

Chase removed a set of keys from his pocket and headed for a set of exterior stairs that led up to the second floor. Benjo followed along behind him. Sarah had lived in Apartment 210. Chase used the keys to unlock the door. He opened the door and stepped aside for Benjo to enter first. Benjo walked through the door into the apartment's living room area. The apartment had been emptied out, save for a dining table with four matching chairs in what would have been the dining room, a couch, and a coffee table. A couple of cardboard boxes with papers and books in them sat on the table. A clothesbasket filled with folded clothes sat in the floor beside the dining room table. The apartment had the empty, dull feeling that all vacant houses seemed to have. With most of the furniture gone, the living room area seemed a lot larger than it actually was. A bar with a countertop separated the dining room from the kitchen. A short hallway led from the living room area to the open door of an empty bedroom. A second door across the hall from the open bedroom was closed. Benjo figured it was a second bedroom, the one Sarah had occupied.

Chase walked in behind him. "What exactly do you hope to find, sir?" Chase asked. His voice echoed off the bare walls.

"Anything that might help me figure out why your sister ended up getting shot by Monica Cole," Benjo replied. "But first, I wanted to talk to you." He walked over to the table, slid the boxes down to one end, and pulled back a chair. "Let's have a seat." He motioned to the chair across the table from his.

Chase sat down apprehensively. "What do you want to know?" he asked.

"Tell me about Sarah," Benjo said. "Make her something to me other than a name on a paper. If any questions come to mind, I'll ask them." He removed a small notepad and a pen from his shirt pocket. "Do you mind if I take a few notes?" Chase shook his head no. "Good," Benjo said. "Tell me about your parents and where you were born."

"Sarah was two and a half years older than me," Chase answered. "Our parents were Rick and Reena Fleming. We lived in a small house out in the country off Highway Ten, also known as Millhouse Road, until I was seven. We then moved into the suburbs. My mom still owned the house when she passed away and I still live there. Sarah and I had talked about selling it, but then everything else happened. My dad died in 2016 of a heart attack. My mom passed away from cancer earlier this year. Actually, she died about two months before Sarah." A stunned look appeared on his face. "My God, I just realized that I'm the last one left from my whole family."

A glance at Chase's face told Benjo that he needed to keep the young man focused. "Tell me about Sarah," he said. "Whatever comes to mind."

"We were typical brother and sister; one moment we were best buddies, the next our mom had to separate us for fighting," Chase said with a pained smile. "She was always a sweet, nerdy girl, all the way through high school. She was very smart and loved anything related to the medical field. I think she originally wanted to be a doctor, but as she grew up it changed to being a nurse. During high school, she had a couple of boyfriends, but nothing serious. She was just an ordinary girl."

"No run-ins with the police or trouble at school, either high school or college?" Benjo asked. "Any odd behavior with the boyfriends you mentioned? Anything that made you think she was possessive or the jealous type?"

"Not at all," Chase said instantly. "There was a breakup with a guy she dated for a few months during her junior year in college. She caught him cheating with another girl. She was hurt and angry, but she didn't do anything weird."

"Would you know if she had?" Benjo asked. "Did she confide in you?"

"Sarah was more like a best friend than a big sister," Chase said. "We were very close. I really think I knew most of her secrets and she knew most of mine."

Benjo looked Chase directly in the face. "Chase, there's no easy way to ask some things, but I need to ask them in order to find out what happened. Did Sarah have a current boyfriend?"

"No," Chase said flatly. "She dated a couple of casual guys from work at the hospital, but nothing serious. She actually complained to me a couple of days before she was killed that she couldn't find any guys who were serious about relationships. She seemed kind of down about it, really."

"Could your sister have been involved with August Cole?" Benjo asked.

"What?" Chase asked, obviously flustered. "No. That's crazy."

"What about with Monica?" Benjo pressed. "Could she have been having an affair with either or both of the Coles?"

"What the hell kind of question is that?" Chase asked angrily.

"A valid one," Benjo retorted. "Something made your sister interact with the Coles. I'm trying to figure out what. If the Coles are to be believed, it was something that made her stalk and physically attack Monica Cole. Now, if she was in her right mind, there had to be a reason. If she wasn't in her right mind, that means that some type of undiagnosed mental or emotional issue prompted the events that resulted in her death. You want me to figure out what happened. I'm trying to."

Chase looked away from Benjo's direct gaze. Benjo gave him a few seconds to compose himself. "I'm sorry," Chase said. "I understand that you're trying to help."

"I am," Benjo replied. "Chase, as a detective one of the first things I learned was that every criminal act committed by a sane person is motivated by the desire for four things: love, money, power, or revenge. Sometimes, it's one of those four things. Sometimes, it's a combination of two or more of them. Regardless, trying to get or keep one or more of those things is always present. The only exceptions to that rule are people under the influence of drugs or alcohol or those suffering from mental illness. Those folks are a whole different ball game."

"I've never thought about that," Chase said softly.

"I know you plan to be a lawyer," Benjo said. "If you plan to do any criminal defense work or family law, you will see it pretty quickly. Now, back to my question, could Sarah have been involved with the Coles in any capacity?"

Chase thought about it for a few moments. "Sarah didn't go to their church and her social circle was mainly friends from work. I really do believe she would have told me if she'd met either August or Monica Cole before. They are kind of minor celebrities, if you know what I mean. As much as we talked, something would have come up if she was involved with them in any way."

Benjo scribbled down some notes. "Tell me about your sister's roommate."

"Her name is Darcy Woodruff," Chase said. "She's been Sarah's best friend since her freshman year of college. Both of them were in the nursing program together. They got this apartment together a few days after they graduated with their Bachelors of Science in Nursing. They both worked at the hospital. Darcy worked in the maternity ward, I think."

"Is there a chance they could have been more than friends?" Benjo asked.

"No," Chase said flatly. "My sister was not gay, Benjo. I am one hundred percent sure of that. Also, Darcy has a boyfriend she's been involved with for at least the last two years."

"Okay," Benjo answered. He pointed to the open door of the empty bedroom. "I take it Darcy moved out?"

"After Sarah's death and the burglary, Darcy moved in with her boyfriend," Chase answered. "They're engaged. The wedding is in the fall."

"Do you have a cell phone number for her?" Benjo asked. "I need to talk with her too."

"She might not want to talk to you," Chase said. "Sarah's death really shook her up. The lead sheriff's detective on the case treated her like she was some kind of accomplice when he interviewed her the day after Sarah was shot. I think he pissed her off with some of his questions. I think he implied that the burglary was faked so she could get rid of evidence of Sarah's involvement. He had a search warrant for the laptop and other stuff, but the laptop was gone. She might not want to talk."

"Detective Marsh, the lead detective, isn't much of a person and even less of a detective," Benjo said dryly. "I'll remind Darcy I'm on Sarah's side. I'll be nice, too."

Chase looked in his phone and gave Benjo Darcy's number from his contact list. "You going to ask her if Sarah was a lesbian?" he asked sarcastically once Benjo had the number.

Benjo never looked up from his notepad. "If I think it will help, yes," he answered. He finished writing, closed the notepad, and stood up. His eyes scanned the apartment. "You said that the person who broke in ransacked Sarah's room and a desk there, but left Darcy's stuff alone."

"Darcy had about twenty bucks in cash on her dresser when she went to work that night," Chase answered from his chair. "That's all they took."

"To go to all the trouble of impersonating a maintenance person, complete with fake uniform, for just twenty dollars in cash and a laptop," Benjo said. "Doesn't make much sense. And why their apartment?"

"The city officer who took the report said he might have seen the story about Sarah's death on the news and figured he could loot the place," Chase said. "The officer said it might have been someone looking for some sort of ghoulish trophy because of how she died."

" Maybe," Benjo said. "You mind if I go into Sarah's bedroom?"

"Go ahead," Chase replied. "It's just as the burglar left it. All I did was close the door. I can't make myself go in there and pack up her stuff. That just seems so final."

Benjo felt a twinge of sympathy for the younger man. "I understand," he said. "When I packed up my wife's stuff, I spent the next two days sitting in a dark room staring at the wall. It's tough."

"David told me a little bit about what happened to you and your wife," Chase said. "That's horrible."

"Presley, my wife, was a very special person," Benjo said. "I miss her every day. The pain I feel from losing her makes me want to help other people who have lost someone. That's why I'm here." He turned toward the hallway. "You can wait here, if you want."

Chase shook his head. "Have at it," he said. "I'm not quite there yet."

Benjo walked to the bedroom door and opened it. The bedroom was furnished with a bed, a dresser, a bedside table, and a desk along the far wall beside a set of windows. The desk had a small lamp sitting on it. The desk drawers had been pulled out and emptied onto the bed. The bed was made but it looked as if the burglar had lifted the mattress to look under it then roughly dropped it back into place. The emptied drawers still lay in the floor near the foot of the bed. Several books- old college textbooks, a couple of romance novels, and a Bible- also lay on the bed. It looked as if someone had held the books open and shaken them in an effort to find something hidden in the pages. Benjo stepped into the room and took a long look around. He stood there for nearly five minutes, scanning the room and its contents, before he began to search.

He started with the bed first, working his way through the papers scattered on the bed. Most of it was bills or paperwork pertaining to Sarah's job as a registered nurse working at the local hospital's emergency room. Benjo looked over each piece looking for anything that jumped out at him as odd. The only odd thing he found amongst the papers was a printed picture that appeared to be an aerial view of the roads in a rural area several miles outside the city, complete with road names. The printed map looked like a screen shot from one of the internet sites you used to get directions. A wooded area off a two-lane highway that ran through the country was circled in blue with a question mark drawn beside it. Another country road intersected the highway before the wooded plot just a short distance away. The printed aerial map had nothing else written on it. There was a date and time stamp showing when it was printed, most probably on a printer at Sarah's workplace. The date and time were approximately two weeks before Sarah's fateful encounter with Monica Cole at the church. The printed map was nothing special at first glance, but its appearance there amongst the other papers on the bed was odd. All of the other papers were either bills or work-related things. The single printed map of a rural area just didn't belong. Given that it was something Sarah had printed out for some reason before her death, Benjo found it intriguing. He set the map aside and kept looking through the room.

The rest of the room was basic, young working female things. The closet contained a variety of the scrubs nurses wore and a fashionable mix of other casual wear. It didn't look like the burglar had gone through the closet, at least not the clothing hanging up, because it was all too neat. Once he was done with the closet, Benjo moved on. There were a couple of framed pictures sitting on the bedside table. One was a full-face photo of Sarah that was obviously taken in a professional photographer's studio. Sarah was a pretty brunette with almond-shaped eyes, a pretty smile, and cheeks that bordered on chubby. A second photo was a family photo showing Sarah, Chase, and an older woman and man that appeared to be their parents. Sarah really stood out in the photo because of her dark hair and her height; Chase and the parents were blondes or reddish blondes and of average height. All four of the family members were smiling and looked at ease in the picture.

Benjo continued his search, even going so far as to lift the mattress to look under it in case the burglar had missed something. There was only one other thing that caught Benjo's attention. Sitting in the corner of the room in the floor beside a wastebasket was an opened cardboard box. The box was slightly smaller than a shoe box but the same shape. It had been opened using a pair of scissors or knife, judging by the neat edges on the packing tape. There were no other labels on the box, but there was a spot where a shipping label had been removed. The box had a printed letter on its side that was printed directly on the cardboard. It was a stylized W. Benjo looked into the box, but it was empty. Like the map, it struck Benjo as odd for some reason. He made a mental note to try to find out what company the W stood for.

Benjo left the box by the wastebasket, picked up the printed map, and walked back out into the hallway. There was a bathroom in the hallway right beside Sarah's bedroom door. "That bathroom was Sarah's," Chase called down the hall when he saw Benjo looking. "Each of them had their own bathroom." Benjo glanced into the bathroom. All of Sarah's personal toiletries were still in there on the bathroom counter. There were a few different hairbrushes, other things girls used for their hair, and some cosmetics. Nothing else that stood out. It was kind of unsettling in a way; it almost looked as if Sarah would be coming back in a few minutes.

Benjo left the bathroom alone and walked into the living room. Chase still sat at the table. He was reading something on the screen of his cell phone. He looked up from it as Benjo came down the hall. "Find anything helpful?" he asked.

Benjo handed him the printed map. "Does this mean anything to you?" he asked.

Chase studied it for a few seconds. "No," he said. "I recognize the highway name and the surrounding roads, though. That's just about two miles from the first house we lived in when we were kids. If memory serves, it's just a patch of woods that borders a farm that belonged to the Pearsons, I believe."

"Hmm," Benjo said as he took the map back from Chase. "Was Sarah looking for a new home or property?" he asked. "Was she thinking about building a new place?"

"Not that I am aware of," Chase replied. "If she was, she would have looked in either the suburbs or the city limits. Sarah liked the convenience of living closer to everything." He looked up at Benjo. "You think it's important?"

"I looked through all of the stuff the burglar poured out of the desk drawers when he ransacked the place," Benjo said as he studied the map. "All of the rest of the papers were bills or work-related memos and stuff like that. This is the only thing that didn't fit in amongst all of the other papers. It's just odd."

"No idea what it could be for," Chase said.

"Another thing that struck me as odd is how the supposed burglar did," Benjo said. "The way Sarah's room was searched, coupled with the fact that the burglar didn't steal anything else but some easily accessible cash and her laptop, kind of makes me think that Sarah was the target and he was searching for some type of documents or something that might be saved on a computer. You sure Darcy's room wasn't tossed like Sarah's was?"

"I came out here the day it happened," Chase replied. "With the exception of the cash, Darcy's stuff wasn't touched."

"Weird," Benjo said. "I think I'm done here, Chase."

"Okay," Chase said as he stood up. He looked relieved. "Anything else I can help with?"

Benjo scratched his chin. "You say you have Sarah's purse and checkbooks and stuff?"

"Yes," Chase replied. "Sarah was a stickler for writing things down and keeping track of her finances."

"I need to get access to her cell phone records," Benjo said.

"You're in luck," Chase said. "Sarah and I shared a cell phone plan. It was cheaper for us to split a plan than for each of us to get our own. The account is in my name and Sarah was listed as a secondary user. I can get all of that just by logging onto my account on the computer."

"That's awesome," Benjo said sincerely. "It makes my job a lot faster and easier. As soon as you can get them, I need Sarah's financial info and cell phone records for the last three months before she killed." He looked at his watch. It was a few minutes past ten in the morning. "I'm going to take a drive out to where this is," he added as he held up the printed map. "Then, I'm meeting one of the detectives who helped investigate Sarah's death for lunch. I want to get his take on everything."

"What do you think you'll find out there?" Chase asked as he pointed to the map,

"No idea," Benjo replied honestly, "but this area meant something to Sarah. Based on the date and time stamp she printed this off just a couple of weeks prior to her death. It might be nothing, but I need to see." He paused. "I don't suppose I could hang on to the keys for this apartment, could I?"

Chase looked puzzled. "Sure," he said. "Why though?"

"I might need to come back here," Benjo explained. "It would save me having to coordinate with you if I need to come back for some reason. It will save us both some time."

"I've got to have them back in a few days," Chase said as he handed Benjo the keyring. "I have to finish moving her stuff by the end of the month."

"I'll get them back to you," Benjo promised as he slipped the keys into his pocket. "I'll lock up behind us."

Thirty-five minutes later Benjo pulled his truck over on the shoulder of State Highway Ten and killed the engine. According to the map he'd taken from Sarah's apartment, he was right where she had circled. He studied the map in his hand for a few seconds, then laid it on the seat and looked around. The patch of forest she'd circled was to his right. It looked like maybe two acres of typical forest for the region, complete with tall pines, a few sprawling oaks, and other smaller trees. Honeysuckle vines and kudzu were tangled everywhere. Benjo also noted a few areas of poison oak and ivy. The opposite side of the road to his left was more of the same tangled woods. There were no houses in sight. The last house Benjo had seen was probably a quarter of a mile back. It was just an empty country road in the middle of nowhere.

Benjo activated the truck's hazard lights and got out. He walked around his truck to where the grassy shoulder started turning into forest. He saw nothing unusual. He cocked his head and listened, but heard only birds and the hum of insects. Turning, he walked several paces along the edge of the woods, staying parallel to the road. He saw nothing, so he turned and walked back. Using his truck as a fixed point. He searched the shoulder of the road and the edge of the woods for about fifty yards in both directions. All he found was some litter and a discarded porn magazine.

Benjo found a spot that wasn't blocked by kudzu and briars and walked about ten feet into the woods beyond the roadside. Once again, he walked a fixed pattern, looking for anything unusual. He found absolutely nothing but pine cones. Now genuinely puzzled, Benjo emerged from the woods and walked back to his truck. An older Ford pickup truck was coming down the highway heading the same way Benjo's truck was facing. As Benjo reached the rear of his truck, the older Ford pulled onto the shoulder of the road behind Benjo's truck. Benjo walked back to the truck's driver's side just as the driver rolled his window down. The driver was an elderly man with the deeply tanned skin of someone who spent a lot of time outdoors, and a bald head covered by a stained baseball cap. He smiled at Benjo as Benjo walked up to the truck window, revealing a few missing teeth. "You broke down, son?" the old man asked.

Benjo shook his head. "No sir," he said. "I just stopped to check on something concerning this plot of land right here. You live in the area, by chance?"

The old man nodded. "You're in luck today, son. I do live in this area. Right down the road here about another quarter mile. That plot of land there actually belongs to me. Well, my family actually. Name's Tommy Pearson, by the way." He cocked his head. "What's concerning you about my land here?"

"Nice to meet you, Mr. Pearson," Benjo said. "It's kind of weird, but let me explain it to you. I have a friend who just passed away unexpectedly a while back. I was helping sort through her effects and we found a map that had this particular piece of land circled and a question mark beside it. We've been trying to figure out what exactly that meant because she lived in the city."

"That is weird," the old man answered. "She didn't have no notes or anything about it?"

"Nope," Benjo replied. "Have you ever had this plot up for sale or had anyone try to buy it from you?"

"Nope," Tommy replied instantly. "My family has owned about three hundred acres here since about 1890. We have a dairy operation." He pointed to the plot of woods Benjo had just walked out of. "If you walk into the woods there and keep going, in about a hundred yards you will come to one of our pastures with a barbed wire fence around it. From then on, it's open land to the barns and my house. Me and my brother live beside each other." He pointed through the windshield at the highway in front of the truck. "Our driveway is up the road there a piece."

"So, you've never had anyone approach you asking about buying this land, like a realtor or anything?" Benjo asked.

"No," Tommy said amicably. "We wouldn't sell it anyway. My daddy made us swear on his deathbed that we wouldn't ever sell any of the family land. He always said 'The Lord ain't making no more of it, so hang on to it.'"

Benjo grinned. "It makes sense," he said. "Is it possible that someone could have talked to another member of your family about selling it and you just don't know?"

Tommy shook his head so hard he nearly dislodged his cap. "No," he said. "It's just me and my wife at my house. Our kids all grew up and moved away for fancy jobs. It's my brother and his wife in his house. They ain't never had no kids. Anyone trying to buy this place would have had to talk to one of the four of us. My wife and sister-in-law couldn't keep a secret if you threatened them with bloody murder. My brother feels the same way about the land as I do. We gave our daddy our word."

"You have to respect that," Benjo said. "I know her family used to live in the area just down the road a few miles. Maybe she wanted to build a house out here and thought it was a good spot. Who knows? I do have one more question, though. Has anything ever happened here? Anyone ever died on this land? Like the police ever found any bodies here or there been a car wreck where someone died here?"

The old man looked at Benjo like he was an idiot. "Nope," he said. "There ain't many people around here, but we'd have heard if anything like that happened. People around here pay attention to things. They love to talk. All the old women huddle up after church on Sundays like a flock of cackling hens. It's a sight to see."

Benjo smiled. "Alright then, Tommy, I appreciate you talking to me and checking on me to make sure I didn't need help."

Tommy nodded. "No problem," he said. "You have a good day, son."

Benjo walked back to his truck and watched as the old man eased his truck back onto the highway and drove past him. As the old man drove away, Benjo got back into his own truck, started it, and did a tight u turn to head back to the city.

4

Sam's Family Restaurant was a bustling restaurant located just a couple of city blocks away from the county judicial complex that housed the sheriff's department and the county detention facility. Housed in a red brick building that had once been a hardware store, the good food and reasonable prices made the place popular with people who worked in the area. Even though it was still a few minutes before noon when Benjo walked through the front doors, the place was already filling up. As he approached the young lady behind the hostess' desk, he caught a glimpse of the fellow he was there to see. "I'm meeting someone," he said to the hostess. The young lady nodded and waved him on past. Benjo smiled and headed for a booth in the back corner of the dining room.

The occupant of that booth was a black male with horn-rimmed glasses, a shaved head that gleamed in the light, and a neat goatee. He wore a gray suit with a white shirt and a yellow bowtie. He was slender and, standing up, he was barely five and a half feet tall. He had that type of smooth, flawless skin that made guessing his age a nightmare. At the moment he was studying his menu intently. Benjo expected that; the man, Deacon "Deke" Jeter, did everything intently. That natural intensity was what made him a great detective. Deacon could focus it at will, whether he was looking at some tiny piece of evidence or interrogating a suspect. Deke was the best detective Benjo had worked with at the sheriff's department by far. He was also a good, personal friend that Benjo could rely on. Even better, he was also one of the investigators assigned to the Fleming case. Dale Marsh was the primary investigator, meaning it was his case, but Deacon was the secondary, which meant his job was to assist Marsh. Benjo knew that had to have rankled Deacon because his opinion of Marsh was similar to Benjo's. Deacon didn't hate Marsh like Benjo did, but he thought Marsh was a bad joke as a detective and he didn't trust the man at all.

Deacon looked up from his menu as Benjo slid into the booth on the opposite side of the table. "I figured you would be early," he said as he looked Benjo up and down. "My God, dude, you look like you've gained about twenty pounds of muscle. And when did you start letting five-year-olds color on your arms?"

Benjo settled down in the booth and smiled. "Probably about the same time you gave up on the baldness creams and just shaved those five hairs you called a hairdo off," he replied. "It's good to see you too, Deke."

Deke smiled and put down his menu. "It's been a while, my friend," he said. He studied Benjo for a few seconds. "You look completely different from when you left the department. What happened to the clean-shaven, short-haired white dude with no tattoos I used to know?"

"Jacob Clement happened," Benjo answered as he glanced at his menu. "Losing someone you love and then being the primary suspect in a murder can make you re-evaluate a lot of things. I realized one day that everything else in my life had changed completely, so I decided to change myself completely."

Deke arched an eyebrow. "Well, it worked," he said. "You went from generic white male to scary white male. I almost drew my gun when you walked in."

"That could be a good thing," Benjo said. "It might be helpful in my new line of work." He reached into his pocket and removed a small leather case. He flipped it open and slid it across the table to Deke. Deke picked it up and studied it. "Private Investigator," he read. He flipped it closed and slid it back to Benjo. "I'll be damned. What brought that on?"

"I needed something to do," Benjo answered. He left off the part about it being his psychologist's recommendation. "Unfortunately, being a detective doesn't prepare you for much except being a detective. I needed a reason to get out of the house, so I'm doing this. I'm working on my first case."

"Oh?" Deke said. "What type of case are you working on?"

Benjo was about to answer, but they were interrupted by the arrival of the waitress. They ordered iced teas and their lunch. They made small talk while they waited for their food. Deke was married with two teenaged daughters that were driving him nuts. The sheriff's department still had some of the same issues it had when Benjo left, only they had worsened. Sheriff Crowe, the county's elected sheriff for the last twenty years and a man Benjo had once greatly admired, was supposedly retiring and not running for re-election for a sixth term. Both men agreed that his retirement might be a good thing. For his first three four-year terms, Crowe had been a lawman first and a politician second. For the last two terms, he'd been more of a political animal first and lawman was a distant second. That was about the same time frame when Dale Marsh and his family's deep pockets had entered the picture. Rumor had it that the sheriff was retiring with plans to run for the state senate and maybe even governor.

Benjo also learned that Dale Marsh was still there and still a detective. Marsh was hired following the sheriff's re-election in 2012. He'd spent one year as a uniformed deputy on patrol, two years in Community Relations, and then been promoted to detective. For everyone else, it could take years to make detective. The running joke at the department was that it only took Marsh long enough for his daddy's check to the sheriff's re-election committee to clear. His lack of the hard-earned experience that comes from being a street cop, combined with natural stupidity and a lazy streak, made him a joke as a detective, to the point that he was only assigned open-and-shut cases that practically solved themselves. Still, he managed to mess those up so frequently that he usually ended up with another, actually good detective, assigned to assist him. There was good news, however. According to Deke, since the Jacob Clement incident, the other detectives treated Marsh like a pariah. Good cops wanted nothing to do with another cop who might have tipped off a criminal. They only interacted with him when they had to.

Their plates arrived and the two men ate in companionable silence. They had worked together many times as both uniformed deputies and as detectives, so there was no pressure to keep up the conversation. As he ate, Benjo noticed a few people glancing at them out of the corner of their eyes. It didn't bother him; he knew that him and the small, dapperly-dressed black man made an odd spectacle. He actually thought it was funny. Once they were done eating, both men pushed their plates away. The waitress hurried over and removed them. Once she was gone, Deke leaned back into the back of the booth and looked at Benjo. "You never did answer me," he said. "What type of case are you working, Benjo?"

"I'm actually working on a case right now for a local attorney named David Whiteside," Benjo said.

"I know David," Deke said as he took a sip of tea. "Good man. He handled my mom's will for her."

"I'm looking into the Sarah Fleming shooting from about two months ago," Benjo said. "You were secondary behind the sheriff's department's answer to Sherlock Holmes, Detective Dale Marsh. I have a few questions about the case."

Deke's demeanor changed instantly. "I should have known that you needed something when you invited me to lunch," he said with a groan. "Why has Whiteside got you looking into the Fleming case? That case has already been reviewed by the prosecutor's office and ruled self-defense."

"Sarah Fleming's mother worked for him for many years," Benjo replied. "Sarah's brother is working for him now before he heads off to law school in a few weeks. Sarah was like a daughter to David. David and Chase asked me to look into it because they have difficulty believing Sarah did what the Coles claim."

"The prosecutor's office reviewed our case file," Deke replied. "They said it was a justifiable shooting. State law says you can use deadly force to defend yourself or the life of another person. You know that."

"I know the law," Benjo said. "I also know that the prosecutors just review the case file the investigating officers send them. The only time they ask questions is when something isn't clear in the file. I know our prosecutor well enough to know that his office isn't going to try a case like this, especially against someone like the Coles, local pastors with money and influence. You know as well as I do that they're not going to court unless it's a surefire win for them."

Deke looked at Benjo. "I must admit the county prosecutor seemed very happy with Marsh's report. Marsh made it abundantly clear that, in his learned opinion, it was a clear-cut case of self-defense."

"We both know that Marsh got the case because it looked like an easy one and the sheriff wanted his golden boy to feel like a real detective," Benjo said with a trace of bitterness. "The only real investigator that got anywhere close to this case was you. That's why I'm talking to you, Deke, I want to know what you thought. Not what Marsh's so-called investigation found, but what you thought."

Deke turned and looked out the window by their booth. He stroked his goatee thoughtfully for a few seconds before looking back at Benjo. "What do you know about the case so far?"

"David had a copy of most of the case file he got through the state freedom of information laws," Benjo said. "With the case being officially closed following the prosecutor's justifiable homicide ruling, the sheriff's department had to release it to him. I've read the initial reports and I've seen the video evidence from the church's security system. I've also read the medical examiner's report. I've read the statements from the Coles, as well."

"So, your file doesn't have copies of the official statements from the church's secretary who called it in or from the church's security guy, a man named Paul Tucker?" Deke asked. He reached up and touched his right ear lobe casually as he spoke.

"No," Benjo admitted. "David told me that he thought his file was incomplete. What was in those statements?"

"A whole lot of nothing," Deke said. "The church secretary had a doctor's appointment that morning. It was supposed to take a couple of hours, so she wasn't supposed to come in until around eleven AM. Her treatment got canceled, so she came in a full hour earlier than expected. She found Sarah Fleming already shot and the Coles over her. Marsha called nine one one. Tucker, the church's security director, claims that he was way on the other side of the building taking a dump in the bathroom there. Tucker claims he didn't hear a thing until he got a call on his cell phone from Marsha West, the church secretary. He rushed over there to Monica's office, but the damage was done."

"I plan on talking to both of them soon," Benjo said. "Any way you can get me their statements? It might be helpful when I talk to them."

"Give me your email address before you leave," Deke said. "I'll email you copies of them as soon as I get back to the office."

"I appreciate it," Benjo said. "Now, Deke, tell me what's bothering you so bad about this case."

Deke cocked his head." What makes you think something is bothering me about the Fleming case?" he asked with a slight smile.

"I've known you for fifteen years, Deacon," Benjo said. "If there's one thing I've learned in those fifteen years, it's your body language. You reached up and touched your ear lobe. You do that when something is bugging you. If you're getting mad, you clear your throat and shuffle your left foot."

Deke looked surprised. "Really?" he asked. "I've never noticed that I do anything like that."

"Most people don't notice their own body language," Benjo said. "Go home and ask Charlotte if she's ever noticed any quirks like that. She's been married to you for twenty-four years, so I know she has. I noticed them the first time I ever worked with you."

Deke smiled broadly. "Damn, I miss having you around," he said. "You were Doctor Watson to my Sherlock Holmes."

"Don't flatter yourself," Benjo countered with a smile. "You were Watson. Now, between me and you as personal friends, talk to me, Deke."

Deke sighed and looked Benjo directly in the eyes. "This conversation never happened," he said in a low voice. "If I'm asked, I was eating lunch, you walked up and sat down, and two old friends shot the breeze for a while. We talked about football."

"Roger that," Benjo said. "You know you can trust me, Deke."

"I know," Deke said, "but that's my version and I'm sticking to it if asked. Now, before I tell you what I think, I know you read over everything and you said you watched the videos. Tell me, did you notice anything? This is a pop quiz to see if you're still up on your game."

"The first thing I noticed was on the video footage. On the video footage from the outside security cameras, Sarah Fleming drove up, parked at the side of the building, and walked straight to the side door, the side door that happened to be the straightest path to where Monica Cole's office was located," Benjo said. "That door was unlocked because she turned the handle and went right in. If memory serves from the times I went there when it was a store, that's a big building. How did she know to go to that particular door? If she was some deranged stalker looking for an unlocked door, logic says she would have gone to the main entrance doors of the building first. If she tried them and found them locked, then she would have moved on to try other doors."

"Bingo," Deke said, smiling like a proud father. "If you go check out the building- which I know you will- you will see that the door Sarah went to is the only door on that side of the building. She went straight to that door, a door that not even the staff who work at the church use regularly, and it happens to be the one that's accidentally left unlocked, even though the rest of the doors are normally kept locked. That's weird, to say the least."

"Agreed," Benjo said. "Now, your turn, Deke."

Deke leaned forward in his seat. "Sarah, this alleged stalker, happens to show up at the perfect time to attempt to kill Monica Cole," he said. "She shows up the day that the church secretary, Marsha West, happens to have a doctor's appointment that has her coming in at eleven instead of eight thirty like usual. Also, the church's security director happens to be way on the other side of the building in a remote bathroom dropping a load when all of this goes down. There are numerous bathrooms in the building, including one right down the hall from the church offices and one literally next door to the church security office where Tucker, the security director, works."

"Maybe he just likes his privacy," Benjo opined.

"You think Tucker, the security director, would be used to a lack of privacy, considering the amount of time he's spent behind bars," Deke added. "August Cole is a couple of years younger than Paul Tucker. They served time in prison together for a few months in 1997. Both were in for drug charges. Cole stayed on the straight and narrow after he got out. Tucker was in and out for the next seven years. He hasn't been arrested for anything since 2008. He says it's because Cole preached the Gospel to him and helped him straighten out."

"So, Tucker is a convicted felon," Benjo said as he rested his elbows on the table.

"He's stayed out of trouble since 2008," Deke said. "He's been on the church's payroll since 2012."

"Or he just became a better criminal who's learned how to avoid getting caught," Benjo said.

Deke smirked. "Benjo, are you trying to say a man can't find Jesus while he's in prison?" he asked sarcastically.

"Plenty of men find Jesus while they are doing time in prison," Benjo answered. "You know as well as I do that ninety-nine percent of them leave Jesus standing at the prison gate once they get out, though."

"Damn, you white people are a cynical bunch," Deke replied. "The other thing that troubles me about this is Sarah's medical records. More specifically, the lack thereof. I personally scoured Sarah's medical records. For someone who was supposedly mentally troubled enough to harass and then attack a woman in her office, there were no medical records that indicate Sarah ever sought any type of mental health treatment. I checked with every mental health professional and treatment center within driving distance. I even subpoenaed her health insurance company to see if they had ever paid out for any type of mental health treatment. Nothing."

"Maybe she paid cash," Benjo suggested.

"Even then, the doctor she was seeing would have records," Deke replied. "There's nothing out there. She could have used a fake identification when she was seen. Or, she could have been undiagnosed. However, you know that people who are troubled enough to do what Sarah allegedly did have a few behavioral red flags. I interviewed countless people who knew Sarah, either professionally or personally. If there was anything there, about fifteen different people missed it. Some of those people were trained medical professionals she worked with at the hospital."

"Her brother swears that he would have known if something was up with her," Benjo said. "He's pretty adamant about it." He took a sip of his iced tea. "Did you notice the papers?"

Deke looked puzzled. "What do you mean?"

"On the video, when Sarah got out of her car after she parked, she had a couple of folded papers in her hand," Benjo said. "She has them in her hand when she opens the side door. Nothing in the report I've seen says what those papers were or if they were recovered at the scene in Cole's office."

Deke was silent for several moments, lost in thought. "Benjo, I'm going to be honest with you," he finally said. "I didn't exactly kill myself on this case. It was Marsh's case and you know I hate working with his ass anyway. Per Captain Mason's orders when he called me to let me know I needed to respond with Marsh to the scene, my job was to not let Marsh screw it up too bad. Outside of helping with the paperwork and pointing out a few issues that bothered me, like the perfect timing, I stayed in my lane on this one. I'm kind of ashamed to admit that I didn't follow up on some things like I could have because I felt like Marsh should do it."

"I understand the feeling," Benjo said. "Marsh is the law enforcement equivalent of the kid in high school who was assigned to a group project, did absolutely nothing, and still got an 'A' from everyone else's hard work. I get it, Deke. Watch the video. Sarah took papers in the building with her. Nothing I've seen in the reports or the statements says what those papers were or what happened to them."

"Maybe it was just a ruse to get by the secretary," Deke said. "An 'I'm delivering these to Mrs. Cole' kind of thing."

"Then why didn't the Coles mention that in their statement?" Benjo asked. "Monica Cole said that Sarah wasn't carrying anything when she came into the office. Check her statement."

"Sarah could have dumped them into a trash can once she realized no one was there to stop her," Deke said.

"That's possible," Benjo conceded. "But it does make you wonder, doesn't it?"

Deke turned and looked out at the crowded dining room for several seconds. "You've got my curiosity up now, Benjo," he said as he turned back to look at him.

"I've got your curiosity up because this whole thing was still bugging you, Deke," Benjo replied. "Marsh investigated this case for literally four days, based on the dates on the reports. Straight up, if you were primary investigator on this case, what would you have done?"

"There are a few things I would have wanted more detail on before I turned it over to the prosecutor," Deke said. "It might legitimately be a case of self-defense. The timing issue and the straight path to the unlocked side door could just be weird coincidences. I saw the telephone records for Sarah Fleming as well. There were three telephone calls from her cell phone to Monica Cole's office during the two weeks preceding the shooting. One call lasted about five or so minutes, another one lasted just a few seconds, but there was also one that was almost twenty minutes. Monica Cole claimed she was trying to reason with Sarah and minister to her, but who wants to do that with a deranged stalker? Speaking for myself, I would have looked a lot closer at them than Marsh did."

"Did you know Sarah's apartment got broken into and ransacked the day she was killed?" Benjo asked. "A white male impersonated a maintenance worker for the apartment complex where she rented an apartment, broke in, and searched Sarah's stuff. Just her stuff, too. The roommate's stuff wasn't touched. The only thing stolen was some of the roommate's cash and Sarah's laptop."

"Really?" Deke asked. "I didn't know that."

"The city police have the report," Benjo said. "That's another weird coincidence, making a total of three by my count. Three coincidences in a row on the same case? The chances of that are about mathematically equivalent to winning the lottery." He looked across the table at his friend. "This case has more red flags than a red flag factory. I'm going to stay on this case until I've got some answers. I just want you to know that it's not my intention to make you to look bad if I turn up anything."

Deke shrugged nonchalantly. "As luck would have it, I have a copy of the email I sent to Captain Mason and Sheriff Crowe the day before the case was turned over to the prosecutor's office where I expressed my concerns with the investigation," he said. "Brother, I was born at night, but it wasn't last night."

Benjo breathed a sigh of relief. Before he could say anything else. the waitress returned to bring them their check. Benjo grabbed it as soon as the waitress put it down. "Lunch is on me, Deke. I appreciate you taking the time," he said as soon as the waitress was gone.

"Not a problem," Deke said. "I do have one question, though. Are you sure the way you feel about Marsh isn't affecting how you're looking at this case? I don't like Marsh, but you despise him. Is that a factor?"

"I do despise Marsh," Benjo answered honestly. "The man is responsible for Presley being murdered. He tipped off a criminal that he was the subject of an investigation. Granted, he probably had no idea that Jacob Clement would hire people to try to kill me, but that doesn't excuse the fact that he tipped the man off."

"After you left the department, Marsh called a meeting with everyone in the detective division," Deke said. "The gist of it was that he and his family did have a business relationship with Clement and that he had met Clement on a few social occasions, but he had never told Clement anything about being the target of an investigation. He claimed that he never knew you were investigating Clement."

"That's a damned lie and you know it," Benjo said irritably. "You know how the detective division worked; everyone knew what everyone else was doing."

"I'm just curious as to how you're so sure it was Marsh," Deke asked.

Benjo pulled out his wallet and left some cash on the table as a tip for the waitress before looking his old friend in the eyes. "Who else could it have been, Deke? " he asked. "It amazes me how Marsh gets the benefit of the doubt from everyone."

Deke held up his hands in a placating gesture. "Calm down, big boy," he said. "I've been on your side from the get go. Remember?"

Benjo took a deep breath. "You're right, dude," he said. "I'm sorry if I came across with an attitude."

"All I'm saying is don't let your hatred of Marsh and the chance to make him look stupid cloud your judgement," Deke said calmly. "Investigate this thing the way I know you're capable of. If it blows back on anyone, including me, then it does." He glanced down at his watch. "I've got to run, brother. I'm due in court in twenty minutes."

"Be careful out there," Benjo said.

Deke stood up. "On a side note, you still got that saber-toothed tiger you claim is a house cat?"

Benjo smiled. Deke and his wife had come to Benjo's house for dinner a few times before Presley's death and Benjo's resignation. Both Deke and his wife, Charlotte, had been amazed by Harley's size. The cat would lay in Charlotte's lap and she would pet it and fuss over it the whole time. "Leave my wee kitten out of this," he said. "That's my buddy."

Deke just shook his head. "Looking at you, with the beard and tattoos, you would assume that you had a pit bull or a big-ass Rottweiler with a spiked collar as a pet."

"Shouldn't a black man be the last person in the world to stereotype somebody?" Benjo asked innocently.

Deke laughed out loud. "Well-played, my friend," he said as he turned and headed for the door. "Appreciate the lunch."

Benjo sat there and watched his friend leave. His conversation with Deke had been fruitful. He knew how good a detective his friend was, and if Deke was troubled by certain things in the case, then those things were worth looking at. He couldn't judge Deke harshly for not doing more with his concerns before; sometimes you had to play political games if you wanted to keep your career on track. He knew Deke well enough to know that, politics and career aside, the man would do what was right if he found evidence that Sarah Fleming's death was anything but what it seemed to be on the surface.

Once Deke was gone, Benjo headed for the counter to pay for their food. He had one more place he wanted to check out before it got too late.

5

Benjo studied the building that was now Hope Springs Church on Highway 40 as he approached it in his truck. The building located just outside the city limits had started life as a huge retail store owned by a national chain that sold electronics. The building sat along a stretch of the highway that was lined on both sides with similar types of big-box retail establishments, strip malls, and chain restaurants that sold everything ranging from hamburgers to lobster. The former electronics superstore had undergone an extensive exterior renovation, with a new paint job, an awning with the church's name, and stonework bordering the four sets of double doors that were the front entrance. Flower gardens and landscaping, complete with a flowing water feature, took up most of the front exterior wall. According to what he'd read on the church's social media pages, the water feature and the church's name came from a biblical verse about God being an ever-flowing spring of hope, love, and mercy. The water feature was a nice touch. He could tell that the architect, builders, and landscapers had tried really hard, but the building really didn't look that much different from the huge home improvement store it shared a parking lot with. Other than the water feature, the only other really eye-catching thing about the building was a giant metal cross attached to the roof. The cross stood at least twenty feet above the roof. Benjo had never been inside the church, but based on what he'd seen in videos posted online, the interior of the church seemed like it was a different story. The interior was all state-of-the art sound and lighting equipment, gleaming wood, and upholstered benches with stadium-style seating that offered great views of the stage and pulpit area.

Benjo turned his truck into the parking lot and headed for the church. The parking lot was huge and newly-painted with arrows and new signs directing traffic flow. Several sections of parking spaces were marked for new visitors. Another section was marked specifically for bus parking, seemingly indicating that people came by the busload every Sunday. As he drew closer to the church's main entrance, he noticed three signs mounted on a sign post where the sidewalk met the parking lot. One sign said Main Lobby and had an arrow indicating that a person should go through the glass doors ahead. A second, smaller sign said Church Offices Inside. It also had an arrow pointing toward the four sets of double glass doors that served as the church's main entrance. The third, smaller sign below that one said Office Hours, Monday-Friday, 8:30 AM until 5 PM.

Benjo noted the signs, but didn't stop to enter the building. He kept driving past the front of the building to the front corner of the building. He turned the corner and drove on around the building. He counted entrances as he drove down the side, around the back of the building, and then to the other side. Not counting the garage door at the rear loading dock area, there were seven other doors. On the final side as Benjo approached the front of the building again, there were two doors. The door closest to the front of the building on that side was the one Sarah had found unlocked and used as a point of entry according to the police report. The side of the building he was on had one line of parking spaces near the wall of the building, a lane for travel, and then a grass embankment and a six-foot-tall wooden privacy fence. On the other side of that privacy fence was an apartment complex. Benjo drove into one of the parking spaces closest to the door Sarah had entered, killed the engine, and hopped out.

He noticed the black half-dome mounted several feet high up on the wall near the door. That was the camera that had caught the video of Sarah parking, getting out of her car with the papers in her hand, and walking to the door Benjo was now approaching. There was no sign on the door or anything else that made it stand out above any of the other doors that were on the two sides and back of the building. "Why did you come to this door, Sarah?" Benjo muttered to himself as he walked. The door had a handle instead of a knob, so Benjo walked up and tried the handle. The door was locked. He noted that there was no keyhole in the center of the handle where a keyhole should be, meaning the door locked from the inside and couldn't be accessed from the outside with a key. Back when the building was a retail store, the door had probably been an emergency exit only.

Benjo stood there for several seconds rattling the handle. It didn't give a bit. Benjo released the handle and stood there for a few moments looking around and thinking. The front corner of the building was about twenty feet away. Based on what he'd seen as he drove to and around the building, if he went around that corner, he would have to walk about another fifty feet or so to the sidewalk that took him to the main church entrance and the signs that pointed to the main lobby and the church entrance. One of those signs clearly indicated where the church offices, including the Cole's offices, were located and when they were open. For some reason, Sarah had ignored that main entrance, the signs there, and all of the other doors to come to this more secluded side of the building. The opposite side of the building faced the home improvement store across the parking lot. The front of the building faced the main highway. The back of the building faced another parking lot exit and a street that was one of the main roads to the apartment complex on the other side of the privacy fence. If she had wanted to try to sneak in without being seen by someone on the outside of the building, this was the side to come to. However, the security camera mounted on the wall was blindingly obvious, so that kind of ruled out the sneaking part.

Benjo was pondering it all when he heard footsteps on the other side of the door. There was a loud squeak as the handle turned and the door was opened from the inside. A skinny, older man who looked in his late sixties pushed the door open and stood in the doorway. He wore black pants and a white shirt with a gold badge and patches from a private security company. The old man was bald and wore wide-framed glasses that covered nearly half his face. He wore a gun belt with a holstered revolver that looked like it had once belonged to Jesse James. The patches and name tag on the shirt identified him as John from American Federated Security. He was glaring at Benjo like he'd just caught him climbing out of his wife's bedroom window. One hand was resting on the butt of the old revolver. "Can I help you, sir?" the old man asked. There was a hint of nervousness in his voice.

Benjo smiled disarmingly. "Perhaps you can, sir," he said in his most friendly manner. When all else fails, nothing works like the truth. "My name is Benjo Lane, sir. I used to work for the county sheriff's department, but now I'm a private investigator."

"You here from that lady at the television station?" the security guard asked suspiciously. "I know Pastor Cole has already threatened Channel Seven with a lawsuit if she didn't stop coming around here. Did she hire you to pester them instead?"

"You mean Kathy Miller, the reporter that does the investigative stories for Channel Seven news?" Benjo asked, taking a stab in the dark. He knew her name simply because he'd seen her face on commercials for WTLN, the local station which aired on channel seven. She hosted an investigative reporting segment called Getting Answers. It was very popular and a couple of segments had even won major awards for investigative reporting. The security guard nodded. "No sir, I don't work for Channel Seven," Benjo replied calmly. "I've been hired by the family of a woman named Sarah Fleming. Does that name ring a bell?"

John nodded. "That was the crazy lady that came here a couple of months ago and tried to kill Mrs. Cole," he said gruffly. "That incident is the reason why the church hired us to patrol their building." He looked at Benjo like Benjo smelled bad. "What's there to investigate? Police already said shooting the girl was self-defense."

"John, I told them the same damned thing," Benjo said with feigned exasperation. "You know how people are, though. They think they can sue and get some money, even when there's not a case or they were the ones in the wrong. The family is paying me pretty good, so I've got to make it look good, if you know what I mean."

"You got any identification?" John asked as he held the door open with one hand and kept the other one on his gun.

"I do," Benjo said. "I'm going to reach into my back pocket and get my state private investigators license. I'm going to move nice and slow, okay?"

"Don't try anything funny, son," the old guard warned.

"Wouldn't even consider it," Benjo said, even though he'd actually weighed his chances in case the old man got crazy. Considering the distance between them, the old man's age and physical condition, and that the guard was having to hold the door open because it was designed to close automatically, Benjo knew that disarming him wouldn't be an issue if the need arose. However, at the time, there was no need for anything so drastic. Instead, Benjo slowly removed the leather case holding his license. He opened it to show his credentials and held it up for the old security guard to see.

The old man visibly relaxed when he saw Benjo's identification. "I'm going to need to call this in to Mr. Tucker. He's the director of church security. He's here today."

"That's great," Benjo said. "I was hoping to get a chance to talk to him anyway. Do you want me to hold the door for you while you grab your radio off your belt?"

John looked down and realized that the hand he needed to grab the radio in the holder on his belt was indeed occupied with holding the door open. The door had an automatic closing mechanism at the top. "Go ahead," he said.

Benjo stepped forward and grabbed the door to hold it open. The guard stepped back to grab the radio on his belt. As John retrieved his radio and started using it, Benjo studied the inside handle on the door. The door had a panic bar on it, meaning that someone had to push the handle mounted about waist high across the door for it to unlock and open. There was a keyhole on the panic bar to the left of the handle. Benjo was familiar with this type of hardware. The door would normally stay closed and locked, but if you used a key, you could lock the latch back so that the door could be opened from the outside by turning the handle.

John put his radio back on his belt. "Mr. Tucker will be right out," he said.

"Good," Benjo said. "So, John, if they hired your company after the incident here where the girl got shot, who did security before that?"

"Mr. Tucker was the fulltime security director," John said. "On Sundays and for special events, they hire off-duty sheriff's department personnel to watch the parking lots and the lobby. I just work Monday to Friday eight to five. At night, there's no one. The building has an alarm system."

The news that the church hired off-duty sheriff's personnel to work extra duty surprised Benjo, but he kept it hidden. "I imagine you need armed security now, especially with some of the mass shootings happening at churches I've seen on the news."

Before John could answer, the sound of footsteps hurrying down the corridor behind John distracted them. A few seconds later, a man that Benjo assumed was Paul Tucker turned the corner from a hallway that intersected the hallway where they were. Benjo studied Tucker as he approached. Tucker was a couple of inches taller than Benjo's six feet and weighed maybe thirty pounds more, most of it around the mid-section. His hair was short and he had a full beard that came to a point a few inches below his chin. He had deep-set eyes with a scar over his left eye. He wore khaki pants and a golf shirt with the Hope Springs logo embroidered over the left breast. He had a big chest and thick arms with several tattoos visible on his forearms and the back of his hands. He looked like a brawler. He did not look happy to see Benjo.

"Mr. Tucker, this is him," John said when the man reached them. "This is Mr. Tucker, the church's director of security," he added, speaking to Benjo.

Tucker stepped forward and leaned against the door to hold it open. "Hit the road, John. I've got this," Tucker said harshly. The old security guard nodded, turned, and walked away down the hallway. Judging from the stiffness in his shoulders, the security guard was not happy with how Tucker had spoken to him.

Benjo smiled and offered his hand to Tucker for a handshake. Tucker ignored Benjo's proffered hand. "Who are you and what do you want?" he asked brusquely.

Benjo retracted his hand. According to the biography on the church's website, Tucker had once been a prison inmate with a rough past. Thanks to the preaching of Pastor August Cole through his prison ministry, Tucker, a man August had served time with in his earlier, rougher days, had found Jesus Christ and Jesus had changed him into a better person. If that was so, Benjo wondered what kind of person Tucker must have been in the past, because the current version of him came across as a complete ass. According to the website, besides being over security, Tucker also ministered to prison inmates and was quite a soul saver himself. Benjo didn't see it. He immediately didn't like the man and he could tell the feeling was mutual.

"My name is Benjo Lane," Benjo said politely. "I am a private investigator. I have been retained by the family of Sarah Fleming to investigate her death at the hands of Monica Cole."

Tucker glared at him and crossed his arms across his chest. Benjo noticed that he had words tattooed across the knuckles of each hand in black, block letters. The left hand had the word Rise and the right hand had the word Again. The words looked professionally done, unlike some of the other tattoos Tucker had visible on his forearms. Some of them were very obviously amateur and probably done in prison. "What's there to investigate, man? The police already investigated it and the prosecutor closed the case," he said with a hint of anger in his voice. "It's pretty simple. Don't stalk somebody and then try to kill them and you won't end up dead. Seems like someone who wasn't an idiot would realize that."

Benjo couldn't decide if the idiot comment was directed at the dead girl or him. Regardless, he didn't take the bait. The last thing he wanted was to brawl with Tucker. Benjo felt like he could win the fight, but it would be ugly. Tucker looked like the type you would have to beat nearly to death to get him to stay down. Benjo didn't need that drama, at least not right now. "The family hired a lawyer because they feel like there might be more to it than that, sir," he said. "The lawyer, David Whiteside, hired me to review the facts of the case and decide if there was anything there."

"There's not," Tucker growled. "The cops were very thorough. As a matter of fact, there was this gay-looking black detective that really put poor Monica and everyone else who was here that day through the ringer. He pissed a lot of people off with that stuff. Even with that flamer trying to make something out of nothing, it was still ruled justifiable."

For a man who was allegedly a minister of the Gospel, Tucker certainly didn't show it through his words. Benjo was familiar with the Bible, having sought solace in its pages following his wife's death. He certainly hadn't seen the adjectives 'gay-looking' and 'flamer' used to describe anyone in its pages. He wondered if Deke would be offended by hearing himself described in such a way. He doubted it; he knew Deke had been called worse to his face by better quality people than Tucker seemed to be. "Well, Mr. Tucker, I know that," Benjo said with forced pleasantness. "I was just hired to review everything and make sure it was what it looks like. That's all."

"Let me guess, they want to sue the Coles," Tucker said. "It's always about money."

"I don't know what their intent is," Benjo replied. "I simply would like to talk with you, and eventually the Coles, to go over everything again. If there's nothing there, there's nothing there."

"The Coles are good people and they are both still torn up about what happened," Tucker said. "That's all I have to say about it. I'm not talking to you and I'll bet they won't either, so hit the road. If you want to ask them yourself, they have an attorney that represents them and the church."

"Fair enough," Benjo said. He reached into his pocket and removed a couple of the business cards he'd had made when he got his private investigator's license. The card had Benjo Lane, Private Investigator, and his cell phone number on it. Nothing else. He offered Tucker a couple of the cards. "Will you take a couple of my cards in case you or them change your mind?"

"We won't," Tucker said flatly as he ignored the cards in Benjo's hand.

"Look, Mr. Tucker," Benjo said calmly. "I'm going to do my job and investigate what happened here. Just so you know, I'm really good at what I do." He glanced at his wristwatch. "For example, I've only been at it for a little over five hours now, but I've already found a couple of things that just don't quite set right with me. Can you even begin to imagine what I might find if I *really* start looking hard?"

"Oh yeah?" Tucker said defensively. "What could you possibly find that the police didn't?"

"Have you even wondered for a moment why I came to this door instead of coming into the church offices through the lobby?" Benjo asked. From the confused look on Tucker's face, Benjo knew it had never even crossed the man's mind. "I came to this door because this is the door Sarah Fleming used to come into your building to confront Monica Cole. The first question that popped into my mind when I got this case is why this door? Why not just stroll in through the lobby like anyone else?"

"She was sneaking in, Einstein," Tucker said sarcastically. "Read the police report."

"That's very good theory," Benjo said, "but it still doesn't quite explain why this door and not one of the seven other doors. What do you think the chances are of her picking this one out of all of those others and it being unlocked? I noticed that this door has to be manually unlocked with a key or it locks automatically. If it's not unlocked from the inside with a key, the handle on the outside won't even turn. On the video, Sarah comes straight to this door, turns the handle, and walks in. What are the odds?"

Tucker's face turned a deeper shade of red. "Like I told the police the day it happened, it's not against the law for one of our staff to mess up and leave a door unlocked. One of the staff accidentally left it unlocked. The girl just got lucky."

"Why would the staff unlock it?" Benjo asked. "There's nothing on this side of the building like a trash can or delivery area, nothing to make someone need to unlock it. So, why did they unlock it? Actually, who left it unlocked? Surely, there's a limited number of people with a key to this lock. Did anyone admit to leaving it unlocked? If that's in the police file, I missed it."

"There are several people who work here who have keys," Tucker retorted. "The police and I asked the people with keys to the doors who might have unlocked it. Do you think anyone admitted it, knowing they might lose their job or be in trouble with the cops over it?"

"See, that's a reasonable response," Benjo said. "That's why it's important that I talk to people; getting their side of the story can help you see things another way. You sure you don't want to talk to me or take my card to give the Coles?"

Tucker's reply was to smirk, step back out of the doorway, and release the door. As the door started to close, he raised his hand and extended his middle finger to Benjo. "Get off our property before I have you arrested for trespassing," he said.

"What would Jesus think?" Benjo asked as the door closed the final few inches. If there was a reply, Benjo couldn't hear it through the thick metal door. He slipped his business cards back into his pocket and walked back to his truck. He got in, started the truck, and drove across the parking lot. Once he was off of the what he assumed was the church's property, he pulled over, parked, and took out his cell phone. He hummed to himself as he dialed a number from memory.

Deke Jeter answered on the second ring. "Hey, Deke, it's me. Does Captain Forrester still handle sheriff's department personnel working off duty assignments?" Per sheriff's department policy, any sworn officers who worked a side job as security had to get approval from the department. Captain Forrester, the captain over the Uniformed Patrol Division, was the man who kept up with the off-duty work opportunities and either approved or denied them.

"Yes," Deke said.

"I need a favor," Benjo said. "I just left Hope Springs Church. I met Paul Tucker, whom I might add is a positively charming individual."

"Ain't he though," Deke said. "I'll bet after about five seconds of talking to him, you were wondering how the man is supposedly a minister."

"I was," Benjo said. "He remembered you from when you interviewed him after the shooting. While I was there at the church, I learned that they employ off-duty sheriff's personnel as security on Sundays. Can you call Forrester and ask him if he handles security jobs for Hope Springs Church? If he does, ask him if Dale Marsh has ever worked for Hope Springs."

Deke was quiet for so long that Benjo was starting to wonder if he had lost the connection. "There's no way Marsh is stupid enough to not tell anyone that he was working extra duty at a place run by someone he's assigned to investigate," Deke finally said.

"It's Marsh," Benjo said. "We need to make sure. You know Marsh has a history of not revealing conflicts of interest,"

"I'll call Forrester right now," Deke said. "I'll bet you fifty bucks that not even Marsh is that shady, especially not after what happened with Clement. He came dangerously close to getting indicted for obstruction of justice for that fiasco. The only thing that saved him was the state police couldn't find solid evidence he told Clement anything." Benjo said.

"I'll take that wager," Benjo said. "Getting paid about fifty bucks an hour to sit in a parking lot and direct traffic is just the type of easy money Marsh would jump on. Call me when you know."

Benjo ended the call and drove away from Hope Springs. He had barely made it two blocks when his cell phone rang again. It was Deke. Benjo grabbed the phone out of the holder on his console and answered it. "What's the word?" he asked.

"Marsh worked for them regularly," Deke said. From the tone of his voice, Benjo could tell that Deke was fuming. "He hasn't worked for them since the shooting there, but he did about two Sundays a month before that."

"And he didn't mention that when he was assigned the case, did he?" Benjo asked bitterly.

"I'm going to go talk to Captain Mason right now," Deke said. Captain Dan Mason was the captain over the Investigations Division. He had once been Benjo's boss. Mason was a good man who tried to do what was right most of the time. Mason had wanted Marsh gone after the facts about his relationship with Clement came out, but the sheriff had overruled him. "The whole Fleming case just turned into a crap sandwich with an extra helping of crap."

"Let me know how it goes," Benjo said. "I'm on my way to talk to Kathy Miller, the investigative reporter at Channel Seven."

"Why her?" Deke asked.

"Apparently, she is as interested in the Coles as I am," Benjo replied. "I'm curious as to why."

6

WTLN Channel Seven News occupied the first two floors of a five-story concrete and glass building in the center of the city. Across the street from the main entrance of the building was a town square with a fountain, benches, a few trees, and a nicely-manicured lawn. Benjo sat down on one of the park benches shaded by the limbs of a spreading oak and waited. He glanced at his watch and saw that it was few minutes until three. Kathy Miller was supposed to meet him there at three. He settled back onto the bench and watched a couple of young children run around the fountain. Their mother, a pretty redhead who was pushing another smaller child in a stroller, watched from another bench on the opposite side of the fountain. Every so often she would glance across the fountain at Benjo and watch him for a few seconds. Benjo couldn't tell if she was doing it out of interest or fear. With his hair, beard, and tattoos, he elicited one or the other from most people, even if they wanted to admit it or not.

Much to Benjo's surprise, Kathy Miller had proven very easy to get in touch with. Once he'd finished his call with Deke, he'd looked up the television station's number and called it. A pleasant receptionist had put him through to Kathy Miller's office where he'd gotten a message asking him to leave a voicemail. His message was simple: "My name is Benjo Lane. I'm a private investigator looking into the Coles at Hope Springs Church. I hear you might be doing the same." He'd ended that message with his cell phone number. Kathy Miller had returned his call within five minutes. They had arranged to meet here in the park across from her office at three PM. He'd given her a brief description of himself to help her find him.

At three o'clock on the dot, a tall, willowy blonde in khaki slacks, a pink blouse, and aviator-style sunglasses emerged from the main entrance to the building across the street. She waited until traffic cleared and then crossed the street to the park. She paused to look around for a moment before she saw him on the bench and headed his way. Benjo stood up as she approached him. When she reached him, she stopped, slid the sunglasses down, and looked him over. To Benjo, it didn't seem like he was being judged by appearance as much as he was being weighed and measured as a human being. "Mr. Lane, I presume?" the woman asked.

"Yes," Benjo said, "and you would be Kathy Miller, investigative reporter."

She pushed the sunglasses back up on her nose and smiled at him. She was much prettier in person than she was on television and she had the prettiest, whitest teeth that Benjo had ever seen. "That's me," she said. "Mind if I sit?" she added as she pointed to the bench.

"By all means," Benjo said. "Do you mind if I sit beside you?"

Kathy sat down and patted the bench beside her. "That's what benches are made for," she said. "You're very polite. First, you stand up as I approach, then you ask permission to sit beside me. You don't encounter many gentlemen nowadays."

"Manners are important," Benjo replied with a smile as he sat beside her. "I imagine you're busy, so I appreciate you taking the time to meet with me. I'm sure my call was unexpected."

"To be honest, I wondered if you might have been sent to set me up, Mr. Lane," Kathy said. "I've spent the last hour or so making a few calls and checking up on you."

"Please call me Benjo," Benjo said. "I assume I must have checked out because you're sitting here beside me."

"And I'm Kathy," Kathy replied. "Your name seemed familiar as soon as I heard it on my voicemail,"

"It does stand out," Benjo conceded. "It's a family name that's been passed down on my mother's side, according to my mother. Either that or she was high from the pain medication after delivering me. Sometimes I can't decide which one it was. "

Kathy chuckled. "I searched your name on the internet first. I came across several news stories about you. As soon as I saw the first story, I remembered you. You won quite a few awards as a police officer and detective, including a couple for valor. It also seems you were quite the detective. The majority of the stories were about your wife's death and Jacob Clement. I'm sorry about your wife."

"Thank you," Benjo said. "I left the sheriff's department following her death and now I'm a private investigator. I've been retained to look into the death of Sarah Fleming. She's the young woman who was shot by Monica Cole after allegedly attacking her in her office at the church."

"I'm familiar," Kathy said. "We covered the story. Supposedly the girl had been stalking Monica Cole with harassing phone calls and approaching her after a service. She sneaked into the building and tried to stab Monica. Monica shot her in self-defense. Our crime reporter, Jesse, reported on the story when the prosecutor ruled it justifiable homicide and closed the case."

"I have started digging into the case," Benjo continued. "It didn't take me long at all to find several troubling things that make me wonder if the official version might be wrong."

"What do you mean by 'wrong?'" Kathy asked. She reached in her pocket and removed a small digital recorder. She held it up. "You mind?" she asked.

"I prefer to be off the record for now," Benjo said. "I think we can help each other. I'll tell you what I've got. You tell me why you are looking into the Coles."

"What makes you think I'm looking into the Coles?" Kathy asked innocently.

"I went to Hope Springs Church today," Benjo said. "I wanted to see the building in order to determine if a theory I have is possible. I met a security guard there who asked me if I was working for you and your station when he found out I was a PI. He said you had been pestering the Coles."

Kathy smiled. "If trying to expose them for the frauds they are is 'pestering', then I guess I am," she said as she slid the recorder back into her pocket.

"You think the Coles are frauds?" Benjo asked.

"And you seem to think they might be murderers," Kathy retorted. "If Sarah Fleming's death was not justifiable self-defense, then it was murder."

"Fair enough," Benjo said. "I'll go first. I don't think what happened with Sarah Fleming is anything like what the Coles have portrayed it to be. Granted, I'm early in my investigation, but I have yet to find anything that leads me to believe Sarah was struggling with any mental health issue that would have made her fixate on Monica Cole. Everyone I've interviewed says she was normal and happy. I have yet to figure out what her connection with the Coles was, but I will." He continued, listing all of the things he'd found thus far that struck him as odd about Sarah's trip to the church and her death. He ended his monologue with the revelation that the lead detective on the case had actually been on the Cole's payroll prior to being assigned the case.

"Wow," Kathy said once Benjo was finished. "We were led to believe that it was an open and shut case. Sarah Fleming was a deranged stalker who targeted Monica Cole for some unknown reason and then tried to kill her." She shook her head. "Detective Marsh handled the case, even though he had worked for the Coles in the past? How is that not a conflict of interest?"

"That's a valid question that deserves an answer," Benjo said. "It seems like a determined investigative reporter could get an answer."

"Oh, don't worry," Kathy said with a slight smile. "What do you think really happened with Sarah Fleming? What led to her confrontation with Monica Cole?"

Benjo shrugged. "No idea," he said with complete honesty. "At least not yet. I will find out though."

"I'll bet you do," Kathy replied. "You strike me as the type who finishes what they start. I wish you luck, though. Nothing is ever what it seems with the Coles."

"Now your turn," Benjo said. "Why is an investigative reporter from the local news looking into the Coles?"

"A source of mine came to me a little over a year ago," Kathy said as she settled back on the bench. "He has a friend who works for the Coles at the church. We'll call the friend Anonymous, just for safety's sake. Anonymous was at a private party with my source and got wasted. Anonymous started running their mouth about the Coles, claiming that their private persona is completely different from what the public and their church members see. Supposedly the people who actually work at the church hate the Coles because they treat their employees like trash. Anonymous, who my source says works in a position at the church where they would know, claimed that the Coles do some really creative bookkeeping with the money that they take in at the church. A lot more goes into the Cole's pockets than ever goes toward the various ministries they claim the money is for when they ask for it on Sunday. Also, Anonymous had an interesting fact about Paul Tucker. Paul Tucker, the church's head of security and an associate pastor, is actually a founding member of the Southern Devils, a motorcycle gang based in this area."

"What? A righteous and holy man like Tucker? Tell me it ain't so," Benjo said sarcastically.

"I know, right?" Kathy replied with a smile.

"I'm familiar with the Southern Devils from when I worked with the sheriff's department," Benjo said. "They have about eighty full members of the gang scattered throughout the Southeast. Their name kept coming up during drug and prostitution investigations. I think we arrested a couple of low- level members over the years for some minor stuff, but never any of their top people, to my knowledge. I also think they rent themselves out as muscle for other motorcycle gangs. I've also heard that they sometimes work with Mexican drug cartels." Suddenly, a light bulb flipped on in his mind. "Damn it, I knew I had seen that tattoo before, but I just couldn't place it."

"Beg pardon?" Kathy asked with a confused look on her face.

"Paul Tucker had the words Rise Again tattooed on the knuckles of his hands," Benjo said. "The moment I saw that, I knew that I'd seen it before. Now, I remember. Full members of the Southern Devils have it tattooed on their hands. It's supposed to stand for the Confederacy rising again. I've seen it on the knuckles of a couple of the guys I questioned who belonged to the club."

"Really?" Kathy asked excitedly. "I met with Tucker about three months ago when I first started sniffing around to see if the financial allegations might actually be true. I never noticed the tattoos. If he has those tattoos and that's a sign of membership in the biker gang, then the other part of what Anonymous claimed during their drunken rant might be true."

"And what was that?" Benjo asked.

"Anonymous, who works for the Coles at the church, claimed that Tucker regularly brings in wads of money to the church in gym bags. Anonymous said that the Coles would then mix that money in with the regular cash donations they got on Sunday to hide its source."

"That sounds like it might be money laundering to me," Benjo said. "If Tucker is high up in the Southern Devil's leadership, it might be his job to help launder the money they are making from whatever illegal things they are involved in. If you think about it, a church would be an excellent way to hide dirty money."

"Exactly," Kathy said. "Churches are exempt from federal and state taxes. The IRS and state tax authorities are usually very hands-off when it comes to auditing a church's financial records. Also, if a church is registered as a non-profit charitable organization, they can be fairly lenient with their records on disbursements. They can give money away to people or organizations fairly freely as a part of any charity the church operates. They have a huge amount of discretion regarding who gets money and how much. It's nuts. A church can get away with stuff that would get a person or any other type of business audited mercilessly."

"So, Hope Springs Church could take in a bunch of unexplainable cash, claim it came from the collection plates, and then disburse that money as a donation to another person or organization?" Benjo asked.

"Yes," Kathy said. "Let's say I'm the chief financial officer at a church. You give me twenty grand in dirty cash. I take that twenty grand and mix it in with the money gathered from collections on Sunday. Then, I put that money in the bank. You have a fake company that I can claim my church does business with. You give me a fake invoice so I can write you a check for that twenty grand a few days later. Granted, you will have to pay taxes on that twenty grand through your fake company, but that money will be all nice and legal with no questions as to where it came from. Or, you set up a fake charity and my church writes you a check to help your charity minister to those less fortunate. Once again, you have a nice explanation for where that twenty grand came from."

Benjo gave a low whistle. "That's actually pretty smart," he said. "I know money launderers love businesses that handle a lot of cash because it makes hiding the money's source easier. They still have to be careful because the federal and state tax authorities keep an eye out for anything that looks too shady. The same tax authorities won't give a church a second glance, however. Also, there's no way any government investigator can tell you how much money someone put in the collection box. You're talking hundreds of people putting bills of various denominations in there. It could be five bucks, ten bucks, or two thousand dollars. It's completely untraceable."

"Did you know that August and Monica Cole are the chief financial officers for Hope Springs Church, including the separate ministries the church runs?" Kathy asked. "There is no other church of comparable size and membership numbers that has the senior pastor as the chief financial officer. Most of them have an accountant or team of accountants. The Coles have a team of low-level employees that count the collections on Sunday, but the Coles actually handle the paperwork and make the bank deposits. The Coles also wrote every check the church disbursed."

"I can't believe that no one has any concerns about that," Benjo said. "You would think that some of the church deacons or members would at least have a few questions about that."

"You would think," Kathy said. "Have you ever been to the church, Benjo?"

"No, I haven't," Benjo replied.

"When the church first started getting big, I went to a couple of services," Kathy said. "I was curious to see what my friends and coworkers were raving about on social media and in our breakroom. The closest thing I can compare a Sunday service there to is a rock concert. There's a seven-piece band with concert lighting and a sound system that would do a major concert venue proud. The Coles are both really good-looking and charismatic people and August Cole has very dynamic way of speaking that draws you in. You can look around during his sermons and people are just staring back in awe. It's almost like watching those old 1940s newsreels of Hitler giving a speech. It's actually a little creepy. I swear if Jesus Christ Himself were to show up at one of their services, He would get second billing behind August and Monica Cole."

"You said you only went to a couple of services," Benjo asked. "Why did you stop going?"

"It's because it seems like the people there worship the preacher more than the God he allegedly speaks for," Kathy said after a few moments of trying to find the right words. "The way the people who attend that church act, I think the Coles could perform a human sacrifice on the altar and nobody would bat an eye. That's why I think no one has called them out on the way they run the business part of the church. It's a cult of personality." She looked sideways at Benjo. "Does that make sense?"

"It does," Benjo said. "Have you been able to substantiate any of the things Anonymous claimed while drunk?"

Kathy's face fell. "Yes and no," she replied. "I approached the person I've been calling Anonymous one day after they had left work at the church offices. I asked them if they wanted to talk about the claims they had made at the party. Anonymous turned as white as a sheet and nearly fainted. I mean I literally thought they were about to collapse. They said that everything they had said at the party in question was nothing but the liquor talking. They claimed that they had no idea what I was talking about when I asked about the allegations of financial mismanagement. Anonymous then literally begged me to leave them alone and to not proceed with my investigation."

"Do you think that was fear of the Coles or because they didn't want to lose their job?" Benjo asked.

"I think it was fear," Kathy replied. "Maybe not of the Coles, but of Paul Tucker. You talk about someone who doesn't belong; Tucker is a convicted violent felon who did about fifteen years in prison for a number of crimes. He belongs in a church about like a fox belongs in a hen house."

"Supposedly, August Cole witnessed to him and made him change his evil ways," Benjo said.

Kathy cocked an eyebrow behind the sunglasses. "You met Tucker today. Was there anything about his personality that led you to believe he's a good man?"

"Not in the least," Benjo answered instantly. "Actually, I left with a terrible feeling that me and him are going to tangle again and I don't mean verbally. Call it a hunch."

"Be careful," Kathy warned. "I think he might be a dangerous man on his own. If he's still actively involved in the Southern Devils Motorcycle Club, he most likely can get other dangerous men to do things for him as well." She looked him up and down. "You look like you could hold your own in a fair fight, but I suspect Tucker isn't one to fight fair."

"I'll be okay," Benjo said. "When Anonymous recanted, did you try anything else?"

"I went to the state department of revenue's main office and checked out the church's yearly financial records. As a registered non-profit, they have to file those records every year. Luckily, once they are filed, they are public record. I got to see the church's financial records for the previous three years," Kathy continued. "There were the normal business expenses like utilities, insurance, and payroll. There were also a lot of checks written to fund the different ministries and charities the church claims to support. There were several large checks written to a construction company that's allegedly renovating a building the Coles own that's going to be a halfway house for released inmates through the church's prison ministry, Fresh Start. I located the building that's being renovated. It's a rundown warehouse off of Interstate Twenty about ten miles outside the city limits. There are no signs of any type of construction or renovation work being done there, even though they've been getting checks for nearly two years. I've been checking on the place for two months. Absolutely no progress at all. If someone is actually working on that building, they are the slowest carpenter who ever lived. The construction company's office address is a single room in a dingy building where you can rent office space by the week. The construction company, Ace American Builders, is owned by a limited liability corporation that's owned by another shell company. It would take a good forensic accountant with unlimited resources months to figure out who owns what."

"I'd be willing to bet that Tucker or the motorcycle club are the ones who end up with the money," Benjo said.

'There were also a lot of checks written to a beauty salon here in the city," Kathy said. "They are only for about two hundred bucks a pop. That one struck me as odd because I found out that the Coles have hair and makeup people on the church payroll so they can look good for their services, social media, and on their television show. There's actually a salon in the back of the church on the same hallway that houses the studio they use for the television show and social media. No ordinary beauty salon for the Coles, no sir! Anyway, it turns out that the woman who owns that salon has a brother who is in the Devils MC."

"They are writing checks to the salon for supposed services, then the salon owner cashes them, and passes the rest to her brother in the club," Benjo guessed. "Classic money laundering trick. The salon owner keeps enough to cover the taxes and keeps a cut for herself. Two hundred dollars a week doesn't seem like it would help much, but if they do that with four or five other small businesses, it adds up quick."

"Exactly," Kathy said. "There were a few other really questionable expenses in their records as well. Supposedly, they are leasing all of their audio-visual equipment and lighting for the studio there at the church. They are paying several thousand dollars a month for that to a company based in Charlotte, North Carolina. The company's office address is a laundromat in a strip mall on the bad side of Charlotte."

Benjo whistled. "It sounds like you're a much better detective than I am," he said. "You've got some pretty solid information. Why haven't you aired a story about them?"

"There's a couple of reasons," Kathy said. "I went to the church a few times trying to speak with the Coles. As soon as they found out what I wanted, they clammed up and had Tucker toss me out. Once they hired that private security company following what happened with your girl, I can't get anywhere near the Coles. The building is locked up tight as a drum. Then, they had a pack of lawyers descend on our station with threats of lawsuits for slander and restraining orders. Our corporate office nearly crapped their pants. I was basically told that, unless I had ironclad, undeniable proof that the Coles were doing something illegal, to stay the hell away from them. Unfortunately, I don't have the resources to uncover the kind of proof I need to convince our lawyers to let me proceed. And, to be completely honest, I'm afraid to keep going on it."

"What do you mean you're afraid?" Benjo asked. "Based on what I've always heard about you, you never give up on a story."

Kathy's whole demeanor instantly changed. She glanced around them before she continued. There was no one around them; the mother and kids had left a few minutes earlier. "Within twenty-four hours of me first approaching the Coles to request an interview regarding the church's financials, someone slashed all four of my car's tires," she said. "Since then, I've had numerous death threats called in to the station, not to mention someone tried to break into my house. Thankfully, I have a good security system and my husband owns several guns. The good Reverend Cole also used me as an example of evil trying to stop the spreading of the Gospel. Since then, I've had people approach me in the grocery store accusing me of being an atheist and of hating Jesus Himself."

"Do you think it's just members of his church being weird or do you think it's someone else trying to derail your investigation?" Benjo asked.

"I think the vandalism to my car and the attempted break-in was an attempt to scare me away from looking into the church," Kathy said. "The rest of it was so-called Christian members of the church. Like I said, that church worships the Coles, not the God they claim to represent. Still, I have to be very careful, no matter who might come after me. That's why we met here out in public. That's also why I have at least two of my coworkers watching us now through the windows on the third floor."

"Wouldn't it have been safer to meet me in your office?" Benjo asked.

"If the station manager found out I was even talking to someone about the Coles, he would probably fire me," Kathy said with a tight smile. "I don't remember the name of the bigshot lawyer the Coles hired, but he put the fear of God in the bosses."

"How can you be sure I'm not secretly working for the Coles?" Benjo asked.

"That was a question I asked a few of the people I talked to about you," Kathy answered. "They told me that anything was possible, but they seriously doubted it. They said you would have very little tolerance for people like the Coles."

"Based on what I've found out about them in just the first day, I have to agree with whoever told you that," Benjo said. "I would also take that as a compliment."

"The Coles- both of them- are bad people," Kathy said fervently. "Before I even approached the Coles, I dug into their backgrounds. It was eye-opening to say the least. The biographical stuff they put on the church website has been sanitized and edited to hide a lot of dirt. For example, August Cole went to prison on drug charges when he was just eighteen while sweet Monica waited at home for her man, if you believe their website. After interviewing several people who knew both of them during that time frame, I discovered that both August and Monica were involved in crimes together. They acted like they were a late-nineties version of Bonnie and Clyde. They were both into drugs and numerous other crimes. I spoke with one man who used to run with them during those days. He swore that Monica was just as involved in several violent crimes as August. The only reason Monica never ended up in jail with August was a combination of pure luck and love. One of the witnesses who could put her at the scene of an armed robbery died of a drug overdose before the police could interview him. August agreed to plead guilty to some things in exchange for the cops leaving Monica out of it. Stuff like that."

Benjo was quiet for several moments as he digested this information. "It's amazing that two decades later, they are pastors of a thriving church."

"I agree," Kathy replied. "When I first started hearing about the Coles, I thought their story was a marvelous example of people's ability to change for the better. It was story of spiritual redemption worthy of a Hollywood movie. However, once I started learning more about them, I started feeling like maybe it was just one long con job. August Cole is charismatic, handsome, and a natural public speaker who was brought up seeing how a church worked. I think he realized being a preacher was easier than a regular job, so he used what he learned as a preacher's kid and ran with it. I think Monica is along for the ride."

"I have to admit that, so far, I haven't discovered anything that would make me want either of them to give me spiritual guidance," Benjo said with a slight smile. "I also have to admit that I don't care what the members of his church believe. My main concern is finding out why Monica Cole shot a twenty-five-year-old woman to death in her office."

"How do you plan to do that when the police and prosecutors have already ruled it justifiable?" Kathy asked.

"If I can find evidence the police missed that calls that ruling into question, the prosecutor can re-open the case and file charges," Benjo said. "I would have to prove to the police and the prosecutor that the shooting was not what it appeared to be."

Kathy pondered this for a few seconds. "To do that, you would have to prove that either Sarah never tried to kill Monica or that it was a set up and Sarah was lured there and murdered."

"Yep," Benjo said. "To do that, I have to figure out a motive for the Coles to want Sarah Fleming dead. I have to do that without the Coles cooperating and all of the evidence seeming to point to a case of justifiable self-defense."

"That's a pretty tall order," Kathy said as she glanced at her watch. The time must have surprised her because she jumped up off the bench. "I've got to get back and get ready to go on the air later," she said. "Please keep me informed of what you find out. This could be a huge story if you discover it actually was a murder." She handed Benjo a business card. "This has my personal cell number on it. Stay in touch."

"I will," Benjo said as he stood up and took the card. "It was a pleasure meeting you, Kathy. If there's anything else I can do for you, please call me."

"Likewise," Kathy said. She gave Benjo a long look that could have been either concern or pity. "Listen, you be careful. I think the Coles could be dangerous if you back them into a corner."

"Most people are," Benjo said as he turned to walk away.

7

Later that evening, Benjo sat in an old, wooden rocker on the front porch of his cabin mulling over the things he'd learned that day. The rocking chair on the front porch overlooking the lake was his favorite place at the cabin. When Presley was alive, the two of them would sit out there on the front porch in two matching rocking chairs and watch the sun set. Sometimes they would have lively discussions about whatever came to mind. The topics could run the gamut from their day at work to current events to whether there was life on other planets and everything in between. Following her murder, he had avoided the front porch for weeks, simply because the sight of her empty chair was just too painful. However, with the passage of time, he'd eventually worked up the nerve to start sitting out there again. He still missed Presley more than words could express, but the porch had become his go-to place to sit in the silence and think. Sometimes he would even talk to the empty rocking chair beside him as if she were still there listening. It probably seemed a little insane, but it also kept him from going a little insane.

It had been a day full of surprising information and unexpected twists. At the moment, he had a head full of new facts and pieces of evidence that didn't quite make sense. It was like having pieces of a giant jigsaw puzzle, all jumbled up in a pile on the table in front of him, with no picture of what the puzzle was supposed to look like. All he could do was to start looking at each individual piece and seeing if it connected to any other piece. If he could connect enough small pieces of information, eventually the small pieces would end up forming a recognizable piece of the big picture. With enough recognizable pieces of the big picture, eventually he could tell what the picture actually was. Sitting there in the silence and combing over everything he'd learned would help him see which pieces might actually connect to each other. If none of them did, he would keep digging until he found pieces that did connect.

After nearly an hour of turning things over in his mind, Benjo had to admit that he was no closer to figuring out the connection between Sarah Fleming and the Coles. He still couldn't figure out what had brought them together and resulted in such a deadly outcome. Based on what Kathy had told him, the Coles were bad people and faking the whole preacher thing for the money and prestige. They were also probably laundering money for an outlaw biker gang. One or both of those things could be connected to Sarah's death, or neither of them could be. It could be exactly what it looked like: a troubled young woman who fixated on another person for some reason that made sense only to her. However, something in his gut told him that wasn't the case.

Benjo was still sorting through it all when he heard the sound of a vehicle approaching up his driveway. The sound of the approaching vehicle disturbed the ducks swimming on the lake, prompting all of them to fly off together toward the west and the setting sun. He felt a touch of irritation as he watched the ducks fly away. Apparently, he had a visitor coming. This would make two visitors in two days. In Benjo's opinion, that was two too many. With a sigh, he stood up and walked across the porch to the steps that led off the porch to the side of the cabin that faced the driveway. He stood there, waiting for the vehicle and whoever was driving it to come into view.

As he stood there waiting, there was a loud beep and the automatic pet door mounted in the cabin's side door flipped open. Harley slinked through the door and sat there on the side porch watching the driveway. The big cat turned her head and looked at Benjo like the approaching visitor was somehow his fault. "I don't know who it is," Benjo said defensively to the cat's scowling look. "I don't like visitors either." Harley's reply was a look somewhere between disgust and pity before she turned and strolled casually down the steps. She vanished around the corner of the house with her tail swishing behind her.

A black Ford Explorer came into view and headed up the driveway. Benjo recognized it instantly as an unmarked police vehicle because nothing in the world looked as much like an unmarked police vehicle as an unmarked police vehicle. The front windshield was tinted so darkly that he couldn't see who was driving the vehicle or how many occupants it had. As the vehicle got closer, Benjo could see the emergency lights concealed under the front grill and along the top of the windshield, confirming his assumption that it was a police vehicle. Benjo swore under his breath. There was a good chance it was another visit from the state police investigators assigned to the Jacob Clement case. They had questioned Benjo three times since Clement was found dead. Supposedly he was no longer a person of interest in the case, but that could have changed. Something had brought them to his door this late in the evening.

The Ford Explorer stopped a few feet away and the driver shut off the engine. The door opened and a single figure emerged. It was not anyone from the state police; it was a man who'd been Benjo's boss for nearly fifteen years, Sheriff John Crowe. To say that Benjo was surprised to see the sheriff in his driveway was an understatement. It had over a year since he'd seen Sheriff Crowe in person. That was the day he'd resigned from the department after learning that nothing would be done to Dale Marsh and that he was going to be moved out of detectives to patrol. He had not seen or spoken to the man since. "Hey, Benjo," Sheriff Crowe said.

Benjo took a moment to study the man. The sheriff looked the same as he did a year ago, tall, slender, with short, gray hair, rugged features, and a gray mustache. The only thing that had changed on him was his eyes. His eyes looked old and tired, like they had seen too much. He was dressed in jeans, boots, and a black shirt with the sheriff's department badge embroidered on the breast. He carried a Glock semi-automatic pistol in a holster on his side. "Sheriff," Benjo replied politely. "What brings you out my way?"

"I drove all this way because I wanted to talk to you face to face," Sheriff Crowe said. "Somewhere we can go sit down and chat?"

"If you don't mind sitting outside, we can sit on my front porch," Benjo said.

"That'll work," Sheriff Crowe said. "I'll follow you."

Benjo led the way back up onto the front porch. He took a seat in the rocking chair he'd been occupying previously. The sheriff took a seat in the remaining one, the one where Presley used to sit. The sheriff settled back into the chair and took in the view. "Nice place," he said. "I could sit out here for hours on end."

"I have before," Benjo said. "I've slept out here a few times, actually. A couple of times it was even intentional."

Sheriff Crowe smiled. "Is the lake natural or manmade?" he asked as gazed out across the water.

"Natural," Benjo replied. "Presley and I got lucky when we found this property for sale. We had always dreamed of having a log home and this place was perfect for it. Presley actually designed this cabin."

Sheriff Crowe looked at Benjo with sympathy. "How are you doing since her passing?" he asked.

"Her passing?" Benjo asked as he settled back in his chair. "Passing makes it sound like she died peacefully in her sleep. She didn't pass away, Sheriff. She was gunned down because the two assassins sent to kill me were lousy shots." Even now, a year later,he had to focus on keeping the anger and pain out of his voice.

Sheriff Crowe visibly flinched and looked ill at ease. "I didn't mean to offend," he said. "Maybe I should have phrased it better, but is there a good way to ask that question?"

Benjo suddenly felt like an ass. "I apologize," he said. "As you can tell, I'm still a little touchy on the subject of my wife. I'm doing okay, Sheriff. I have good days and bad days."

"You ever hear anything else from the state police about Clement's death?" Sheriff Crowe asked.

"After the third time they questioned me about Clement's murder, my attorney sent them a letter basically telling them to either arrest me or leave me alone," Benjo said. "About three months ago, they notified him that I was no longer considered a prime suspect. I'm still a suspect, technically, but I'm on the list below several other people."

"Good for you," Sheriff Crowe said.

Benjo cocked an eyebrow at the sheriff. "You really going to sit here and act like you didn't already know that?"

Sheriff Crowe sighed. "I was hoping my coming here wouldn't re-kindle hard feelings, Benjo. This is a peace mission."

"The last time we spoke a year ago, it was to inform me that you weren't going to do anything to your golden boy, Marsh, even though there's about a ninety-nine percent chance that he tipped off a man suspected of numerous serious felonies that he was being investigated, prompting that man to go about destroying evidence, intimidating witnesses, and murdering my wife in hopes of getting me off his trail," Benjo said fiercely. "During the same meeting, you also mentioned that you were reassigning me to uniformed patrol on night shift because I was considered a suspect in a state police investigation." He turned to face Sheriff Crowe. "So, am I supposed to forget that and we're buddies now?"

"I did what I felt was right at the time," Sheriff Crowe said calmly. "There was no way I could confirm that Marsh told Clement anything, much less if he did it intentionally. Marsh admitted that there was a chance that he could have inadvertently let something slip to Clement in a social setting. There's a world of difference between tipping some-one off in an attempt to obstruct justice and accidentally being over-heard. On the other side of the coin, you were the prime suspect in the murder of a man who probably killed your wife. Try to put yourself in my shoes, son."

"I've tried to, Sheriff," Benjo said honestly. "I've always liked and respected you, but if there's one thing you've always had a blind spot on, it's Dale Marsh. That man has been with your department for several years and he's been a joke for all of them. The fact that you coddle him has cost you a lot of people's respect. I know politics makes for some strange bedfellows, but damn!"

"Actually, Marsh is one of the reasons I am here," Sheriff Crowe said. "Earlier today, Captain Mason and Deke Jeter came to my office. I understand that you're a PI now and that you've been hired to dig into the Sarah Fleming shooting that happened at Hope Springs Church."

"I have," Benjo answered.

"May I ask why?" Sheriff Crowe asked. "What are you supposed to be looking for?"

"Some friends and family members don't believe that Sarah was stalking Monica Cole," Benjo answered. "They also don't believe for a minute that Sarah would try to attack anyone. They want me to find out the truth."

"I know you reached out to Deke," Sheriff Crowe said. "He told me as much in my meeting with him today. He told me that you have some of the same questions regarding the events at the church as he did. My lead detective on that case felt like those discrepancies were explainable. That's why we closed the case and turned it over to the prosecutor's office."

"Your lead detective was Marsh," Benjo answered simply. "Given his history, that should be explanation enough."

"I reviewed the file," Sheriff Crowe answered. "He did a good job. I signed off on him closing it and turning it over."

"Wow," Benjo said. "That sucks for you."

"Why does that suck for me, Benjo?" Sheriff Crowe asked.

"Where should I begin?" Benjo asked. He glanced at his watch. "I've worked on this case for literally eight hours and I've already found holes in the Cole's statements about the day Sarah died that you could drive a truck through. I've also discovered that your boy, Marsh, actually worked for the Coles prior to investigating them for a possible murder."

"That's why Mason and Deke were in my office today," Sheriff Crowe said. "That looks terrible. I did not know he had worked security duty there before I put him on the case. He should have disclosed that, but he didn't."

"Oh, shades of Jacob Clement," Benjo said as he pressed a hand to his forehead and faked swooning. "I think you saw what you thought was an easy case that not even Marsh could screw up, so you stuck him on it. You had a pastor's wife admitting she shot the dead girl in her office, a dead girl who couldn't tell her side of the story, and some evidence that at first glance looks like the dead girl might have been a stalker. Marsh got to feel like a real detective for a few minutes, so he could brag to his daddy, and you got a quick, closed case. A one-and-done, if you will. The problem you have now is that this one isn't nearly as done as it looks. If this justifiable homicide turns out to be anything but that, you and the department are going to look like fools."

"I don't know what you think you've found," Sheriff Crowe said as a touch of anger crept into his voice, "but my department stands by what it found. I have faith in the investigator I assigned to the case."

"No, you don't," Benjo replied casually. "That's why you came out here this evening. You want to see what I've found out."

"Is that what you think this is, a fishing expedition?" Sheriff Crowe asked.

"That's part of it," Benjo said. "What's the rest?"

"I got a call today from August Cole at Hope Springs Church," Sheriff Crowe said. "He complained about a private investigator who came to his church asking questions about a matter that he'd been assured was closed. He wanted to know how that was possible, given the police and the prosecutor's office had closed the case. I had to explain to him that there was nothing illegal about what you were doing, unless you started stalking or harassing anyone. He wasn't happy about that."

"Well, bless his heart," Benjo said. "As I explained to Paul Tucker, their security director, I would love to hear their side of the story."

"I came out here to see you today for two reasons," Sheriff Crowe said. "One was to tell you that I've ordered all of my personnel to stay away from you and this case, including your buddy, Deke. I'm not going to have my people help you try to make me and my department look bad. The second reason is to warn you to stay away from the Coles and

Hope Springs Church. I'm officially trespassing you from their property at their request."

Benjo looked at the sheriff with disgust. "So, not only are you not interested in truth, you're going to actively interfere in me finding it?" he asked.

"Not at all," Sheriff Crowe replied. "I'm simply honoring the request of a concerned citizen. The Coles requested that you be trespassed from their property."

"But what if I need spiritual guidance?" Benjo asked sarcastically. "I could go to hell without their intervention. What would Jesus do?"

The sheriff ignored Benjo's sarcasm. "If you find evidence that might warrant re-opening the case, you're more than welcome to bring it to our attention."

"I find it stunning that the Coles have enough power to make the sheriff himself come out to my property to threaten me," Benjo said, "but then I realize they have a lot of influence. Those votes would be important for a man who wants to keep his career in politics going." He shook his head in disgust. "You've completely changed, Sheriff Crowe."

"Me?" Sheriff Crowe asked in disbelief. He motioned at Benjo. "Have you looked in the mirror, Benjo? With the tattoos, that hair, and that beard, you look like you ought to be in a prison gang. You used to be Mr. Clean-cut. What made you decide to go from the way you looked to this?"

Benjo was silent for a moment. "Well, I think my attitude about some things changed because the person who kept me on the straight and narrow is now in an urn on the mantel inside," he finally replied. "My whole life, including who I am and how I look, changed because your pet, Marsh, put me and the one thing I cared about most in the world in a killer's crosshairs." He turned to look the sheriff directly in the eyes. "He's the reason Presley died and you didn't do a thing about it. Shame on you, Sheriff."

"Like you did something about Jacob Clement?" Sheriff Crowe spat back as he stood up from his chair. "Everyone, including the state police investigators, think you're the one who killed Clement. You were just smart enough to not leave any evidence. You got lucky because the neighbor's security camera was poor quality and it was raining enough to make positively identifying you impossible."

Benjo continued to rock casually in his chair. "Can you or the state police prove any of your allegations?" he asked calmly as he looked up at Sheriff Crowe.

"Son, if I could, you would have been in handcuffs a long time ago," Sheriff Crowe answered grimly.

"Well, Sheriff Crowe, I'll tell you what," Benjo said. "I'm going to stay on the Fleming case because my gut tells me that it was not a case of self-defense. Also, since you came out here to officially give me a notice to stay off church property, allow me to give you a couple of notices. First of all, if I see one county sheriff's department vehicle in my rearview, if I suddenly start getting tickets, or a deputy starts showing up at places I'm at, my attorney, Billy Cleveland, is going to get so deep in your ass that you'll need a colonoscopy to see him. Second of all, I have a great, new friend named Kathy Miller from Channel Seven News. She's really interested in the Fleming case too. She was also really intrigued by how the lead detective investigating Fleming's death was on the Cole's payroll prior to investigating them. I suspect you will be hearing from her shortly. Last, but not least, get the fuck off my property. If you come back, you better have a warrant."

"Are you threatening me?" Sheriff Crowe asked fiercely.

"No sir, I am advising you that I know my Constitutional rights as an American citizen," Benjo said politely. "Have a good evening, Sheriff."

Sheriff Crowe's face turned about three shades of red as he turned and walked back off the porch to his vehicle. Benjo stayed in his chair and continued to rock. He listened as the sheriff's truck door slammed, the engine started, and the truck turned around and drove away down his driveway. He continued to sit there, lost in thought, staring at the lake as darkness started to fall.

Benjo continued to sit there until a huge shadow came slinking up the porch steps and approached him. Harley strolled casually up to his chair and rubbed against his leg, nearly pushing him out of the chair and breaking his reverie. He reached down and rubbed the huge cat's catcher's-mitt-sized head. The cat began to purr loudly, a sound not that much different from an idling chainsaw. "I think the Coles are worried about me," Benjo said to the cat. "Why would they be if what happened with Sarah was on the up and up?"

Harley's answer was to cock her head back and rub her chin on his knee. "You're right," Benjo said as if the cat had answered his question. "Let them worry."

8

On Sunday mornings, Pastor August Cole cut quite a dashing figure as he preached from the stage at Hope Springs Church. At the age of forty-two, he was tall and well-built, with broad shoulders, a narrow waist, and a powerful chest. His black hair reached to just past his collar and was flecked with just enough gray to make him look distinguished. He was also strikingly handsome, with a square jaw, sharp features, piercing blue eyes, and a smile that would have made an orthodontist swoon. As if his physical attributes weren't enough to win over most people, especially women, he also radiated charisma and charm. Each Sunday as he preached, he drew people in with his quick, easy smile, a good, folksy sense of humor, and friendly, approachable demeanor. After every service, Pastor Cole would stand at the church doors along with his beautiful wife, Monica, to speak to everyone as they left, shake hands, and even give out hugs to those wanting one. That same quick smile and charming personality were on display any time he was out in public, making people wonder if the good pastor ever lost that warm, peaceful smile and good mood.

The answer to that question would be an emphatic yes, especially if those same people could see August Cole's face as he sat behind the massive mahogany desk that occupied his spacious office in a hallway just off the church's main lobby. At the moment August's smile was gone, his face was beet -red with anger, and he was openly glaring at the two people who sat in the leather chairs in front of his desk. One of those chairs was occupied by his wife, Monica, a pretty woman with reddish-blonde hair, a statuesque figure, and beautifully-tanned skin.

Like her husband's public persona, Monica was normally all smiles, charm, and gab. At the moment, however, Monica was quiet, her face was pale, and her expression was somewhere between fear and anger. The other chair was occupied by Paul Tucker. Tucker just looked bored and impatient. August's anger did not faze Paul at all, even though August was technically his boss.

"So, tell me what this private investigator said one more time," August said. "I want to know his exact words."

Tucker rolled his eyes. "Jesus Christ, August, I've already told you three times," Tucker said. "He'd apparently seen the security camera footage from the day that girl died. He had the same questions that black detective had about why she came in through the door she did instead of through the lobby. I told him the same thing we told the police, that she was trying to sneak in and got lucky. It's not against the law for someone to accidentally leave a door unlocked. Her going straight to that door could be a coincidence. There's no way anyone else can prove otherwise.'"

August slapped his hand down on his desk. "I should have figured that would look weird," he said. "We should have had her come in through the lobby like anyone else would."

"We couldn't take a chance on her parking up front and being seen coming into the church. The outdoor security cameras on the store across the parking lot can see the front clearly," Tucker replied gruffly. "Granted, there were probably better ways we could have handled the situation, but hindsight is always twenty-twenty." He shrugged. "Either way, the cops bought it and the prosecutor ruled it justifiable. That's a perfect outcome considering the plan went all to hell when Marsha showed up early."

"That private detective poking around could find something that makes the police realize they might be wrong," August said.

"That's very doubtful," Tucker said. "Obviously, the girl didn't tell anyone else about what she found because you two would most likely be in jail right now. The guy I sent to search her apartment didn't find anything else tying her to you two. The documents she brought in with her, we destroyed. Both of you need to chill out. This is over. This guy is going to milk the clock, act like he's looking hard, and then get a fat check from whatever lawyer hired him. This stuff will be over in two weeks. A month, tops."

August ran a hand over his face, then turned to look out his office window. It was dark outside, but the street lights in the parking lot made it as bright as day. "We've worked so hard to build all of this," he said softly. He stood up from his chair suddenly and walked over to look at the pictures sitting in frames on the shelves behind his desk. All of the pictures were of either him or him and Monica meeting with various wealthy or important people. Several of the larger pictures showed August on stage with a microphone in his hand and sweat pouring down his face as he preached a sermon to a stadium full of people during a revival service a couple of years ago. "You ever think back to twenty-four years ago when the two of us were sitting in a prison cell?" he asked Tucker over his shoulder. "Did you ever imagine I would be here? That I would be preaching to thousands of people at a church I ran and on television? That I would have money and everything else?"

"Everybody dreams of something better when they are sitting in a prison cell, Gus," Tucker answered, using the nickname he used for August that August hated. "Most of them never pull it off. If you recall, I was in and out of prison for several more years after you started this. All I wanted was some cold beer, maybe some weed, a woman to screw my brains out, and to take my bike out on the open road."

"I'm sure you got that as soon as you got out. Each time you got out," August added as he continued to stare at the pictures. "You got what you wanted and I got what I wanted. Two wildly different things, yet here we are together again." He shook his head as if amazed by it all. "All of us, all three of us, seemed to be linked together by something bigger than us. What do you think, Monica?"

Monica didn't answer. Tucker shifted in his chair and glanced out of the corner of his eye at Monica. Monica sat still and stared off into space with a dazed look on her face. Monica was not taking what had happened with the girl well. Actually, she had been acting weird since the Fleming girl had reached out to her the first time. Since the shooting in her office, Monica had been taking some medication prescribed to her by her doctor to help her with anxiety and the trauma of the girl's death. The medication and the stress from what had transpired had turned the normally bubbly and outgoing Monica to a quiet and withdrawn woman who was sleeping way too much. August had continued services and producing their television show without her, blaming the trauma of the girl's tragic death for Monica's absence. Ironically, the whole thing had resulted in a decided uptick in attendance to their church, visits to their social media pages, and an increase in their television show's ratings.

August turned and walked over to his wife. He looked at her with concern. He placed his hand on her shoulder and shook her gently. "Yes?" she asked dazedly.

August frowned. The medication the doctor had given her was powerful enough in its own right. The fact that Monica was helping it along with steady glasses of wine had really turned her into a zombie. "Honey, I said it seems like God has brought us together. I asked what you thought."

Monica just looked around dazedly as if the question was far beyond her to answer. Tucker answered to end the awkward moment. "Gus, you know I've never believed in that stuff," he answered loudly. It was a running joke between the two men. On paper, Paul Tucker was an associate minister at the church and the director of church security. He would go up on stage every so often and share his testimony of how God had changed his life and made him a better person. In actuality, Tucker was an atheist, the job title was just a way to keep him on the payroll, and that touching testimony had been written by August for Tucker to use during services. Tucker hadn't changed a bit since getting out of prison; he was just a better criminal than before. "The only thing that brought us together was good, old-fashioned greed. I had a bunch of money I needed to make legit and you had a way I could do that. I kept hearing about my old buddy, August, and the way his church was growing in leaps and bounds, so I came to one of your little tent services. When I saw all of that cash going into those plastic buckets you used for collection plates, I knew you could help me out. Since I knew you hadn't changed that much from the guy I shared a cell with, I knew you would help me out. That's what brought us back together."

"I built all of this and I have no intention of giving all of this up. I'll die first," August said grimly. "I can't believe this mess is happening now, just when everything is going perfect."

"God is punishing us," Monica said suddenly. Her voice was soft and distant. "That's why the girl showed up. God sent her to punish us for what we did."

August went over to his wife and rubbed her shoulders. "Baby, you know that's not true."

"Then how did she pop up out of nowhere?" Monica asked in a much stronger voice. "She shows up just when everything is so perfect. She was sent to us and we should have listened to her. Instead, we did what we did. We thought we got away with it, but now someone else has come. God is going to destroy all of this."

August looked at Tucker behind his wife's back and rolled his eyes. "That's not true, baby," he said. "I don't know if she was telling the truth or if it was some weird attempt to bluff us and blackmail us."

Monica shrugged her husband's hands off her shoulders and jumped to her feet so fast that it startled both men. "You saw the papers she had," she said angrily. "How could she know what we did?"

"Monica, someone could print something like that off on a home computer," Tucker said calmly. "It's amazing what someone resourceful enough can figure out."

Monica spun to look at her husband. Her body was quivering and her face was a mask of fear and anger. "You caused all of this," she said as she pointed her finger right in August's face. Spittle flew from her lips and her eyes were wild.

August stiffened as his own, fierce temper flared. "No, Baby, *you* caused this," he retorted. "All because you got bored one day and decided to do something a bunch of your lady friends were doing. You should have just lived in the present instead of worrying about the past."

Monica cursed and drew back like she was going to throw a punch at her husband's face. Tucker jumped up and got between the husband and wife. "That's enough," he growled. "Both of you sit down and lower your damned voices. The last thing we need is for someone to overhear you two."

August spun and walked back to sit down behind his desk. Monica glared at Tucker and then sat back down. Both of them still looked furious. Tucker couldn't even begin to imagine what would happen when the two of the got home alone. Tucker stood there, towering over Monica. "Monica, you need to get yourself together," he said firmly. "I'm telling you that you're the one I'm worried about in this equation. What's done is done and we can't take it back. If we don't keep ourselves and our story together, we all three could end up in prison for the rest of our lives." Tucker stepped back and turned sideways so he could see both August and Monica. "Both of you listen to me good." He made sure both of the Coles were watching him. "I am NOT going back to prison," Tucker said menacingly. "They will have to kill me before I will let them put me back in prison. I'll also kill anyone I think might be putting me in danger of going back. Is that understood?"

"I don't like being threatened, Paul," August said.

"And I don't like wondering if I might go back to prison for life or to death row because of you two," Tucker said. He walked back and sat down in his chair. "Look, I don't like threatening two people I consider good friends and even better business partners," he said as he softened his tone. "We're all in this together, the money, the church, and what happened with the girl. We've got to keep our heads about us. This private detective is sniffing around and doing just enough to justify his bill to the lawyer that hired him. This will pass if we play it cool. Hell, the police and the prosecutor are actually on our side."

Monica's face crumbled and she began to cry softly. "I never wanted this to happen," she said. "I didn't want her to die. We could have done something else."

Tucker reached over and rubbed Monica's shoulder gently. "Like what, Monica?" he asked softly. "How would you have even started to explain everything to the people who come to church here? To the people who follow you and August? Do you really think you could convince them that what you did back then was okay? How could you justify it? How many of those people would never come back to this church? Never give any more money? That six- hundred- thousand- dollar horse farm you and August just bought in the mountains? Gone! Your Mercedes? Gone!"

"He's right, you know," August said from his chair behind the desk. "We would lose it all, honey."

"If there was no more money coming in from collections and donations, then we couldn't funnel the money from me and my business partners through the church," Tucker continued. He spoke softly, as if he were consoling a small child who had skinned a knee. "They would not be happy at all, Monica, and when they get unhappy, people get dissolved in acid and vanish forever."

"I never wanted any of that!" Monica whined. "It was never supposed to get so complicated." She glared at Tucker and then at her husband. "Paul, you were the only one we were supposed to be helping out. You were never supposed to involve other people."

"You never had a problem with the ten percent of it that went into your and your husband's pockets," Tucker replied reasonably. "As a matter of fact, when I first told you how much money that could mean for you and August, you were very excited about it." He released her shoulder and sat back. "Aside from our friends from the other side of the border, how would you explain it to the police? There's no statute of limitations for some crimes in this state."

"We could have paid her to go away," Monica said as she wiped at her eyes.

Tucker rolled his eyes. "Think about the secret she had hanging over you, Monica" he said. "You and August would be a living, breathing ATMs for her for the rest of her life. Anytime she needed or wanted something, your phone would be ringing. Even if she did take the money and go away, all it would have taken is for her to run her mouth one time in the wrong setting and it would be over. It could be something as simple as pillow talk with a boyfriend or running her mouth while drunk at a bar. You and August are high-profile people. If she did that, how long do you think it would take for the word to spread? What would happen if some investigative reporter got wind of her story and some network offered her money to talk? What if something you did or said made her mad and she got vindictive? Have you even considered that?"

Monica looked down at her lap and shook her head. "No," she said softly.

August took that moment to get up from behind his desk and come to his wife's side. He knelt beside her and slipped an arm around her shoulders. "He's right," he said. "I know the way we had to handle it bothered you, but it had to be done, my love. If we were ever going to breathe another breath without fear, it had to be done. You know I love you more than life itself, and I would never lie to or mislead you, especially about something this important."

Monica's shoulders began to shake and the tears increased. "You're both right," she said. "I know it, but this whole thing just shook me up." She shrugged off her husband's arm and stood up. "I need to use the restroom and compose myself," she said. "I'm sorry."

"Of course," August said as he stood up. Monica staggered over to the door that led out of August's office and into her own office, which had an attached bathroom. She closed the door behind her as she left August's office.

"Dude, you better keep her on a tight chain," Tucker said in a low voice as soon as the door was shut. "Either get her some better pills or take her on a vacation. I don't care, but her head's all messed up about that girl. She sees it as some divine punishment; I see it as a weird fluke, like when a jetliner crashes and everyone is killed except for one person that survives without a scratch on them."

"I know," August said. "I've never seen her like this."

"Get her out of town," Tucker said. "We can't have her talking to anyone, much less that private detective. There's no telling what she could say with all of that dope in her."

"I talked to Sheriff Crowe today personally about this private detective," August said. "The sheriff told me that we could trespass him so he can't come on church grounds or our personal property. The sheriff offered to personally deliver the message to Lane. That should keep him away from us. However, that won't stop him from approaching whoever else he wants to talk to. That worries me. It seems that Lane used to work for the sheriff's department. The sheriff told me that Lane used to be one of his best investigators. If he digs long enough and hard enough, he might get lucky."

Tucker thought for a moment. "I've got a couple of guys I could send to talk him out of continuing the investigation via a few weeks in the hospital."

August thought for a moment. "That might make him more determined," he said. "But, if the poor man happened to get injured in, say, a road rage incident or mugging, that might change his mind."

Tucker smiled a little. "I'll make some calls and see what I can do," he said. "I'll handle Lane. You keep your old lady in line. If I think she's the weak link, I will have to deal with it."

"If that happens, I'll let you," August said. "I have no desire to be dissolved in acid."

9

Because he had a busy day planned, Benjo started his morning bright and early. He rolled out of bed at five AM, dressed in his normal workout clothes, and hit the gym he'd built in his garage. He spent the next two hours working out hard with a combination of bodyweight exercises, free weights, and mixed- martial- arts-sparring with a heavy bag and a practice dummy. Unlike most men, Benjo's time in the gym wasn't meant to build big muscles to impress others, mainly women, or to meet some unrealistic image promoted by dietary supplement makers or fitness magazines. Benjo worked out hard because the physical exertion kept him physically fit and ready for whatever situations life might throw at him. Besides the positive physical effects, getting the blood and sweat flowing also kept him sharp mentally and emotionally. As he worked out his body, he also used the time to sort through his thoughts and keep his mind clear and focused. Hitting a physically-challenging goal and venting his anger and grief on the practice pads and heavy bag had also helped him through the process of trying to get over his wife's brutal murder. Venting those feelings in the gym and the physical tiredness of pushing himself to the limit helped him fall into a deep and dreamless sleep each night instead of staring at the ceiling or reaching over to feel the empty side of the bed where his wife once slept.

Once his workout was done, Benjo went back into the cabin where he showered, dressed in jeans, boots, and a nice shirt, and headed for the kitchen. As usual, Harley met him there, meowing to be fed like the poor thing had been left starving for days when in reality she'd eaten less than twelve hours earlier. He opened a can of cat food and dumped the whole thing into the cat's bowl near the refrigerator. The beast went through two cans of cat food a day, one in the morning and one at night. "I suspect it might be cheaper to raise a horse," Benjo said to Harley as he cooked his own breakfast. Harley replied by completely ignoring Benjo and continuing her meal.

Once his breakfast of scrambled eggs, toast, and bacon were done, Benjo sat down at the table in the breakfast nook and ate. As he ate, he pulled up Marsha West's statement on his email and read it again. Deke had emailed him the statements from West and Paul Tucker late last night just as he'd promised. However, he'd enclosed a message with the attached statements. The message was basically that the sheriff had ordered him to not help Benjo in any way, just as the sheriff himself had told Benjo earlier. Deke's message made it clear that Benjo was on his own and wished him good luck. The message angered Benjo, but not at Deke. His anger was reserved for Sheriff Crowe.

Benjo skimmed over the statement again in preparation for his meeting with Marsha. Marsha was the church's secretary who'd walked in on the aftermath of Sarah Fleming getting shot and called nine one one. Actually, as Benjo had learned after calling her yesterday evening, she was the former church secretary. She'd quit her job working at the church a month after the shooting and taken another job at a doctor's office dealing with medical records. After some initial reluctance, she'd agreed to speak with Benjo this morning at eight thirty before she went to work at ten AM. Despite agreeing to talk to him, Marsha, a thirty-three-year-old, married white female according to the police report, hadn't exactly sounded thrilled at the prospect of re-hashing the events of the day.

With that reluctance in mind, Benjo finished breakfast quickly, grabbed his cell phone and the Fleming file, and headed for his truck. He paused long enough to lock the cabin up before getting in his truck and driving to Marsha's address. Fortunately, it was just a twenty minute or so drive to an area he was familiar with from his time with the sheriff's department. Traffic wasn't bad at all and he arrived at Marsha's address, a nicely-restored Craftsman style home with red shutters and a concrete driveway in an older neighborhood in a small town several miles outside the city limits. A Honda sedan and an older Ford pickup truck sat in the driveway, so Benjo parked at the curb in front of the house near a mailbox bearing the home's number and the name West on the side in reflective black letters. A flagstone and concrete walkway led from the curb to the front door. Benjo got out and took the walkway to the front door. He rang the front doorbell.

The front door was opened almost immediately by a somewhat plump woman with dark, curly hair and glasses wearing purple scrubs. She wasn't bad-looking, but she would have been much more attractive if she'd just tried a bit harder and if she wasn't looking at him as if he had the plague. She had a name badge clipped on the front of her scrubs that identified her as Marsha West. "Mrs. West?" Benjo asked. "I'm Benjo Lane, the private investigator you spoke with on the phone yesterday evening."

"Yes sir," Marsha said. "Please come in." She stepped aside and waved Benjo in. Benjo stepped in to a living room full of comfortable furniture arranged around a big screen television mounted on the wall over a small fireplace. There was a small plastic table with two child-sized chairs around it. The table was covered with coloring books. "Excuse the mess. We have two kids. My husband just left to drop them off at school on his way to work." She pointed to the couch. "Have a seat."

Benjo took a seat on the edge of the couch and Marsha sat down in a chair across from him. Benjo gave the living room a quick once over as he settled down on the couch. He noted an empty wine glass sitting on the part of the kitchen counter he could see through the open archway that separated the kitchen from the living room. "Thank you for taking the time to see me," Benjo said. "I could tell my phone call yesterday caught you off guard."

"It did surprise me," Marsha said nervously. "I've already talked to the police a couple of times." She looked at Benjo suspiciously. "What exactly is your involvement in this again?"

"Some of Sarah Fleming's family and friends hired me to look into her death," Benjo said. "They are very suspicious about her death and what led to it. There are some things about her death that just don't quite make sense to them. I'm digging into the police investigation to see if there's anything they might have overlooked."

"And you're a real private investigator, Mr. Lane?" Marsha said as she arched an eyebrow at him. "Like on television?"

Benjo smiled and reached into his pocket to remove his PI credentials. He opened the small leather case to show her his official state PI license. She studied it intently. "I'm a real private investigator," he said. "Although I'm afraid it's nowhere near as exciting or glamorous as they make it out to be on television." He closed the case and slid it back into his jeans pocket. "If you don't mind, you can just call me Benjo."

"You don't look like a private investigator," Marsha said as she looked him up and down. "With the tattoos and the beard, I mean."

"What's one supposed to look like?" Benjo asked rhetorically. "Would you feel better if I had on a suit and tie?"

"No offense," Marsha said hastily. "You're just, well, different."

Ma'am, you have no idea, Benjo thought to himself as he smiled and tried to look extra-friendly. "I get that a lot," he said. "Despite looking a little different, I'm very good at my job. Right now, as I said, my job is to figure out if the shooting of Sarah Fleming was a real case of justifiable homicide as the Coles and the police say, or if it was something else entirely."

"What else could it be?" Marsha said as she sat back in her chair. "Do you think the Coles murdered that poor girl?" She suddenly looked a lot more interested.

"Do you?" Benjo asked. "You were one of the three living people who were there at the scene the day it happened."

"This is amazing," Marsha said. "I love true crime documentaries and podcasts. Now, just by pure coincidence, I'm in the middle of a murder investigation." She shook her head. "Awesome."

Benjo was tempted to tell her that Sarah probably wouldn't think it was awesome, but that might embarrass or anger the woman enough to make her stop talking to him. Instead, he decided to play to her excitement. "That's why I'm here, Marsha," he said. "I need your help. You were there the day it happened. You walked in on the scene of the crime just a couple of minutes after it happened. The Coles have their version of what happened, but they are involved and trying to stay out of trouble. You, on the other hand, are what we call an impartial witness. You have no vested interest in a particular outcome."

Marsha sat up straighter and squared her shoulders like she'd just heard a rousing motivational speech. "That's right," she said. "I would love to help you, Benjo, but I've already told the police everything that happened. If you've read my statement, you know what I told them."

"I've read your statement, Marsha," Benjo replied. "However, I spent over fifteen years as a detective for the sheriff's department. During that time, I investigated a lot of cases and interviewed hundreds of people. One thing I learned doing that was that a person's memory does odd things, especially if the memory is traumatic. During the traumatic event, a person can notice way more than they realize. They notice the big, important details first and foremost, obviously, but their brain also notices little things that the person didn't realize they noticed. Some of those weird, trivial things can pop up hours, days, even months later. I've interviewed people who were robbed at gunpoint who could barely tell me what race the robber was a couple of hours after the crime. However, two weeks later they call me to tell me that they remember the guy was white, he had a scar on his chin, and one eye was blue and the other was green."

"That's amazing," Marsha said.

"Marsha, I would like for you to tell me what happened the day Monica Cole shot Sarah Fleming," Benjo said. "Take your time and really think about it, okay? If something pops into your mind, no matter how trivial, tell me about it." He took out his notepad from his pocket. "I'm going to take a few notes, if you don't mind."

"Okay," Marsha said, nodding. "It was a Tuesday morning. I normally come into work around eight thirty, but I had the morning off to go to a doctor's appointment. I have psoriasis and I take an infusion treatment the doctor administers in his office. I was not supposed to come in to work until eleven that morning, but when I got to the doctor's office, I found out that the infusion machine they were going to use was not working. I was forced to reschedule, so I left the doctor's office and went straight on in to work. I always come in through the main doors of the church. My office, along with the Cole's offices, Paul Tucker's office, and another couple of spare offices are located down a hallway that runs off the lobby. A set of double doors separates that hallway from the lobby area. We normally have a receptionist who comes in to unlock the main doors. She has a desk there in the lobby so she can monitor who comes in and out of the building and help anyone who comes in."

That was the first Benjo had heard about a receptionist with a desk in the lobby. "Where was this receptionist that morning?" Benjo asked. "I don't recall seeing anything about a receptionist working in the lobby on the police incident report."

"Her name is Theresa Satterfield," Marsha said. "She was lucky enough to be on vacation that week. Her and her husband took their kids to Disney World that week, I believe."

"Is Theresa still working for the Coles?" Benjo asked as he jotted down a few notes.

"Yes," Marsha replied. "The poor girl took my job when I resigned after the incident with the girl."

"I take it her vacation had been planned for weeks?" Benjo asked. "This wasn't a spur-of-the-moment thing, was it?"

"No," Marsha said. "That's why I had the keys and had to unlock the main doors when I came in that morning."

"Okay," Benjo said. "Without Theresa there, who would man her desk in the lobby?"

"No one," Marsha said. "We have an alarm on the front door that lets us know when someone enters or leaves through those doors. It dings on my computer, as well as the Coles' and Paul's computer in his office. It also pops up a live video feed from the security camera we have in the lobby that looks at the front doors."

The file David had given him was limited, so Benjo had not had access to a lot of the information he was now getting from Marsha. He hadn't known anything about an alarm system that alerted people in the back offices of the church that someone had entered through the front doors. "Marsha, did any of the other doors at the church have that alarm on them to let people know that a door had been opened?"

"No, just the main entrance doors," Marsha said.

"Interesting," Benjo said. "Please continue."

"I unlocked the main doors with my keys and walked into the building," Marsha continued. "I had just opened the doors leading to the hallway where the offices were when I heard a loud pop. Just a few seconds later, I heard another pop."

"Did you know they were gunshots?" Benjo asked.

"No," Marsha replied immediately. "I thought someone had dropped something or that one of our maintenance guys had come in on his day off for some sort of emergency and was fixing something."

"Were the maintenance guys for the church off on Tuesdays?" Benjo asked.

"With the exception of myself, Theresa, and the Coles, everyone else was always off on Tuesdays," Marsha said. "Tuesday is the slow day for the church. Sunday is always busy because of services and Monday is spent cleaning up the building and handling things from Sunday. Tuesday is kind of a break from all of that stuff. It picks back up on Wednesday with Wednesday evening services, prayer groups, and other social activities for the elderly and stuff. On Thursdays and Fridays, the Coles film their television show and do a lot of their social media stuff."

"So, all of the other church employees are off on Tuesdays?" Benjo asked. Marsha nodded. "How many other employees work for the Coles?"

Marsha took a few seconds to count in her head. "Counting the people who work part-time handling production for their television show and their social media stuff, maintenance staff, me, Theresa, and Paul Tucker, there's maybe twenty-two people."

"That many?" Benjo said, surprised. "I wouldn't have thought that many."

Marsha rolled her eyes. "Let me let you in on a secret, Benjo," she said. "The Coles are what my mama used to call 'high-falutin' people'. A bunch of those people's sole job is to make the Coles look good and make their lives easier. They have a girl they pay a bunch of money just to come in and make sure the Coles always look great. She does their hair and makeup before they post anything on their social media and before they film their show."

"Really?" Benjo said, just to keep Marsha talking. "I never would have thought that. Anyway, you said you heard two pops."

"Yes," Marsha said. "I went down the hall to my desk, which is in an open area outside the two offices that are Monica's and August's. I put my purse down on the desk and then went to Monica's office to let her know I was in early. As I walked to her door, which was closed, I heard a commotion inside. I knocked on the door and then I heard Monica yell for me to come in." She crossed her arms and then rubbed them as if she had caught a chill. "I opened the door and that's when I got my first look at what had happened."

"What's the first thing you saw?" Benjo asked.

"The girl laying in the floor in front of her desk," Marsha replied. "She was still moving like she was trying to get up. Monica was standing a few feet away right beside her desk with a pistol in her hand. August was behind Monica's desk. He had just rushed into her office from his adjoining office."

"How do you know that?" Benjo asked. "How do you know he had just come into Monica's office from his adjoining one?"

"There's a door that joins the two offices," Marsha replied. "August was between Monica's desk and the door which is in the wall to the left of Monica's desk if you were facing it. Monica's desk faced the door I had just opened. The door between the two offices was just closing as I was coming in."

"Okay," Benjo said as he pictured it in his mind. "What happened next?"

"August rushed around the desk, took a look at the girl, and then turned his attention to Monica. He took the pistol from Monica and put it down on the desk. He asked her if she was hurt and Monica shook her head and started crying. He told me to go out to my desk and call nine one one. I ran out to my desk and called for help. After I answered a bunch of questions for the dispatcher that answered the telephone, I left the phone off the hook and went back into Monica's office. August was kneeling beside the girl. Monica was standing in the corner gawking."

"Marsha, did you see anything in Sarah's hands? Benjo asked. "Where was the letter opener she was allegedly trying to stab Monica with?"

"As I came back in, August was kneeling beside the poor girl," Marsha continued. "She was unconscious by then and there was blood everywhere. As I walked in, August was taking the letter opener out of the girl's right hand. He took it and tossed it to the side. He then looked at me and ordered me to go out into the hallway and call Paul. I stepped back out into the hallway and used my cell phone to do that. Then I went back into the office to see if I could do anything to help."

"When did Paul Tucker show up?" Benjo asked as he scribbled a few notes.

At the mention of Tucker's name, Marsha frowned slightly and a look of distaste flashed across her face. Benjo made a mental note of that. "I ran out into the hall and called him. He said he was on the way. A couple of minutes later, he popped out of the door between the offices," Marsha recalled. "He said he had run into August's office first, then come through the door when he realized what was happening was in Monica's office."

"Tucker said he was in the rear of the church building using the bathroom near the production studio when you called him on his cell phone to come to Monica's office immediately," Benjo said. "Did you tell him specifically Monica's office or did you tell him to just get to the office?"

"I told him Monica's office," Marsha said. "That's one of the things about it that struck me as weird once everything calmed down and I had time to think about it."

"What do you mean?" Benjo asked. Early in his career as a detective, Benjo had learned that sometimes it was best to just let people talk and not interrupt. Doing that often produced more information than a bunch of pointed questions.

"About two days later, when I got to thinking about it, I couldn't figure out why he came through August's office and not directly to Monica's like I told him. If he was where he said he was, he literally had to run by Monica's door to get to August's office door," Marsha said.

"Did you ever ask him about that?" Benjo asked.

Marsha nodded. "About a week later, I asked him about it at work," she said. "He told me that I was remembering it wrong and that he came through Monica's office door right behind me. When I tried to argue, he told me to drop it because it might upset the Coles."

"Did you tell Detective Marsh about Tucker coming through the door that linked the two offices?" Benjo asked.

"I tried to," Marsha said. "He told me that I had told him in my original statement that Tucker came through the door behind me. I might have, to be honest. Detective Marsh interviewed me just a couple of hours after the shooting. I was a mess emotionally and mentally. I mean, I'd just watched a young lady get shot and lay there suffering. I saw the paramedics try to save her and it not work. That girl was about my younger sister's age. It tore me up."

"That would be hard for anyone to see," Benjo said sympathetically. "What did Detective Marsh say about changing your statement?"

"He basically told me that he wasn't going to do that," Marsha said with a touch of bitterness in her voice. "He gave me a speech about how adrenaline can mess with your mind when you're scared or excited and that he wasn't going to change my statement because my original statement was in line with what the Coles and Tucker had said. Changing it would just complicate things. He made me feel like an idiot, to be honest."

"Marsha, I worked with Detective Marsh for years," Benjo said. "Between the two of us, he's not much of a detective. I think he was being lazy and just trying to close a case with minimum effort. He didn't listen to you because changing your statement might complicate things and make him have to work."

"He was not a nice man," Marsha acknowledged.

"Marsha, I want to ask you a hypothetical question," Benjo said. "It might seem kind of out there, but it's one that I feel needs asking. You said you saw the door between Monica's office and August's office closing when you first entered Monica's office."

"That's right," Marsha said.

"Does that door have an automatic closer or something similar on it?" Benjo asked.

"No," Marsha replied flatly. "I have seen Monica and August leave that door standing open so they could go between the offices without opening it."

"You assumed that August had just come through that door in response to the commotion in his wife's office. Correct?" Benjo asked. Marsha nodded. "Could the door have been closing because someone else was leaving the room and didn't want you to see them?"

"Who else would have been in the room with…?" Marsha started to ask, but then her eyes widened. "My God, you think Paul was in the office with Monica when Sarah was shot, don't you?" she asked.

Benjo shrugged. "You say Tucker came into Monica's office through the door from August's office, even though you told him to come to Monica's office. You also say he had to come past Monica's office door to go into August's office. Who's to say that he wasn't already in there? You worked with them, Marsha. In your opinion, who would be more likely to shoot someone, Monica, August, or Paul Tucker?"

"Tucker, by a country mile," Marsha said instantly. "That man gives me the creeps. There's just something off about him."

"It's just an idea that came to me," Benjo said, "It's one of several possible scenarios. The hard part is figuring out which one might actually be what happened. You said August removed the letter opener from Sarah's hand as she was lying in the floor. Is that right?"

"Yes," Marsha said.

"Had you ever seen that letter opener before?" Benjo asked. "Was it something that Monica normally kept on her desk?"

"I never knew she even had a letter opener," Marsha replied. "It makes sense that she would have one, though, because they were adamant that I never open their mail."

"You were their secretary for how long?" Benjo asked.

"Four years," Marsha said.

"And they wouldn't let you open their business mail? I can understand personal mail, but wouldn't one of your responsibilities be opening business mail?" Benjo asked.

"Monica and August were very weird about stuff like that," Marsha admitted. "They wouldn't let me near anything pertaining to the church's financial situation like the bills or bank statements. There were days I would spend hours shopping online or messing with social media because I didn't have anything to do. I even asked August a few times if he wanted me to help them out with bank deposits or anything and he always said no."

"Did he ever give you an explanation as to why?" Benjo asked. "I would think letting the church secretary handle some of the lesser financial things would be a help for a busy couple like the Coles."

"August told me one time that, early in his career as a traveling minister, a person they hired to handle money for them stole a bunch of it," Marsha said. "He said he was never going to put himself or his church in that situation again. That's why they never had a chief financial officer there. The Coles handled it all."

"When you first went into Monica's office after the shooting, what did the office look like?" Benjo asked. "Were there signs of a struggle? Knocked-over furniture or papers in the floor?"

Marsha closed her eyes as if trying to picture it in her mind. "Just that poor girl lying there bleeding," she finally said after several seconds. "Nothing looked too out of place. August did have some papers in his hand when I went back in after calling for help. I don't recall what he did with them." She glanced down at her watch. "How much longer will this take? I've got to leave for work in about fifteen minutes."

Benjo smiled at her. "I appreciate you taking the time to meet with me," he said sincerely. "I just have two more quick questions and then I'm done. The first one is kind of weird. Did you have a trash can by your desk outside of Monica's office?"

"A trash can?" Marsha asked in confusion. "You mean, like, a waste basket by my desk?" Benjo nodded. "No, the trash can for my desk was inside a cabinet where it couldn't be seen. Monica always said that having a trash can visible didn't look professional, so my desk was one of those with a built-in cabinet to hide the trash can. What's that got to do with anything?"

"Sarah Fleming had some papers with her when she came in the building that day," Benjo answered. "The police said that the papers were a ruse to get in to see Monica. I'm trying to figure out what those papers were and where they went. I was wondering if she might have tossed them in a convenient trash can. One at your desk right outside Monica's door would be convenient."

"Maybe those were the papers August had in his hand when I came back into the office after calling for help," Marsha replied.

"They are not mentioned in the police reports anywhere," Benjo said. "Did Monica ever say anything to you about someone stalking or harassing her? Did you ever get any regular telephone calls from a female demanding to speak with Monica?"

"Detective Marsh showed me the girl's cell phone number," Marsha said. "The phone system we used saves ingoing and outgoing numbers for several months. We were able to find where the girl's number had called the office three times before. I remembered the calls then. A female asking for Monica Cole. The caller was always very polite.

Monica took the first one and talked for maybe five minutes, if memory serves. Another time the same number called and Monica spoke to her for close to twenty minutes I think."

"That agrees with the records I have then," Benjo said. He closed his notebook and stood up. "I think that's it, Marsha. Once again, I appreciate your time."

Marsha turned and led him to the front door. As he reached the front door, he turned to Marsha. "Marsha, if I may ask, why did you resign from the church? You were there for four years."

She opened the front door. "The Coles are hard to work for. They pay very well, but they treat the people who work for them terribly. Everyone who works there hates them. The only reason they stay is that the Coles pay way more than they could make doing a similar job elsewhere."

"That bad, huh?" Benjo asked as he stepped out onto the front porch.

"They treated me better than most, and that wasn't that great," Marsha said. "I've seen Monica make some of the other employees cry. The ones who worked behind the scenes on their television show caught the worst of it. Everything had to be perfect. The Coles are all about how people perceive them."

"Interesting," Benjo said. "Have a good day, Marsha."

Benjo left the house and walked back to his truck. He got into his truck and sat there while he used his cell phone to call Chase Fleming's cell phone. Chase answered on the second ring. "Chase, it's Benjo, did you get Sarah's cell phone records and the financial records I asked for?"

"I've got them here on my desk," Chase said. "I was expecting your call."

"I'm on my way to get them," Benjo said. "On the cell phone records, I need a favor."

"I'll help anyway I can," Chase replied through the phone.

"Go over the cell phone records and highlight the numbers you are familiar with," Benjo said. "For example, your number where you called her or she called you, relatives, friends you recognize, etcetera."

"I can do that," Chase said.

"Excellent," Benjo said. "I don't suppose you could spare a few minutes to meet with me? I have a few follow-up questions."

"That shouldn't be an issue. David is tied up in court, so I'm just reading over some law briefs," Chase answered. "How's the investigation going?"

"Steady," Benjo replied. He did not want to elaborate any further. There was still a long way to go. "I'll be there shortly." He ended the call, put his cell phone in the holder on his dash, and started his truck. He pulled away from the curb and headed for Whiteside's office.

As Benjo drove away from Marsha West's house, a blue Hyundai sedan with darkly-tinted windows pulled away from the curb about fifty feet behind him and started following his truck.

10

When Benjo arrived thirty minutes later, Chase was waiting for him in the lobby of the three-story brick building that housed David's law offices. Chase showed him to a small conference room on the second floor that wasn't being used. Chase had two folders waiting on a large table of polished wood in the center of the room. One was labelled Financial and the other was labelled Cell Phone. The cell phone folder was open and several papers were neatly laid out on the table. Several markers of different color were laid out beside the papers on the table. The papers laid out there had markings corresponding to the different colored markers.

"I did what you asked," Chase said as he closed the conference door behind Benjo. "All of the marked numbers are numbers I recognize personally or numbers that were in her cell phone's contacts list. Most were friends, myself or other family members, or work-related."

Benjo leaned on the table and studied the pages. "You got a lot done in thirty minutes," he said.

"Me and Sarah shared a lot of the same friends," Chase said. "Sarah wasn't a social butterfly; she had a small circle of three or four really good friends she talked to or texted regularly. She didn't have a boyfriend. The last guy she dated was a at least six months ago. In between work and helping out with our mom, she didn't have time for a boyfriend or much of a social life."

"Is it okay if I sit?" Benjo asked as he slid a chair out from beneath the conference table. The chair was made of the same dark wood as the table.

"Sure," Chase replied. He walked to the closest end of the table and sat down himself.

Benjo took a seat and began to skim over the pages laid out before him. It took just a few minutes for him to find what he was looking for. He found the three calls the police had cited in their report as examples of Sarah harassing Monica Cole. Sarah had called Monica's cell phone three times over the course of three days a week prior to the confrontation with Monica Cole at her office. The first call had lasted barely over five minutes. The second call was just a few seconds, most likely indicating that Monica had hung up on Sarah. The third call had lasted slightly over eighteen minutes. Monica's explanation for the length of the third call was that she had tried to reason with Sarah, the unknown caller at the time. There were no other calls from Sarah's cell phone to the church's number for seven days prior to the shooting in Monica's office. During the seven days prior to Sarah's death, there were numerous other calls or texts from numbers Chase had high-lighted with markers. There was one unknown number that appeared three times, twice as an incoming call made to Sarah's phone and once as a call Sarah made to that unknown number. Sarah had received a call from that unknown number at seven ten PM the evening before she was shot in Monica Cole's office at the church.

"You didn't recognize this number?" Benjo asked as he circled the unknown number with his pen. The number had a local area code, but the first three digits of the telephone number were not ones Benjo recognized from local cell phone service providers.

"No," Chase replied. "I dialed it just a few minutes before you walked in. I got a recording stating that the number is no longer in service."

"Okay," Benjo said. He pulled his own cell phone out of his pocket and dialed a number from memory. The call was answered on the second ring by a man with a voice deep enough to sing bass in a barbershop quartet if he wanted. The voice belonged to a man named Colton Goodman, a friend of Benjo's since high school. Colton was a tall, gangly young man with glasses and long brown hair he kept pulled into a ponytail. He looked like the type who would work in the information technology field and he did. He worked in the IT department at a local college, at least as his day job. In the evenings he owned his own technology consulting company where he specialized in building gaming consoles and repairing or upgrading other electronic devices. His favorite devices to mess with were cell phones. Colton was something of an evil genius and a great resource for when Benjo had a technological question.

"Colt, it's Benjo," Benjo said. "I need a quick favor, my friend. It involves a cell phone number."

"What do you need?" Colt asked. His deep voice, which was a startling contrast to his lean frame, was so loud through Benjo's cell phone that he might as well have been on speaker phone.

"If I give you a cell phone number, can you tell me who it belongs to?" Benjo asked. "Before you even ask, I'm not an idiot; I've dialed the number to see who answers. It comes back as not in service. I have a suspicion about it; I just want to see if you verify it or not."

"Benjo, you know that doing such a thing is highly unethical, probably illegal, and a major violation of someone's privacy," Colt replied immediately. "Only the government or a major law enforcement agency would have the resources to build a program that could immediately tell you anything worth squat based on just a cell phone number."

"Or an evil genius I know could build such a thing for a twelve pack of beer and a large pizza," Benjo said patiently. "Now that that's out of the way, I know who I'm talking to. I know you can do it, Colt. I've seen you do more impressive things."

Colt sighed. "Give me the number," he growled. Benjo rattled off the ten-digit number. "I'll call you back within ten minutes." Colt replied. There was a soft beep as he ended the call.

Benjo put his cell phone down on the table and leaned back in his chair. "You seem to know some interesting characters, Benjo," Chase said.

"I do," Benjo replied honestly. "Colt, the guy I was just talking to, is really a genius with anything electronic. I suspect one day he'll either be on a list of the richest people in the word or in prison somewhere. He's a great guy, but he's also a little odd."

"What are you trying to find out about that cell phone number?" Chase asked.

"I don't want to say until I can get my suspicion confirmed," Benjo answered as he leaned forward to rest his elbows on the table.

"Well, then, how's your investigation going?" Chase asked with a frustrated sigh. "Are you making any headway at all?"

"I am," Benjo replied. "I've been to the church where I met their security director, Paul Tucker. He was there the day Sarah was killed. He's a piece of work and it was hate at first sight between us. While I was there, I learned that Kathy Miller, an investigative reporter for the local news station, had been looking into the Coles. I met with her and she thinks the Coles are up to all kinds of illegal shenanigans. However, her bosses have called her off until she can get something more solid against the Coles than rumors and maybes. I also found out that Dale Marsh, the sheriff's detective that worked the case, had a major conflict of interest that he never disclosed. He had worked security for the Coles at their church. I also met with the church secretary who was there the day Sarah died. I learned that all of the Cole's employees hate them because they're obnoxious assholes."

Chase sat back in his chair with a dazed look on his face. Benjo sat back and waited in silence for what he knew was coming. Out in the hallway outside the conference room, someone hurried by. Benjo could tell that whoever it was had on high heels by the way they clicked on the hardwood floor. Benjo thought it might be one of the female paralegals, but with the way the world was going, he wasn't going to assume anything. The air conditioning clicked on with a slight hum. There was a nice painting on the wall across from Benjo. It was a seascape with a towering, three-masted ship cutting through the waves near a rocky coastline.

"That's...That's great," Chase finally said. "What does all of that mean in regards to my sister's death?"

Before Benjo could answer, his cell phone rang. He picked it up and answered the call. "Colt, talk to me," he said as he looked at Chase. He listened to what Colt had to say. "You sure?" he asked flatly. Satisfied with the answer, Benjo thanked him and ended the call. He casually laid his phone back on the table. "It's just what I thought," he said.

"What?" Chase demanded anxiously.

Benjo held up the page of the telephone records that had the unidentified number that had called Sarah in the week before her demise. "That number comes back to a burner phone," he said. "Someone bought a cheap, untraceable, pre-paid cell phone from a store and used it to call your sister three times in the week before she was killed. The final call was the evening before she went to the church and was shot by Monica Cole." He looked at Chase intently. "Chase, is there anyone Sarah knew who would do that? Someone who might have lost their regular phone or something like that?"

"No," Chase replied. "I called everyone on their cell phones to let them know she had died. They all answered, which means they all had their regular phones."

"As soon as I leave, I want you to call all of them and ask them, just to be sure," Benjo said. "It's very important that we confirm that this number wasn't a friend or coworker."

"Why?" Chase asked. "What does it mean if it's not one of them?"

Benjo tapped the phone records. "I think the person who used this phone wanted to communicate with Sarah in a way that could not be traced back to them. That's why a lot of criminals use burner phones; they can use them, throw them away, and there's no way for law enforcement to know who made the call, even if they have the number and a location. The police can track the phone's location and literally find it laying on the ground because someone dropped it and walked away. The other great thing about burner phones for bad guys is that you can buy them practically everywhere from convenience stores to Wal-Mart. I've even seen displays of them in grocery stores."

Chase looked confused. "I'm still not getting it," he confessed.

"I think Sarah was in contact with Monica Cole," Benjo said. "The three phone calls from Sarah's cell to the church the police used as evidence of harassment were Sarah reaching out to Monica Cole for some unknown reason. The first call from Sarah was just over five minutes. That's just enough for an introduction and maybe a brief discussion about the reason Sarah was calling. The second call from Sarah was just a few seconds. That was the church secretary transferring the call to Monica's office phone, Monica seeing who it was, and hanging up on her. The third call was almost eighteen minutes. That's Sarah calling, Monica answering, and then the two of them having a fairly lengthy conversation about something. That doesn't fit with Monica's claim that Sarah was calling her and threatening and cursing her. Think about it, are you going to talk with someone who is obviously mentally disturbed and cursing you out for nearly twenty minutes?"

"No," Chase said. "Monica claimed she was trying to reason with Sarah and get her to get help."

"That's what I would say too, especially if I was the assistant pastor of a church and wanted my followers to see me as a victim," Benjo said. "After that call, the calls from Sarah's phone to the church stop. There are no other calls to Sarah's cell phone to the church or from the church number or a cell number that could be tracked to Monica Cole. However, the calls from the untraceable burner phone to Sarah start. Out of those three calls, the shortest one was nearly ten minutes. Someone reached out to Sarah and was talking to her for a pretty decent amount of time all three times. Who was calling her and why?"

Understanding dawned on Chase's young face. "Monica Cole didn't want a record that she was talking to my sister," he said. "She bought a burner phone so there would be no record that she talked to her."

Benjo nodded. "All the police would have is what we have," he said. "They have the three traceable calls from Sarah to the church. The other three numbers, the ones from the burner phone, could be anybody."

Chase thought for a moment. "But why would Monica Cole want to hide that she was talking to Sarah?"

"There's no easy way to say this, Chase," Benjo said. "I think the Coles were setting your sister up to kill her. I think they used the burner phone because they didn't want anyone to know they were talking back and forth to Sarah. I think they had her come to the church under some false pretext and, once she was there, they murdered her. It's the only plausible explanation that fits."

The color drained from Chase's face. He turned and stared at the wall for several seconds while he fought to control his emotions. "Explain to me why you think that," he said. His voice was a little shaky.

"There was no contact between any number linked to the church or to the Coles for a week prior to Sarah's death," Benjo explained. "However, the calls from the untraceable burner phone started. After those calls start, Sarah goes to the church on a Tuesday morning. It just so happens that Tuesday is a slow day for the church staff, a day when most of them come in later in the afternoon or not at all. Usually, the only ones there on a Tuesday are the Coles, the church secretary, and a receptionist who mans a desk in the lobby there at the main doors. The Tuesday Sarah was killed, the church secretary was off for a doctor's appointment that was supposed to keep her out of the office until at least eleven AM. The receptionist was off for a week of vacation. That meant that the only people there in the church were the Coles and their shady, convicted- felon -security director, Paul Tucker. August Cole has a criminal record for assault and drug offenses, Tucker's record is even longer and full of violent assaults, and Monica wasn't exactly an angel when she was younger either, according to one of my sources. The only reason Monica doesn't have a record, according to my source, was pure luck and the fact that August pled guilty to some things in exchange for the police dropping charges on Monica.

"Sarah arrives at the church and, for some unknown reason, goes directly to barely-used side door. That side door happens to be on the side of the building that is hidden from potential witnesses passing by on the highway or shopping at the store the church shares a parking lot with," Benjo continued. "I learned that the church has cameras on the lobby and an alarm that pops up on their computers when someone comes through the main doors. Their computers beep and a live camera feed pops up showing the person entering the building. There's no way Sarah knew about that camera on the main doors or the alarm system, so why did she go directly to that side door and not any of the other doors? There were eight other doors on different sides of the building. If she was trying to sneak in, as the Coles claim, then why isn't she on video trying any of the other doors?"

"She went straight to that door because someone told her to," Chase answered. "That makes a lot of sense."

"The person who lured her to the church wanted to keep the chances of her being seen coming into the building to a minimum," Benjo replied.

"But that side door had a camera on it as well," Chase said. "That's where the video of Sarah entering the building came from."

"Camera footage can be erased," Benjo explained. "An eyewitness loading lumber on his truck next door at the home improvement store they shared a lot with seeing a pretty girl parking up front and going through the main doors of the church couldn't be erased. A passerby in the parking lot or out on the highway out front who remembered seeing Sarah couldn't be erased with a click of a button. The home improvement store's security cameras couldn't be erased by the Coles or Tucker either. Having Sarah park on the side and enter through that side door cut down the chances of an eyewitness or a camera they couldn't control seeing her by, what, ninety percent at least?"

Chase thought for a moment. He still looked a little dazed. "If they were setting her up, why not cut off the camera on the side door as well?" he asked. "There would have been no record that she was ever there at all."

"I think that the Coles lured Sarah to the church without a plan on how to handle her," Benjo said. "They wanted Sarah out of the way for some unknown reason. I don't know if their plan was to make her death look like self-defense or if they planned to murder her and get rid of her body. Maybe killing her was a spur-of-the-moment thing after something went south during their meeting at the church. Maybe their plan to kill her and get rid of the body was interrupted by the church secretary coming in when she wasn't supposed to. It could be something as simple as they forgot about that camera on the side door. Trust me, I've seen cases solved because of something simple and stupid like that."

Chase stood up and paced the room. "That still doesn't explain why the Coles would want to kill Sarah," he said. "They had the means and opportunity, but what was the motive? WHY were they meeting my sister? Why were they secretly communicating with her? Why did they decide to kill her?"

"I still don't know," Benjo said. "Just like I still don't know if they planned to kill her or if it was a spur-of-the-moment thing. Those are still questions I need answers to. I do know that Sarah had some papers in her hand when she went into the building. That's on the video footage. Those papers are unaccounted for. The police thought those papers were a ruse for getting in to see Monica. They thought that Sarah discarded them once she was inside. My gut tells me something was on those papers. Whatever that something was, the Coles ended up killing her over it."

"I've gone through all of her stuff," Chase said plaintively, "looking for anything unusual. Unless there's something I'm missing, I haven't found a thing. I also feel that Sarah would have told me whatever the secret was."

Benjo thought about that for a few moments. "It depends on the secret," he said. "If it was something very personal, she might not tell anyone, especially if that secret might hurt them. Maybe she was wait-ing to get more proof of whatever it was before she said anything and the Coles killed her before she could," he said. "I think the Coles got rid of the papers Sarah had because they didn't want what was on them getting out. That also explains the burglary at her apartment where her laptop was stolen. Someone was making sure that what was on those papers wasn't on her laptop. They swiped the laptop just to be safe."

"If that's true, then wouldn't something have happened with Darcy or with me or her other friends?" Chase asked. "Wouldn't they worry that she might have told one of the people in her life this secret? If it was something they would kill her over, then it has to be something pretty bad. They would worry that she told someone else."

"Maybe, during her conversations with, we assume, the Coles, she told them that she hadn't told anyone the secret," Benjo argued. "Perhaps Sarah knew that if she told anyone, word might get out and she might lose whatever hold she had on the Coles. For all we know, she could have been trying to blackmail them and they decided to kill her instead."

"Really, Benjo?" Chase asked. "My sister was an extortionist?" He shook his head in disgust.

"The Coles are public figures in a position where they have to uphold certain moral standards," Benjo retorted. "I've learned that they are very conscious of their public image. They also have boatloads of money at their disposal. Both Monica and August also have shady pasts. It's not that hard to imagine, Chase, especially if you accept that Sarah might not have been a saint."

Chase bristled at that. "You know, you need to work on your people skills," he said. "I know you didn't know my sister, but if you had known her you would understand why even thinking she was doing something illegal is outlandish. Also, like I just said, if she knew something on the Coles that was that terrible, it seems like anyone in her life she might have told might be in danger."

"They would potentially have to kill several people in that case," Benjo replied. "That's a lot of killing, Chase. It would not go unnoticed. I personally believe that something happened the day Sarah was killed at the church that convinced the Coles that their secret would die with her. If Sarah was really the kind of good person she seems to have been, then she maybe didn't realize the kind of people she was dealing with."

"You really think August and Monica Cole would murder a girl over some stupid secret from their past?" Chase asked.

"Considering what they might lose? Absolutely," Benjo answered instantly. "I've seen people killed for reasons so petty it boggles the mind. If Sarah knew something that might bring down the Coles and their church, then that's plenty of reason to kill her. If they are actually laundering drug money through the church as my source claims, then the people they launder the money for could have made them kill your sister. I've met Paul Tucker face to face. I can tell you right now that he's a killer. He's got the look."

Chase ran his hand over his face in frustration. "This is insane," he said bitterly. "This whole twisted mess is nuts."

"Look, Chase, something brought your sister into contact with the Coles," Benjo said. "It was something so bad that it possibly made the Coles murder her."

Chase slapped the table in frustration. "Benjo, honest to God, I have wracked my brains trying to think of how Sarah could have been connected to the Coles. I've spent the last two days on the phone with or talking in person with our mutual friends. I've talked to some of her coworkers. If there was something, no one knew anything about what it could be."

"My source believes that the Coles are secretly laundering dirty money for an outlaw motorcycle gang through their church," Benjo said. "Could Sarah have learned about that somehow?"

Chase looked at Benjo like he'd just grown a third eye in the center of his forehead. "She had nothing to do with Hope Springs Church. None of her friends go to church there. If she had found out something like that, do you think she would have confronted the Coles with that knowledge? Why on earth would she do that?" he asked angrily.

Benjo held up his hands in a 'calm down' gesture. "Easy, Chase, I'm brainstorming here, okay?" He thought for a moment. "Is there a chance she could have learned something from her job in the emergency room?"

Chase shrugged. "Like what? The Coles secretly host orgies and they both have the clap? Trust me, nurses gossip worse than a bunch of old women. If something like that had come through the ER, a whole lot more people would know it than just my sister."

"Think, Chase, before Sarah's run-in with the Coles, did you ever notice any kind of changes in her?" Benjo asked. "Was she going out more socially? Was she hanging out with different people than she normally did? Anything you noticed, no matter how trivial, could be important."

"The only thing I saw with Sarah that was any different was right after our mom died," Chase said.

"Then tell me about that," Benjo said.

"Our mom, Reena died two months before Sarah was shot," Chase said. "She was diagnosed with stage four ovarian cancer. It had spread to her lymph nodes and liver. It took three months from diagnosis until she was in a hospice center. When Sarah wasn't at work or sleeping, she was taking care of our mom. During the last two weeks of our mom's life, Sarah and I alternated time at the hospice center. You ever had anyone go through cancer and hospice?"

"No," Benjo replied. "My mom died of a stroke when I was nineteen and in the Marines. My dad died three years ago when a twenty-two -year-old college girl with triple the legal limit of alcohol in her blood decided that she was okay to drive home from the bar. She wasn't. My dad happened to be on the road with her when she decided to drive in both lanes. She survived and is a quadriplegic. My dad didn't."

"Going fast like that is a blessing," Chase said. "Hospice is hell for the family. Of course, I don't imagine it's a walk in the park for the patient either. Anyway, Sarah and I alternated spending time at the hospice house with mom. Sarah was there when mom finally passed. In the days following our mom's passing, Sarah was not herself. She was very quiet and withdrawn. I assumed it was exhaustion and grief. As the days passed, she seemed to improve, but I could always tell there was something eating at her. I asked her about it finally. I think it was a couple of days after mom's funeral."

"What did she say?" Benjo asked.

"She told me that she was holding mom's hand and talking to her when she was breathing her last," Chase said. "She kind of implied that mom had told her something as she was dying that really shook her up. Sarah refused to elaborate on what mom said. I told her that mom was out of her mind from the sickness and the powerful drugs they gave her for the pain, so anything she said was probably just the dope talking."

"Did Sarah cheer up afterwards?" Benjo asked.

Chase looked down at the floor. "She seemed to, at least around me," he said. "In between her work, my school, and dealing with mom's affairs, we didn't spend as much time with each other as we normally did."

Benjo reached over and clasped the young man's shoulder. "That happens with any family," he said. "Don't beat yourself up."

Chase's eyes teared up. "That's easy for you to say," he said. "I never imagined that she would be taken so young, especially that she would be murdered."

"I know," Benjo said. "I can think of about ten million things I would have loved to say to my wife, Presley. Losing anyone is hard, but losing them to murder makes it infinitely worse."

Chase nodded. "How do you cope?"

"Knowing that the men who killed my wife paid for it helped tremendously," Benjo answered honestly. "I think I would have gone mad if the two punks who actually fired the shots and the man who ordered it were still walking around free or sitting in a jail cell watching cable television eating three square meals a day."

"I've read that revenge is a dish best served cold," Chase said.

"Revenge is a dish I'll take served any way at all," Benjo replied. "The victim deserves it and those who remain need it."

"I get that," Chase said. "I want someone to pay for what happened to Sarah so bad I can taste it."

"Me too," Benjo replied softly. "That's why I'm going to do everything possible to make sure that happens."

"You've already done more than the police did," Chase said gratefully. "I don't think they even tried to get the truth."

"I know the detective involved," Benjo said. "He didn't. He was just trying to close an easy case. Like I said the day we met, I get answers, good, bad, or ugly."

Chase wiped at his eyes with his hands. "To be honest, the first day I met you I thought you were an obnoxious ass who was trying way too hard to look edgy," he confessed. "I was wrong and I owe you an apology."

Benjo grinned. "You actually weren't wrong. I am an obnoxious ass. The edgy look just happened naturally when I stopped caring. The good news is that this obnoxious, edgy, ass doesn't know when to quit. That's a hell of a combination to aim at a mystery."

Chase smiled. "What's your next move?" he asked.

"I'm talking to your sister's former roommate, Darcy Woodruff, to-morrow morning," Benjo said. He gathered up the telephone records and slipped them in their folder. He picked that folder and the folder containing the bank records as he stood up. "I'm going over these this evening. I'm going to keep at it until I know why Sarah was murdered and who actually pulled the trigger."

"Monica Cole claims she pulled the trigger," Chase said as he stood up and faced Benjo. "That's stated fact."

"That's the official version," Benjo said. "I don't think she did."

"Then who actually shot my sister?" Chase asked.

"I don't know," Benjo answered. "Yet."

11

It was getting close to lunchtime when Benjo emerged from the rear door of the law office building carrying the two folders Chase had given him. The parking lot for David's law office was located on one side of the building and extended around to the back of the building. Benjo had parked in the part of the lot that was at the back of the building because the parking lot was pretty full when he arrived. Now, with many of the people who worked in the building gone to lunch, the parking lot was barely half full. His truck sat by itself in the back corner of the lot near a row of tall hedges that separated the law office lot from an adjoining lot. Tucking the two folders under his arm, Benjo strolled across the parking lot toward his truck.

He was only a feet away from his truck when the two men emerged from an opening between two of the hedges. One of the men was short, maybe five feet six in his bare feet, but stocky and heavily-muscled. He had on a baseball cap pulled low on a head full of curly black hair and a bushy mustache. He wore jeans, sneakers, and a tee shirt with the name of some band Benjo had never heard of on the front of it. His exposed arms were covered with bad tattoos. The second guy was at least four inches taller than Benjo, making him at least six foot five in height, and he looked to weigh at least a good three hundred pounds. His head was shaved bald and he had the face of an angry bulldog. He had small, angry eyes set deep back in his face behind fat cheeks. He wore filthy jeans, black motorcycle boots, and a tank top with grease stains on it. The two men immediately came around the front of his truck to get between Benjo and the truck. They stood side by side and glared at him.

Benjo stopped a few feet away from them and a tense face-off ensued. His body tensed as adrenaline flooded his system. At first, he had no idea who the mismatched pair were or what they might want, but they looked dangerous. Both men were wholly out of place as they stood in the parking lot of the busy law firm. They looked like they would be more at home behind the walls of the local maximum-security prison. He studied each man carefully, looking over both men for weapons and other clues to their identities and purpose. Neither of the two men had any weapons visible, but, judging from the scars of their faces and knuckles, they had dished out a few beatings. They looked like the type who enjoyed dishing out pain and suffering to others.

As the three men stood there, Benjo calculated his odds. The two men were going to attack him; it was obvious from their body language. Benjo knew he had two options: fight or run for safety. If he was going to fight the two of them, then he would have to do whatever it took to end the altercation quickly. Logic dictated that the longer he fought both men, the greater his chance of being overwhelmed and beaten was. That was just basic math. Of the two men, the short, muscular one was most likely the most dangerous, simply because he was in better shape and moved like he knew what he was doing. The bigger man looked like he relied mainly on his weight and power to carry the day. He looked like the type who would try to tackle you, bear you to the ground with his weight, and pound you into the ground with his large fists. The key to fighting him was to not get into a test of strength. The key to fighting his shorter friend would be to take him out fast before his conditioning and speed became a factor. For a brief second Benjo considered running, but only for a second. Running had never been his style.

"Good afternoon, gentlemen," Benjo said warmly. "Can I help you?"

"Give us your truck keys, your wallet, and those two folders too," the shorter of the two men said menacingly. His voice was a low growl.

Hard experience as a funny-looking kid with a weird name growing up, a former Marine who'd seen combat in Afghanistan, and a cop in some pretty rough areas had made Benjo a huge fan of what he'd labelled QDA. QDA stood for Quick Decisive Action. QDA was his personal code, and it was so important to him that he had the letters QDA tattooed on the inside of his left wrist. QDA's meaning to him was simple: If you have to act, then act fast, make that action matter, and carry it through to the bitter end. That personal code had carried him through many a tough situation, whether it was physical, mental, or emotional. With that mindset to guide him, if he was going to have to fight these two thugs, he might as well start wide open. Benjo grinned at the shorter of the two men, the one who'd spoken to him. "That's not going to happen, Half Pint."

The shorter man stiffened and his face turned blood-red. Just as Benjo had suspected, the man had been the butt of a few short jokes in his lifetime and he didn't like them. That was good to know; Benjo wanted the guy furious enough to make a mistake when the fighting started. An angry person was more likely to forget a previously-made plan than a calm one.

The short man took a step forward. "You heard me," he snarled.

Keeping his eyes on the two men, Benjo lowered the two file folders to the asphalt and laid them flat. He didn't want to drop them and scatter the papers when what he knew was going to happen happened. "I heard you," he replied evenly. "Look, we both know this isn't about robbing me. You just want to make it look like a robbery as a cover. My only question is are you full members of the Southern Devils or just prospects?"

The shorter one hid his reaction well, but the big one's jaw actually dropped open in surprise, confirming what Benjo suspected. Both men's arms had that peculiar top-of-the-arms-only suntan that came from long hours spent riding a motorcycle in the sunshine while wearing short sleeves. The bigger man's boots and the worn areas on his jeans near the thighs and cuffs practically screamed biker. As if those weren't obvious enough, the shorter man had Rise Again tattooed on his knuckles, just like Paul Tucker had.

"You talk a lot for a man who's about to get his butt kicked," the short one said.

Benjo's reaction was to step forward and straight kick the big one, the closest of the two, right in the knee. The heel of Benjo's boot hit squarely on the joint, locking it backwards and causing the big man to pitch forward like he had tripped on an invisible rope. As his head and face came forward, Benjo drove his right fist up into an uppercut blow that caught the big man right under the chin. His teeth clicked shut with a loud clicking sound and he went down like a house of cards in a hurricane. As he collapsed to the asphalt, Benjo followed it up with a kick directly into the big man's face. His nose shattered with a crack and a muffled scream. He went limp on the asphalt.

The big man was still twitching as Benjo shuffled back out of range of his arms and legs and turned to face the short one. Benjo brought up his hands in a boxer's pose, but he kept his hands open. "Your partner is out of this," Benjo said. "It's one on one now, but it doesn't have to be. You can pick him up and get lost if you want."

The short one looked at his stricken buddy twitching on the ground with blood rapidly spreading around his head. Obviously the two men had made a plan to attack their quarry, Benjo. Now that plan had flown out the window and taken the shorter man's confidence with it. His readiness to attack had been replaced with uncertainty, at least for a few seconds. He recovered quickly, however. He ignored his buddy and focused on Benjo. He brought his hands up in a boxer's pose and shuffled toward Benjo. As Benjo had suspected, he had some moves, probably learned from a life spent brawling.

"I figure Paul Tucker sent you," Benjo said as he and the short man circled each other like two lions on the plains of Africa. "A blind man could tell that you two were bikers. Or, in your case, mini-bikers. Does Harley make a bike in your size?"

"Never heard of him," the short man said with a snarl. "You're a funny man. I'm gonna make you regret that smart mouth."

"Of course, you don't know him," Benjo said sarcastically. "Me getting the crap beat out of me during a robbery gone wrong would be a good way to get me off the case I'm on, though. Unfortunately for you, I can't let that happen. I figure he sent you two to send me a message, so I'm going to use you to send one back to him."

The short man's reply was to lunge forward and throw a quick jab at Benjo's face. Benjo smacked it to the side and countered with a straight jab to the short man's mouth that rocked his head back. The short man stumbled backwards, but regained his footing. He spit out some blood and what looked like a piece of one of his front teeth. "Okay then," the short man said. "Looks like you know how to fight."

"The only two things in life I'm any good at start with F," Benjo said. "One is fighting. You can ask your girlfriend what the other one is."

The short man apparently didn't have a sense of humor because he snarled and lunged forward to try to grab Benjo's legs around the thighs and take him to the ground. The move was called a double-leg takedown and it was a staple of mixed martial arts fighting. Ever since MMA fighting had become a popular sport, it had become the go-to move for guys to use in fights, especially if alcohol was involved. What a lot of guys didn't understand was that the move was relatively easy to counter for someone who knew how to fight. Fortunately for Benjo, he was one of those people who knew how to fight. As the short biker lunged in with his head down and grabbed for Benjo's legs, Benjo leaned his upper body forward and moved his legs back like he was trying to pull them out of the man's reach. This put him over the short man's back with his weight coming down on the man. At the same time, he drove his elbow with all of the force he could muster into the short man's back in a blow to his kidneys. The short man gave a strangled cry and fell to the ground under Benjo. His grip on Benjo's legs loosened at the same time. Benjo went down on the top of the man and used his chest on the man's back as a pivot point to spin so that he was facing the same direction. He used his forearm to deliver two quick blows to the back of the short man's head and then leaped up off him.

The short man lay there, stunned from both the kidney punch and the blows to the back of his head. Benjo shuffled out of reach of the man's arms and legs. "Your boss, Tucker, sent you on a suicide mission," Benjo said loudly. "He lied to you about me, didn't he? You were expecting some pushover the two of you could beat the hell out of and scare away. This is your last chance, friend. Get up, get your friend, and hit the road."

The short one slowly pushed himself up off the asphalt onto his knees. He glowered at Benjo as he settled back on his knees and tried to stand up. "You beat one of us, you better be ready to beat all of us," he said through bloody lips.

Benjo took this in stoically. "Well, if I'm going to have to fight the whole gang, I might as well start evening out the odds," he said fiercely. "You get to go first." With that, Benjo stepped forward and kicked the short biker right in the face. The biker flopped over onto his back, unconscious. With grim intensity, Benjo followed up that kick by stomping down on the biker's shin. There was a loud crack as the bones broke. The short biker groaned loudly, but didn't regain consciousness. The short biker was still groaning when Benjo stomped down on the biker's other leg. It took two solid stomps before those bones broke. The short biker shuddered, but didn't make any other sounds. Benjo could see his chest rising and falling steadily. The guy was unconscious and would need a good orthopedic surgeon, but he was alive.

With the shorter one disabled, Benjo turned his attention to the big one. The big one's face was a bloody mess and the knee Benjo had kicked at the start of the fight was still bent backwards at an odd angle. He was still unconscious, but was starting to stir slightly. There was no need to inflict further damage on him. Instead Benjo bent down and tapped the big biker lightly with the back of his hand on his badly-broken nose. The big man squeaked like a trapped mouse and his eyes flew open. He recoiled as soon as he saw Benjo standing over him. "I'm out," he croaked. "I ain't fighting you no more." The guy rolled onto his side. "Jesus Christ, my leg."

"How did you two figure out where I would be?" Benjo asked. "Tell me or I swear I'll shatter the other knee."

The big man looked at Benjo like he was the devil incarnate. "We had the church secretary's address," he whimpered. "We were watching her place because they figured you would show up there to talk to her."

"Who is 'they'? Benjo asked.

The big biker's face was a bloody mask, but the fear in his eyes was easy to see. "Please, man, you know I can't rat nobody out. They will do worse than what you've done already."

"Are you a prospect for the Southern Devils or a color-wearing member?" Benjo asked. Prospects were guys who were trying to join the motorcycle club. For the first couple of years, the senior, full-fledged members would haze the prospects unmercifully and use them as little more than errand boys or muscle to do the club's dirty work. Members who had earned their colors- the motorcycle club's emblem to be worn on their clothing- were full-fledged members of the club with all of the rights and privileges that earned them.

"Prospects," the big man croaked. "Doing this was supposed to earn us our patch."

Benjo breathed an inner sigh of relief. Assaulting a full-fledged member of an outlaw motorcycle club invariably meant that the whole club was obligated to avenge their member. If the two men had been full members, he would have had to fight the whole club. He didn't have the time to wage war with an outlaw biker gang. Doing so would probably require a lot of guns and senseless violence. He was not averse to either guns or violence, but at the moment he was busy trying to figure out what had gotten Sarah Fleming killed. With his two attackers being mere prospects, the Southern Devils might just decide to cut ties with them out of embarrassment and call it a day. "Last question," Benjo said. "You don't have to say a word, so technically you haven't ratted anyone out. Did Paul Tucker send you?" The big man looked around, grimaced, and then nodded silently. "Thank you," Benjo said.

Just then a car drove into the parking lot and turned the corner into the back lot. The familiar Cadillac sedan screeched to a halt. A stunned

David Whiteside emerged from the car, leaned on top of the open driver's side door, and looked at Benjo and the two injured men lying a heap on the asphalt. He was quiet for several seconds. "Do I dare ask what in the hell is happening here?" he finally asked.

"These two fellows were taking a shortcut through your parking lot when they were set upon by ruffians," Benjo replied calmly. "I arrived and scared the ruffians away, thankfully, but it was too late. I think they both need an ambulance."

David arched an eyebrow. "I'll call one for them," he said slowly. "Do I need to call the police as well? The gang of, uh, ruffians could still be in the area. I don't suppose you saw what they looked like?"

Benjo turned and looked down at the two men. "We need the police here, guys?" he asked. The bigger one, the only one conscious, shook his head. "No, sir, they would just like an ambulance. It all happened so fast they didn't get a good enough look to help the police, so it would be a waste of time," Benjo replied.

David removed his cell phone from his pocket. "Benjo, would you like to wait inside while I handle this?" he asked. "I have a few questions, if you don't mind."

"Not at all," Benjo said amicably. He bent down and retrieved the two folders from where they sat on the asphalt. "My time is your time. I'll be in the conference room on the second floor if you need me. I know where it is."

"Thank you," David said calmly. "Once you're inside, you might want to swing by the restroom and clean up a little. You have some blood from the ruffians on your knuckles and on your left boot."

Benjo glanced down and saw that David was right. "Damned ruffians," he said. "I'll take care of that, sir."

David nodded and dialed nine one one on his cell phone. Benjo slipped back inside the office.

Benjo was leaned against the window sill looking out the window when David came into the conference room. Benjo watched as the last of the two ambulances pulled out of the parking lot onto the street in front of the building. David closed the door behind him and took a seat at the conference table as Benjo turned around. The lawyer looked somewhat pale and ill at ease as he shifted in his chair. Benjo came over and took a seat at the end of the table. "You okay, Benjo?"

"I'm fine, David," Benjo replied as he settled back into his chair.

"I was hoping you could explain why there were two thugs who look like they lost a fight with a tree shredder laid out cold in my office parking lot," David said.

"I'll be glad to explain," Benjo said. He spent the next fifteen minutes bringing the lawyer up to speed about what he'd learned during his investigation, including his run-in with Paul Tucker, the church's alleged director of security, and his talk with Kathy Miller, the news reporter. As David listened, his eyes grew wider and he began to rub his chin thoughtfully. "Those two men in the parking lot were trying to get into the Southern Devils, the motorcycle club that Paul Tucker is still secretly a high-ranking member of. They were sent to take me out of the Fleming case and make me leave the Coles alone. Those two guys were going to beat me pretty bad, I suspect, and make it look like a robbery gone bad. A few weeks in the hospital would serve as a warning to back off and drop the case."

"That's pretty sinister, Benjo," David said. "I had no idea that asking you to investigate what happened to Sarah would get you tangled up with a biker gang and a money-laundering operation. I thought the Coles would stonewall you or maybe seek a restraining order on you at the worst."

"Fortunately, I was able to defend myself," Benjo said. "Following my wife's death, I had to find ways to keep myself occupied. One of those ways was spending about three hours a day five days a week at a mixed martial arts gym. Nothing distracts you from grief like getting kicked in the head a few times. Kicking back also helps you vent some of the feelings."

"It kind of looked like you did a little more than defend yourself," David replied with concern. "The shorter of the two looked like he was part jelly from the knees down."

"I broke both his legs," Benjo answered casually. The horrified look on David's kindly face prompted Benjo to explain. "Those two men were sent to attack me, an innocent person who has never done them any wrong personally. Until Tucker showed them a still photo of me he most likely took from the church's security camera footage, those guys had never seen me before in their lives. Despite that, they stalked and then attacked me simply because they want to be able to sew a piece of fabric on their motorcycle vest and call themselves members of a gang of hardened criminals. They deserved what they got. Plus, I needed to let Tucker know that I'm not someone to be trifled with."

"I suspect you made that loud and clear," David answered. "One of the paramedics at first thought the two of them had been hit by a truck." He chuckled a little. "Set upon by ruffians? Where in the world did that come from?"

Benjo half-grinned. "One of the other things I did to keep my mind occupied was read voraciously. I came upon that phrase in a book about colonial times in America. I liked it. I have always wanted to use it in a sentence. This fit the bill."

"Chase came outside when the ambulances showed up," David said. "He was completely unaware anything had happened. He told me what you told him earlier. You really think the Coles murdered Sarah?"

"They might not have pulled the trigger, but they had a part in setting her up," Benjo answered with grim certainty.

"Monica claims she pulled the trigger," David countered. "She admitted it as part of the self-defense argument."

"She was also the only one of the three people in the church at the time who wasn't a convicted felon," Benjo replied. "August Cole and Paul Tucker could have been in trouble for simply touching a gun, much less shooting someone with it. Monica was the only one who could claim to have fired the gun and there not be a ton of scrutiny and controversy."

"So, you think one of the men there shot Sarah?" David surmised.

"Yes," Benjo answered. "Unfortunately, we'll never know because the detective investigating the case didn't do a gunshot residue test on the Coles or Tucker. The gunshot residue test would have told us who fired the gun."

"It seems like that would be a pretty standard test to run in such a situation," David replied. "It looks like yet another example of how bad Detective Marsh fouled things up."

"Given the situation, it was his decision," Benjo replied. "He had someone standing there claiming responsibility for shooting someone else, so there was no mystery as to who the shooter supposedly was. If it had been me, I would have done one, but that's me. Now we will never know for sure unless one of them admits it."

David shook his head. "Do you think one of them ever would?"

"Nope," Benjo replied. "Too much money and prestige at stake. Plus, if you think about it, they've already gotten away with it. Once the prosecutor ruled it a case of self-defense, it's an uphill battle to change that."

This news obviously disturbed David because he looked down at the table in front of him. "It would take some pretty substantial evidence to get the prosecutor's office to reconsider. They would have egg on their face and nobody likes that," he finally said softly. "Are you any closer to finding out why Sarah went there? Why was she killed?"

"I'm working on that," Benjo answered as he leaned forward and rested his elbows on the table. "It's a complete mystery right now; I can't find anything that would have made her reach out to Monica Cole. I have no idea what made her go to the church that day. I have no clue what made the Coles or whoever it was decide to shoot Sarah." He tapped the two file folders Chase had given him earlier. "I've spent the first couple of days digging into the Coles and Tucker. It obviously spooked them because they sent those two guys to make me go away. I think I've gotten all I can out of them for now. Now I start digging into Sarah to see what I can find."

"I will be absolutely floored if you find anything bad about that girl," David said gruffly. "She was an absolute peach of a human being."

"Well, since I've got you here alone, maybe the issue wasn't something Sarah did," Benjo said. "I talked to Chase earlier when I came here to pick up these folders. We sat in here and I got him to really rack his brain for anything different about Sarah's behavior in the weeks leading up to her death. As I told him, absolutely anything, no matter how trivial, could be important. He told me that Sarah and he took care of their mother, Reena, when she was sick."

David nodded. "They did. Reena was diagnosed with ovarian cancer. It had spread to the point there wasn't much they could do for her. She refused the chemotherapy and radiation because the potential benefits were far outweighed by the sickness and pain it would cause. Reena was put into a hospice center just a few weeks after she was diagnosed. She didn't linger long, mercifully, but Chase and Sarah did everything possible to take care of her. It was tragic."

"Chase told me that Sarah was there with her mother alone when Reena passed away," Benjo said. "He said that Sarah started acting a little strange the day after their mother died. She seemed distant and out of it, as he described it."

"Well, she had just lost her mother," David said. "Their dad died of a massive heart attack six years earlier. Now, her mother, the only surviving parent, has just died after an extended period where Sarah helped with her care. I know exactly what Chase is referring to because I noticed it following Reena's death as well. I assumed it was grief and being exhausted from the time spent caring for her."

"But what if it wasn't?" Benjo asked. "What if her mother revealed something to Sarah that really shook her up mentally and emotionally. What if it was something that led her to the Coles and what happened in their office?"

David considered this quietly. "I guess anything is possible," he conceded. "I have no idea what it could be, however. Reena was a great person. Her husband, Rick, was fine man before he died in 2016 as well."

"Tell me what you know about Reena," Benjo said as he removed his notebook and pen from his shirt pocket.

"She came to work for me in early 2000," David said. "I had just opened my own practice and I needed a legal secretary. I posted an ad in the local newspaper's jobs section. What I could offer pay wise at the time was not that great, so I wasn't exactly swamped with quality applicants. Reena's application stood out because she had medical experience and also administrative experience from where she was working at the time."

"Where was that?" Benjo asked.

David thought for a moment. "She worked as what they called a ward secretary in the maternity ward at the local hospital," he said. "That job involved doing the medical records for mothers and new babies and other administrative- type things. She told me she did everything from file records to making sure the right baby went home with the right parents. The administrative background and the medical background worked for me because at the time I was doing a lot of personal injury cases. I need someone who had a background in medical terminology so they could read the medical records on the injury cases."

Benjo scribbled this down. "How long had she worked there?"

"About three years, if memory serves," David said. "She was about twenty-one when she came to work for me. I believe that the hospital was her first fulltime job. The rest were part-time positions she worked at to get through high school and to simply survive."

"What do you mean by 'simply survive'?" Benjo asked. "That's an interesting turn of phrase. Was her background a little rough?"

"Reena and I spent a lot of time working together in my first office," David said. "It was in a strip mall on the edge of a bad neighborhood a few blocks from the courthouse. In the early days, there were times we were sitting around bored, so we talked a lot. I learned a great deal about her. Reena was an only child who was put into foster care because her father killed her mother and then himself when she was nine years old and there were no blood relatives who would take her. She bounced around group homes and foster homes until she graduated high school. Some of the foster homes provided food and shelter, but not much else. That's why she worked part-time jobs to buy clothes and stuff like that. I think she might have been abused at a couple of the foster homes when she was a teenager."

"Physically or sexually?" Benjo asked.

"She never elaborated and I didn't ask," David said. "One thing I can say about Reena, though, was that she came out of all of that a strong person without an ounce of bitterness or anger. Also, she never used it as an excuse to be lazy or anything negative. She worked her ass off for me." He looked around the conference room. "I own this building outright and I have twenty-one people on my payroll right now. I wouldn't have any of it without her help. She was a dear, dear friend and a truly special human being."

"There's no easy way to ask this, but were you two ever more than boss and employee?" Benjo asked.

David looked offended. "No," he said instantly. "I was ten years older than her and married. Never once did our relationship go anything beyond employee and boss or good friends. At first, I think I was almost a father figure to her."

Benjo believed him. "I had to ask," he said apologetically. "Do you know why she left the hospital?"

"She wanted a more regular schedule, I believe," David replied. "She was a single mother at the time. I think Sarah was maybe a year or so old when Reena came to work for me."

"Sarah was born out of wedlock?" Benjo asked in surprise.

"Yes," David said. "Reena swore me to secrecy on that. I think she was dating Rick, the man who would become her husband, at the time. They were a young couple- I think he was a few years older than her- and I think Sarah was a 'whoops' baby. I think Reena missed a birth control pill or something like that. She always seemed kind of embarrassed about it and never really elaborated. She married Rick a few months after she started working for me."

"If Reena told Sarah that from her deathbed, that could very easily be what had her so troubled in the days after her mom's death," Benjo said. "It must have been a shock."

David looked troubled. "Please don't tell Chase that. Reena would be mortified if he knew his older sister was born out of wedlock."

"I won't breathe a word unless I have to," Benjo promised. "Were there ever any signs of domestic troubles between her and Rick, her husband?"

"I think it bothered Reena that Rick waited until after Sarah was born and close to two years old before they got married," David replied. "That's why she kept it secret from Chase. Overall, though, I would say they had a very happy and loving marriage. They seemed to really adore each other. They were also great parents who seemed to really love their kids."

"Is there anything else you can think of?" Benjo asked.

"No," David answered. "What's your next move?"

"Fair enough," Benjo said. "I'm going to go over everything in these files to see if anything jumps out at me. The reason why Sarah died is somewhere in all of this." He tapped the folders. "I'm going to find it." He glanced at his watch. "But first, I need to go see somebody."

12

Kathy Miller was waiting for him in a corner booth when Benjo walked into Mulligan's, a small café just down the street from the television station where she worked. She waved as Benjo came in, looked around, and spotted her. It was way past lunchtime and too early for the dinner crowd, so they had the place mostly to themselves, save for an older couple in a booth by the front windows and a bored-looking young woman sitting at a table tapping on her laptop. Benjo took a seat in the booth across from Kathy. "Hi," she said with a dazzling smile. She wore a blue pin-striped pantsuit and white blouse. Her sunglasses were pushed up over her forehead into her hair.

"Hi," Benjo replied as he settled into the booth. "I appreciate you taking the time to meet me."

"You caught me at a good time," Kathy replied. "I wasn't working on anything particularly important at the moment. Hot leads seem to be sparse these days. I skipped lunch for a meeting and I'm starving. That's why I picked this place. I hope you don't mind meeting here."

Benjo looked around. The café' was small and designed to look like the old train car diners from the 1950s, with a lot of tile and polished metal on the interior. The café had been there long enough for the tile to be faded and the metal a little less shiny, but it was clean. Someone in the kitchen was cooking something that smelled wonderful, making Benjo realize that he had not had any lunch. He was suddenly starving. "That makes two of us," he said. "What's good?"

"All of it," Kathy said. "This place is a hidden gem. It's been run by the same family since the early seventies. Everyone at the station eats here at least once a week."

The waitress, a slender, older woman with her hair pulled back in a ponytail dressed in jeans, sneakers, and a red tee shirt with Mulligan's Café' on the front and back, appeared bearing menus. Kathy ordered a chef's salad with homemade ranch dressing and a sweet tea. "Make that two," Benjo said. The waitress scribbled on the pad she held and headed for the kitchen. A couple of minutes later she appeared with their drinks, silverware, and napkins. Once she was gone, Kathy smiled across the table. "So, what did you need to talk to me about?"

"I talked to Marsha West, the former church secretary for Hope Springs," Benjo said. "I left her house more convinced than ever that Sarah was murdered and the self -defense story was a chance to get away with it."

"Really?" Kathy said as she leaned forward and lowered her voice. "Why do you think that?"

"A few odd things just don't fit in their story," Benjo said. "I think Paul Tucker was already in the office where Sarah was shot. I don't think he rushed over there afterwards. I know Monica claims she fired the shots in self-defense, but I suspect it was either August Cole or, more likely, Paul Tucker."

"But why would Monica claim to have shot Sarah if she didn't?" Kathy asked.

"Because of sexism," Benjo explained. "If a healthy, strong man shoots a girl who weighs fifty pounds less than him and claims self-defense, most people wouldn't believe him. You mean a big, strapping man can't fight off a woman? What kind of wimp are you? If a woman claims self-defense, even against another woman, it's more acceptable. Monica being the one who shot Sarah is just more socially acceptable and believable, especially if you want to say it was self-defense."

Kathy thought about it for a few moments. "You know, I've never really thought about it, but you're right."

"As a cop, I would go to domestic violence calls where some pretty little thing weighing ninety pounds had gotten into a physical fight with her husband or boyfriend," Benjo replied. "The guy, who was a head taller and weighed a hundred pounds more, would look like he'd just lost a fight with Mike Tyson in his prime and the woman would be standing there with bloody knuckles and no other marks on her, but the officers on scene would ask the man what he did to deserve it." He shook his head. "It's as if our brains are hard-wired to believe that a woman is always the victim."

"Why would August or Tucker want Sarah dead?" Kathy asked,

"I'm working on that," Benjo said. "My working theory is that Sarah Fleming somehow discovered something that could bring the Coles and their church crashing to the ground. Sarah confronted the Coles with that information. I don't think the poor girl realized what kind of people she was dealing with; maybe she was naïve or just bought into the public persona the Coles put out there every week. I think August Cole killed Sarah because she was going to expose them or Tucker did it because, if the Coles go down, so does his money-laundering operation."

They were interrupted by the waitress bringing their salads. The salads came in huge bowls and looked delicious. The waitress left their food and their checks on the table and vanished back into the kitchen area. They both dug into their food with vigor. "Have you found any-thing on that?" Kathy asked between bites.

"Yes," Benjo said as soon as he'd swallowed a mouthful of salad. "Paul Tucker is definitely still in a position of authority with the Southern Devils Motorcycle Club and he's definitely using the church to launder money with the Coles' help."

Kathy had a fork load of salad halfway to her mouth that she stopped in mid-air. "You know this?" she asked incredulously. Benjo nodded as he took another bite. He really was starving. "How?" Kathy asked.

"Because earlier today two wannabee members of the Southern Devils confronted me in the parking lot of David Whiteside's law office," Benjo said. "I think their plan was to beat me up pretty badly and put me in the hospital in order to make me stop sniffing around the church. They planned to make it look like a robbery or carjacking that went too far." He paused to take a bite of his food.

Kathy lowered her fork and waited for him to finish the story. When he kept chewing, she lost her patience. "And?" she demanded.

Benjo finished chewing and wiped his mouth with a napkin. "I was able to defend myself," he said nonchalantly. "Actually, I was able to defend myself so well that both of them are currently in the hospital and will probably be there for several days each."

"Two bikers against you?" Kathy asked as she sat back in her chair and stared at him. "There's not a mark on you. What did you do, shoot them? Pepper spray?"

Benjo looked offended. "Nothing like that," he answered. "I beat them up before they could beat me up."

"You beat them up?" Kathy asked. "Both of them?"

"Vigorously and with no remorse whatsoever," Benjo replied. "They were sent with a message for me. I replied with a message of my own. Depending on how good the surgeons are, they'll probably be okay in a few weeks, maybe months."

Kathy's reporter instincts took over. "Did you get their names?" she asked eagerly.

"No," Benjo said. "David, the lawyer I'm working for, arrived for the aftermath. He got me away from the scene and called ambulances for them. If you check with the emergency room at the hospital, it would be two white males brought in by ambulance about two hours ago. They're probably in surgery now, because I broke bones."

"Damn," Kathy said as she went back to picking at her salad. "You don't play, do you?"

"Not anymore," Benjo said calmly. "I think you're missing the big picture. Two Southern Devils' prospects were sent to deal with me by Paul Tucker."

"Did they admit that?" Kathy asked. "How do you know that for sure?"

"One of them already had the distinctive Rise Again tattoo on his knuckles that they are so proud of," Benjo said. "The other one admitted it."

"He just admitted that Tucker had sent them to jump you?" Kathy asked in surprise. "They usually have a code of silence that would make the mafia blush."

"He was in a lot of pain at the time," Benjo replied evenly. "Tucker sending them to attack me essentially proves that the club is using the church to launder money for them. Why else would Tucker send two of their guys to try to stop me from investigating the Coles unless he has a vested interest in making sure they stay free and the church stays open?"

"That's a valid point," Kathy said. She took another bite of her salad. "It's still not concrete evidence, but it's progress."

"It is what it is," Benjo replied. "I just wanted to give you a heads up. Also, I was wondering if you had reached out to Sheriff Crowe to ask about Detective Marsh's prior involvement with the Coles?"

"I have a meeting with him tomorrow morning at ten in his office," Kathy said with a tight smile. "He ducked my calls for a day or so until I reached out to the county commissioner. Once I spoke to the county commissioner, Sheriff Cole called me back in fifteen minutes."

Benjo smiled. The position of sheriff was an elected position. The sheriff served a four- year term and then either ran for re-election or left the position when the new sheriff was elected. Per state law, an elected sheriff could only be removed by a recall by the citizens of the county or by order of the state's governor if misconduct was involved. Because of that, the sheriff was practically untouchable. The county commissioner, however, controlled the purse strings for the entire sheriff's department. That essentially gave him power over the sheriff because the sheriff couldn't have a department if there was no money. "Good move," he said admiringly. "He probably would have ignored you forever if you hadn't done that. He needs to answer for the things he's allowed Marsh to get away with."

Kathy continued working on her salad. "Thank you," she said. "I know how to play the game, Benjo. Now, I have a question for you if you don't mind."

Like Kathy, Benjo continued eating steadily, pausing only long enough to make sure his mouth wasn't full before speaking. "Sure," he said.

"I made a few more phone calls about you after our first meeting," Kathy said. "I talked to some friends who work at the sheriff's department and the state police. I learned a lot about you. Some of it was pretty, uh, intriguing, to put it mildly."

Benjo rested his elbows on the table. He knew what was coming. "I imagine so if you talked to the state police."

"First of all, everyone I talked to, even the ones who don't like you, admitted that you are a hell of an investigator," Kathy said. "Also, the vast majority of them felt the exact opposite about Detective Dale Marsh. One of my sources summed it up as, quote, Dale Marsh is a waste of a badge, end quote. It doesn't take a genius to see that you dislike Marsh. I've heard the rumors, but I'd love to hear your side of the story."

"Are you going to do a story about me?" Benjo asked as he studied Kathy's face across the table. "Am I your new expose'?"

"No," Kathy answered immediately. "I just need to know who I'm working with. I'm curious if your motivation for investigating Sarah's death is a quest for the truth or a desire to make Marsh look bad. The former is noble, the latter is just pure spite. Full disclosure, I don't want to get sucked into someone's desire for revenge. My journalistic integrity is very important to me."

Benjo was silent for a few moments while he searched for the right words. Finally, he decided to go with the truth. "In the spirit of complete honesty, I do hate Dale Marsh," he said. "Dale Marsh is a bad person who's made his way through life solely off of his parents' money and connections. He won the sperm lottery, so to speak, and he has worked it to his benefit. However, he's not the first person to do it and he sure as hell won't be the last. I hate Marsh because he's the reason my wife, Presley, was murdered. He tipped off Jacob Clement that I was investigating him. Clement freaked out, got stupid, and hired a couple of gangbangers out of Florida to assassinate me. They opened fire on me and my wife. I killed them, but not before my wife was shot and killed. Somehow, I didn't get a scratch. Did your sources tell you that?"

Kathy nodded slowly. "One of them gave me the back story," she said. "Marsh's family had a business relationship with Clement. Marsh was friendly with Clement. Marsh allegedly tipped off Clement. Marsh was investigated by both the sheriff's department and the state police, but there was not enough evidence to prove he told Clement anything intentionally to obstruct justice."

"It was a case of knowing it, but you can't prove it beyond a reasonable doubt," Benjo said. "That was why the state police never charged him with anything and that was Sheriff Crowe's excuse for not doing anything to his golden boy."

"But you are firmly convinced that Dale Marsh intentionally tipped off Clement that you were investigating him?" Kathy asked.

"Beyond any shadow of a doubt," Benjo answered unequivocally.

Kathy arched an eyebrow. "How do you know that?" she asked. "How are you so sure when everyone else who looked into it couldn't find anything concrete?"

"I'll just say that I was privy to information that no one else had available," Benjo answered. "Let's leave it at that."

Kathy looked uncomfortable. "I know that some people in law enforcement believe that you killed Jacob Clement," she said. "That you found out he was the one who tried to have you killed, that you beat the state police to him, and that it was revenge for her."

"I'm familiar," Benjo replied. "I know how it looked and I know I was a prime suspect in Clement's death, trust me on that. I figured it out when those nice folks at the state police questioned me several times, searched my property twice, and generally made my life miserable for several months."

"Did you kill Jacob Clement?" Kathy asked tensely.

Benjo leaned forward on his elbows and looked directly into Kathy's eyes. "Kathy, you know me answering that question is a waste of time for both of us," he said sincerely. "If I answered yes, I would be putting myself on death row or in prison for life at the minimum if you told the police. If I answered no, would you or anyone else believe me? I can't prove I didn't do something, simply because most innocent people don't spend their every waking moment making sure they are establishing an alibi. Really think about how much time an average person spends alone or in a place where no one else can verify they were there. Your own home is a perfect example of that. Could you really prove beyond a shadow of a doubt that you were sitting at home all alone on a particular night reading a book if you had to? Now, before you say that your neighbors would see your car parked in your driveway or your lights on, does that prove you were actually inside your house curled up with a good book?" Benjo shook his head. "Not really. It proves your car was parked and a light was on inside. You could have slipped out a side door."

Kathy blinked a couple of times, then averted her eyes. "I've never really thought about it that way," she said.

"That's why our criminal justice system puts the burden on the state," Benjo said. "The authorities have to prove you did something beyond a reasonable doubt. You don't have to prove you didn't do something."

"Some of the people at the state police really believe you killed Jacob Clement," Kathy said. "So do a few at the sheriff's department. To use your words from a few minutes ago, they say it's a case of knowing it but can't prove it."

"And yet, over a full year later, here I sit as a free man, eating a salad in a nice café on a sunny afternoon with a pretty woman," Benjo said. He looked out the window of the café at the street in front of the building. "Not a fence, a set of bars, or a guard in sight. I was a prime suspect in Clement's death. I understand that; I had motive, means, and opportunity. However, as the investigation into his death progressed, a bunch of other people, with a great deal more means, motive, and opportunity, popped up on their radar screen. I don't suppose your sources happened to mention that Clement was a major player in an underground ring swapping stolen cars and car parts for narcotics, did they? Did they mention the lengthy list of other people who might want Clement dead?"

"Not really," Kathy answered.

"I was, and probably still am, a suspect in Clement's death," Benjo conceded, "but I am one of dozens and I'm currently really low on the state police's list of who most likely killed him."

"Are you glad he's dead?" Kathy asked.

"Absolutely," Benjo said. "The first night after his death was the first good night's sleep I'd had in days. His death brought me closure and peace, the closure and peace that only comes from knowing that someone who has hurt you finally paid for it."

"Is that part of the reason you're investigating Sarah's death?" Kathy asked. "Do you want her family to find some peace and closure?"

"Absolutely," Benjo replied. "Now, I have a question for you. The anonymous source who got drunk at a party, talked too much, and was overheard by your source, is Marsha West, the former church secretary, isn't it?"

Kathy's mouth literally dropped open. "How did you….?"

"I talked with her today," Benjo answered. "Once she told me how the Coles are with the church's books, it had to be her. Plus, she looks like the type who would drink a little too much at a party. There was a wine glass with a little bit of wine in it on her kitchen counter. I saw it when I was sitting down in her living room. It could be from the night before or it could have been breakfast. Either way, she likes wine."

"So, what now?" Kathy asked. "You think Sarah was set up and her murder made to look like self-defense. What's our next move?"

Benjo smiled. "Our?"

Kathy returned the smile. "You've sucked me into this now," she said. "My investigative reporter radar is screaming at me."

"You go and get an answer from Sheriff Crowe as to why he let a detective with a proven conflict of interest investigate Sarah Fleming's death," Benjo said as he pushed his now-empty salad bowl away and drained his glass of tea. "I don't think Marsh's prior involvement affected the outcome of the case as much as the fact that Marsh is a lazy, terrible detective did, but I still think a lot of stuff was overlooked to the Cole's benefit. Also, be ready to come running with a camera crew if I call you. I might need you." He picked up his dinner check and then reached across and grabbed her check. "Lunch is on me."

Kathy sat there and watched as Benjo stood up from the table. "You know you never did answer the Clement question," she said. "A simple yes or no would have sufficed."

Benjo grinned. "I know," he said as he turned to walk toward the register. "Have a nice evening, Kathy."

13

What did Sarah Fleming know that made her reach out to Monica Cole? Furthermore, what did she know that was so dangerous it was worth killing her over? These two questions had haunted Benjo for the rest of the afternoon and evening after he got home from meeting with Kathy. Obviously, Sarah Fleming has discovered something that made her first reach out to Monica Cole in her office at the church via telephone. Once that contact was made, someone- most likely Monica Cole- had started using a burner phone to talk to Sarah, most likely to make sure that nothing could be traced back to any particular place or person. It didn't take a genius to see that whatever had prompted Sarah to contact the Coles was something they wanted very badly to keep a secret. The issue for Benjo was that, at the moment, he did not have the slightest inkling what the deadly secret might have been. Benjo didn't like being stumped, but he was truly, epically stumped.

The rest of the afternoon had passed quickly and now dusk was falling outside as Benjo sat at the table in the cabin's breakfast nook and stared out the window at the gathering darkness, lost in thought. Unless Darcy Woodruff, Sarah's former roommate he was meeting with in the morning, had some sort of mind-blowing revelation she planned to tell him, Benjo was genuinely stumped as to what might have brought the Coles and Sarah into each other's orbit. He was even more baffled as to what Sarah, a nurse with no connections at all to the church, the Coles, or Paul Tucker, could have discovered that warranted murdering her to keep her quiet or to get her out of the way. It was a genuine mystery and it had Benjo's mind churning. As he sat there gazing blankly into the darkness outside the window, he rolled the facts he did know over and over in his mind and dissected everything he'd learned since starting the case.

Based on all of the evidence he had, Sarah had only attended Hope Springs Church one time, and that was the time she allegedly grabbed Monica Cole while they were greeting people in the lobby after a service. That was the video clip that the police had seen as evidence that Sarah was a dangerous stalker. However, in the video clip he'd watched, Sarah had barely brushed Monica's shoulder. Actually, it could have been very easily argued that the contact was accidental at most. There were the three phone calls, but three telephone calls over seven days would not be considered harassment by any magistrate in the county. There had to be a pattern of sustained behavior over a certain period of time before a magistrate would sign a warrant for stalking or harassment. No one he had spoken with in the last couple of days had told him anything that made him think that Sarah was struggling with some sort of mental health issue that would have made her randomly fixate on Monica Cole or anyone else for that matter. So, if it wasn't a mental issue, there had to be SOMETHING that made Sarah all of a sudden get interested in the Coles, particularly Monica.

Thus far, the only thing he'd learned about Sarah that was even slightly unusual had come from the talk earlier with Chase Fleming. Sarah's mother, Reena, had told her something from her deathbed that had upset Sarah for a few days. Given what he'd learned later from David, it might be something as simple as the dying Reena, her mind addled with drugs, had revealed to Sarah that she was born out of wedlock. That probably would have surprised Sarah, but in the grand scheme of things it wasn't that big of a deal. Sarah had been raised by a loving father and mother in a good home. In today's society, who cared if she was born before her parents were legally married? Given what he'd learned from David Whiteside about Reena's own childhood spent in the foster care system, Sarah had been very fortunate to have loving parents. Regardless, that news still didn't seem like anything that would explain the Sarah and Coles connection. The Coles had nothing to do with Sarah being born a little early.

He sat there for nearly an hour, staring out at nothing, waiting for something to reveal itself. Nothing popped up. Frustrated, Benjo decided to do something that had worked for him numerous times as a sheriff's detective: Review the evidence he did have very carefully as many times as need be until something revealed itself. Doing that had helped him solve numerous cases because he always noticed something that he'd missed before. Carefully re-reading files, studying photos, and reviewing notes from interviews wasn't glamorous or exciting. No detective in movies or television shows was ever shown sitting at a desk studying notes or reading files simply because it didn't make a good spectacle for viewers, but in real life such things solved way more crimes than a shocking revelation from a surprise, conveniently available witness ever did.

Benjo got up and retrieved the folders Chase had given him earlier containing Sarah's phone records and financial records from the kitchen counter behind him. Those two files were the latest pieces of the puzzle. Benjo set the phone records aside because he'd already looked them over earlier in the day. He took the financial records folder and opened it. It contained several printed pages detailing transactions from Sarah's checking account and a separate savings account. The information on the pages went back ninety days from the day Sarah was killed. Benjo took a seat back at the table and began to scan over the printed sheets. On the day of her death, Sarah had a savings account balance of slightly over five thousand dollars. One hundred dollars was directly deposited into the account every two weeks, leading Benjo to assume that it was put there each time Sarah received her paycheck from the hospital system. For a twenty-five-year-old single female, that was actually a pretty decent amount; Benjo knew some people of the same age that still lived with their parents. He set the savings account record aside and moved on to the checking account. On the day she was killed Sarah had nineteen hundred dollars in her checking account. Sarah had made slightly over fifty thousand dollars a year, based on the payroll direct deposit every other week into her checking account. That was good money for someone so young, but Sarah was a registered nurse. The medical field paid well.

Benjo sat there for the next hour poring over the bank records, concentrating on the debits. You could tell a lot about a person by what they spent their money on. Sarah had gotten groceries at the same grocery store every couple of weeks. She also had a prescription for birth control pills. Around the fifth of every month, she paid her apartment rent and car payment online. She ate out a decent amount and her favorite food appeared to have been Mexican. There were a few debits from a bar that popped up around once a month. Benjo would wager that was a girl's night out, probably with coworkers. He did not see anything indicating any out-of-state trips or any other charges that indicated the girl went anywhere besides work, home, and a few restaurants. In short, there was absolutely nothing that indicated Sarah Fleming was anything other than a perfectly normal, single young woman who worked as a nurse, paid her bills, and had a small social circle of friends from work. There was absolutely nothing there that could help explain why she'd ended up dying the way she had.

There were only two charges on the checking account that weren't for perfectly normal necessities for living. One charge had occurred two months before Sarah's death. It was a charge for one hundred and twenty dollars and it was debited from the account by a company with the name WIA. There was a second charge from the same company just ten days before the day Sarah was shot. The same company had charged Sarah one hundred and eighty dollars for something else. That was it. There were no withdrawals of substantial amounts of cash. No sudden airline ticket purchases. No debits from a sporting goods store where she had suddenly purchased a firearm. Just those two different charges from something called WIA on the bank records and that was it. Those two charges were about three hundred dollars total, nothing extravagant. It was probably something she had ordered online. In short, a whole lot of nothing, at least nothing that would tell him why Sarah had ended up dead.

Benjo looked up from the records and stared out the window. It was pitch dark outside. He glanced at the clock on the stove and was surprised to see that it was nearly ten at night. He had lost all track of time as he sat there examining Sarah's financial records. He suddenly realized how tired he was both physically and mentally. The fight in the parking lot at the lawyer's office hadn't lasted that long, but the aftereffects of that much adrenaline had left him physically drained. The mental exhaustion came from the frustration inherent to trying to figure out what had gone through another person's mind or prompted another person's seemingly unexplainable actions. It was like trying to solve a puzzle where you only had half the pieces and were blindfolded to boot.

As he sat there, Harley strolled into the kitchen and rubbed against his leg. He reached down and scratched her head as she looked up at him. "I'm worn out, old friend," he said to the cat. "I think it's time for this old boy to hit the sack. I've got to talk to some more people tomorrow and I need to be sharp." Harley simply looked up at him and blinked. He stroked her head for another moment or two before she casually wandered off toward the living room.

Benjo reorganized the bank records and slipped them back into the folder. He left the two folders on the table and turned out the kitchen light as he left the room. He made his way through the house, checking the doors and windows to make sure they were locked and activating the cabin's alarm system. He was normally very security conscious to begin with, but the encounter with the two bikers today in the parking lot had him a little more on edge than usual. By beating the two prospects, he had either ended something or started something. Only time would tell if he had a whole new set of dangerous enemies to worry about.

Satisfied that everything on the ground level was secure, Benjo made his way upstairs to the extra bedroom that now served as his home office. He went to the office's closet and opened the door to reveal a gun safe that completely filled the closet. He punched in the code on the digital lock's keypad and the safe's door unlocked with a slight beep. He opened the safe to reveal a neat row of rifles and shotguns and numerous boxes of ammunition for each one of them. Beneath the neat row of rifles mounted in the upright position, there were three drawers that ran the width of the gun safe. He slid open the top drawer and removed a compact Glock nine- millimeter pistol. The black pistol was a compact model that was easily concealable, but at the same time had a magazine capacity of twelve rounds. Benjo checked to verify that the pistol was loaded with hollow-point rounds. Satisfied, he removed a leather holster for the pistol. The holster was specially designed to be concealed at the waist of the pants. Even with the gun in it, it was practically unnoticeable, even with jeans on. Benjo grabbed the pistol, the holster, and an AR-15 rifle from the gun safe and carried them to his bedroom. He placed the rifle by the head of his bed leaning against the wall. He placed the pistol and holster in the drawer of the night stand by his side of the bed. He returned to the gun safe and grabbed one more item he needed and then closed the safe and re-locked it.

Now properly armed just in case, Benjo went into the bathroom and took a long hot shower. The water helped ease some of the tension that was making his neck and shoulders ache. He finished the shower, dried off, threw on some clean underwear, and brushed his teeth. His next stop was his bed. He switched off the bedroom lights and lay back in bed in the darkness. He was very tired and expected to drop off to sleep immediately. However, sleep eluded him. He felt like he was missing something that ought to be obvious. It was like that feeling when you know you're forgetting something, but you have no idea what it is. He lay there in the dark, racking his brain, but nothing came to him. Finally, after nearly an hour of staring at the ceiling, he drifted off to sleep.

While Benjo was sleeping peacefully in his bed, Paul Tucker and August Cole were anything but peaceful. At the moment the two men were seated in Cole's office at Hope Springs Church. Despite the late hour, they were in a meeting with a third man. The meeting was something of a surprise for Tucker and Cole because, up until the third man had called them an hour ago as each man sat at home, Tucker and Cole had no idea they would be meeting anyone, especially someone like the third man in the office. His call had brought both men rushing from their homes back to the church. Upon arriving, they had found their guest and his driver sitting patiently in a BMW sedan in the parking lot of the locked and dark church building. Cole had unlocked the building, shut off the alarm, and escorted their surprise guest back into his office. Their guest's driver had stayed with the BMW outside in the parking lot. Now the three men sat in August's office in tense silence. Cole sat behind his desk while Tucker sat in one of the two chairs in front of the desk. Their attention was focused on their guest, who sat in the other empty chair in front of Cole's desk. The third man was short and fat with olive-brown skin and black hair he kept pulled back into a short ponytail. He wore jeans, a long-sleeved shirt with pearl buttons, and hand-tooled leather cowboy boots. A Rolex watch, gold and studded with tiny diamonds, hung loosely on his wrist. He had introduced himself as Xavier when he called them earlier, but neither August or Paul knew if that name was real or phony. At the moment, Xavier was sitting there quietly and staring back at them.

Based on his short stature and weight, Xavier was anything but an intimidating physical specimen. He looked like he ought to be an accountant or some anonymous office drone for a big company. However, it wasn't Xavier's appearance that had Cole and Tucker sitting there in fear and watching him like a bird would watch an approaching snake. What made them so afraid of Xavier was who he represented. He represented someone whose name had brought Cole and Tucker running from their homes at close to midnight to meet with him. That name was synonymous with a criminal cartel that was responsible for the illegal narcotics worth billions of US dollars that were smuggled into the United States from Mexico annually. Tucker and the Southern Devils motorcycle club helped sell some of the drugs for that cartel. The money from those drug sales were funneled through the church before ultimately making its way to overseas accounts that belonged to that cartel.

"Gentlemen, thank you for making time to see me on such short notice," Xavier said politely in perfect English with no discernible accent. He had a disarmingly pleasant smile on his face. He acted as if either of the men he was talking to had a choice in the matter, but, if they had ignored his call, there was a fair chance neither of them would have seen the sun rise in the morning. "I apologize for the late hour, but my employer insisted that I reach out to you immediately. He is somewhat troubled by some things that have been brought to his attention. When he is troubled, he sends me to look into whatever is concerning him. I'm his problem solver, I guess you would say."

"And what things would he be concerned about?" August asked calmly. "Everything here is running smoothly."

"The death of the young lady who was shot here in your church two months ago," Xavier said. "Your wife shot her because the young woman tried to kill her, I believe?" He shook his head sadly. "It saddens my employer that someone would sink so low as to defile a holy place with violence."

If August hadn't been so scared, he might have laughed in Xavier's face at that comment. The cartel Xavier worked for was responsible for hundreds of deaths from their wars with other cartels and the government. "It was indeed a tragedy," August said instead. "The young lady in question was mentally disturbed. My wife, Monica, was forced to shoot her in self-defense. It broke Monica's heart. She is at home asleep right now because her doctor had to put her on tranquilizers due to the emotional trauma it caused her."

Xavier looked downcast, as if that was the saddest thing he'd ever heard. "I am familiar with the prescription her doctor wrote her," he said woefully. "It is quite powerful. Her mixing it with alcohol makes it much more potent. She should be careful."

August stiffened. Xavier had, in a roundabout way, just told him that Monica was being watched carefully. They knew what medicine she was prescribed and that she was drinking regularly. "It will pass," August said calmly. "It was very unsettling for her."

"Taking someone's life can be traumatic," Xavier said sadly, "at least the first time."

"The police investigated it thoroughly," Paul said. "They said it was self-defense. The local prosecutor agreed. The case is closed. It's over and done. Most people have already forgotten about it."

Xavier casually turned to Paul and fixed him with a sad look. "Apparently someone remembers, because there's a private detective sniffing around you and the church because of her death."

"How do you know that?" Paul asked incredulously. There was a faint hint of surprise in his voice that wasn't there seconds ago. Paul knew that the cartel had the resources to do many things, but he was shocked by how quickly their intelligence network worked. It was amazing how fast they could find out things when they wanted to. Just thinking about it made a cold sweat start to drip down his back under his shirt.

Xavier looked at him as if he were disappointed in him. "Paul, you know we keep tabs on people who are important to us. Your club makes us a lot of money. Your plan to funnel the money through Pastor Cole's church here was brilliant. It was so brilliant that we are looking at using other churches for the same purpose. If something happens that might threaten this operation, my employer gets very concerned. That's why he asked me to come by and check on things."

"There's nothing to check on," Paul said firmly. "This detective was hired by the family of the girl Monica shot. He's trying to find something that they can use to try to sue for some easy cash. There's nothing to find. We're not worried about him."

Xavier stood up and walked over to study some of the pictures August had on his office walls. "You were worried enough about it to send a couple of your soldiers to try to scare him away," he said as he studied a picture of August shaking hands with the state governor during a fundraiser. "Both of the men you sent are in the hospital recovering from that stupid, stupid plan." He turned and glared at both Paul and August. "If you had simply left it alone, he would not have found anything if, as you say, there was nothing to find. Now, potentially, you have made this private detective and the family he works for even more determined to dig into your- and our-business. This is very concerning for us. "

The color drained out of August's face. Paul simply sat there, too stunned to move or say anything. Sending the two prospects to deal with Benjo Lane was his plan, but he had needed permission from the other leaders in the club to send them after Lane. Besides himself, there were four other men who were in leadership roles in the club. Sending the prospects had required a meeting and a vote between the five of them. Since the club was making money hand over fist from the laundering operation through the church, they had agreed to it without question. The meeting was held in the gang's clubhouse in secrecy. Now, obviously, someone in the leadership group was talking to the cartel behind Paul's back. That was not good.

August, seeing the shocked look on his friend's face, spoke up quickly. "The two of us made a decision to take action," August replied with calmness he didn't feel. "The two men we sent were supposed to make what happened look like a robbery or carjacking. We did not want this man coming around our church because he might find something that could make us all look bad."

"I thought there was nothing to find," Xavier said.

"There is nothing to find regarding what we do for your boss," August retorted. "But, there are other things this detective could find that might be misconstrued and used to make my wife, myself, or our church look bad. We did not want to take that chance. A church must uphold a certain image if it is to do well. The faintest hint of hypocrisy or scandal can ruin a church. The detective snooping around freaked us out. Granted, in hindsight, we might have overreacted."

Xavier listened politely. "So, Pastor Cole, what personal things are there that this detective could find? Do you like whores? Drugs? Gambling? You're not Catholic, so I doubt it's little boys."

"Nothing like that," August answered defensively. "I wasn't implying there was anything like that going on. I was just saying that we were afraid this detective might make something out of nothing in an attempt to get a financial settlement out of us for the girl's death. That he would try to make us look bad in the media in order to make us pay the girl's family off. That's what this is all about, sir. Trying to get us to give the family some money to go away."

"Then give them money to go away," Xavier said coldly. "That some crazy girl attacked Monica and forced her to shoot her is just a tragic twist of fate. Such things happen sometimes in this world that we live in. If you think paying this girl's family off will get rid of this detective, do it."

"Our insurance company won't pay them off," August said. "I reached out to them following the girl's death just in case there was a lawsuit. They won't pay a dime to the girl's family. This state has laws protecting people from civil liabilities in cases where it was self-defense. It was written to protect people who had to defend themselves legally from being sued by ambulance chasers."

"Then you pay the family off," Xavier replied simply. "Negotiate with them and pay them to go away. It might not take as much money as you think it will. Even if it does, find the money to pay them off."

"Why don't we just finish the job?" Paul asked gruffly. "Kill the detective. Even better, have some of your people intimidate the family into going away."

Xavier turned and looked at Paul as if he were a small child who had dared to interrupt the adults talking. "That is an option," he said, "but it's the option most likely to backfire. Killing anyone else might bring even more scrutiny to the church. That's the last thing we want. Reach out to the detective and whoever hired him. Make an offer of financial compensation to the family. You can even spin doing it to make yourselves and the church look good. You can say it's to help the remaining family move on."

"That's actually a good idea," August said. "It would be the Christian thing to do. It might solve our problem."

Xavier smiled. "See, I'm a problem solver," he said. "I know you can come up with the money if you're motivated enough."

"What if they want a lot of money?" Paul asked. "I'm talking hundreds of thousands of dollars? No matter how motivated you are, it might be hard to find that much money."

Xavier sighed as if beset by the problems of the universe. "Three days ago, I stood in a warehouse in a small city in northern Mexico and watched a man who disappointed my employer be dismembered and disemboweled using power tools bought at a local hardware store," he said. "My men did it in such a way that the man was alive for three hours before they put him out of his misery. It was recorded as a message to others. I can send you the entire video if you need motivation."

"That won't be necessary," August interjected quickly. "We'll handle it."

"Hold on, August," Paul said firmly. He turned his attention to Xavier. "I've met this detective face to face. What if he won't take the money?"

Xavier shook his head and glanced at the huge watch on his wrist. "I have neither the time nor the patience to go back and forth with you two," he said irritably. "You have my suggestion, but I also understand that sometimes people can be irrational and stubborn. I really don't care how you handle the situation, as long as our operation here remains unaffected. Is that clear enough?"

"Clear as a bell, sir," August answered.

"I'll show myself out," Xavier said. He nodded to the two men. "Gentlemen." With that, he turned and walked out of the office.

August and Paul listened as his footsteps receded down the hallway toward the lobby. The heels of his fancy cowboy boots clicked loudly on the tile floor. A minute or so later they heard the front door open and close. August rushed to the front window and looked out. He watched as the short, fat man walked to the idling BMW and got into the car. He remained at the window until the BMW drove out of the parking lot. Once he was sure Xavier was gone, he spun to face Paul. Paul was still seated. "What in the hell just happened?" August asked incredulously.

"Well, basically, we just got told to fix this mess before anything happens that might result in us not being able to wash their dirty money for them," Paul replied. "Word has gotten back to the cartel. Obviously, I have a rat running behind my back to tell the cartel things that ought to stay club business."

August turned back and stared out the window into the empty parking lot. "What was the name of the lawyer that detective said hired him?" he asked softly.

"Lawyer's name was David Whiteside," Paul replied.

"I'll reach out to him tomorrow," August said reluctantly. "I'll say we want to do the right thing as pastors, it's good for healing, blah, blah, blah. I'll low-ball them. We might get lucky."

"That detective bothers me," Paul replied tersely. "He's a pretty strange dude. I'm not optimistic they'll drop it."

"Make a plan to handle it in case he doesn't," August replied. "If that happens it's him or us. I have no intention of losing all of this, and I have even less intention of getting tortured to death in a warehouse in Mexico."

"I agree," Paul said. "If I have to kill Benjo Lane to stop him from shutting us down, I will. I'll do it in a way that minimizes the police looking at us as suspects. Regardless, I'd rather take a chance with the cops than the cartel."

"Agreed," August said. "Hopefully, I can end this with the lawyer the easy way. If not, everything else is on the table."

14

At nine AM the next morning, Benjo was knocking on the front door of the house where Darcy Woodruff, Sarah's former roommate, lived with her boyfriend. The single-family home sat on a cul-de-sac in a new subdivision where all of the houses looked almost exactly the same: eighteen hundred square feet with an attached garage, vinyl siding, shutters of either black, red, or green, and a small front porch barely big enough for two chairs. Darcy's house was one of the few that didn't still have a realty company's for sale sign on the front lawn. It was also one of only two on the cul-de-sac where someone had planted flowers and taken a few steps to decorate the exterior. Benjo was willing to bet the new flower gardens were the result of Darcy moving into the house with her boyfriend. She had been living there for about six weeks now. The flowers looked freshly planted and the mulch still had that sweet smell that new mulch did.

The door was opened almost immediately by a slender female with short blonde hair, glasses, and startling green eyes. She smiled at him, revealing a set of braces. Darcy was supposed to be around the same age as Sarah, twenty-five, but she could have passed for sixteen. She had pixie-ish features that made her look like she should be flying around in a Disney cartoon. She wore jeans, a tee shirt with a rainbow on it, and sandals. "Mr. Lane?" she asked. Her voice was soft and pleasant to the ear.

"I am," Benjo said as he returned the smile. "And you, obviously, must be Darcy." She nodded vigorously. Benjo suspected she did everything in life enthusiastically. She just had that type of personality. "Please call me by my first name, Benjo," he said.

"Please call me Darcy," Darcy said. "Your name is pretty different. Is it Ben Joe, as in short for Benjamin Joseph?"

"No ma'am," Benjo replied as he stood on the porch. "It's just one word. I don't have a middle name."

"That's different," Darcy replied. She looked him over from head to toe. "You're not what I expected at all when I heard private investigator."

"I get that a lot," Benjo said. "Were you expecting Magnum P.I.?"

"Who is that?" Darcy asked. She looked confused.

Benjo suddenly felt like he was a hundred years old. "He was a private detective that used to be on television in the 1980s," he explained. "He was played by Tom Selleck. You can still catch the reruns on some television channels and on some streaming services. I thought everyone knew who Magnum was."

"I'm not that old," Darcy said. "I'll have to look that up." She stepped back and motioned for Benjo to enter. "Please come in. If you don't mind, we can talk in the kitchen."

Darcy turned and led Benjo into the living room. The house had an open floor plan with the dining room and kitchen separated from the living room area by a half wall with an island attached. The living room area was neat but masculine, with a couple of guitars leaning in a corner, a gun cabinet, and an online gaming setup in front of a big screen television mounted on the wall. The kitchen and dining area were all female, however, with a definite sunflower and butterflies theme going on. The kitchen still smelled faintly of eggs and bacon from breakfast earlier. "Have a seat," she said. "Coffee?"

"No thanks," Benjo said as he took a seat at the table. The table sat right in front of set of double windows that gave him a good view of the backyard. The backyard was surrounded by a wooden privacy fence. Sunlight filtered through the windows and flooded the kitchen and dining room. Overall, it was a very pleasant place.

Darcy sat down at the table. "I called Chase after I got your call yesterday," she said. "I was just checking to make sure you were legit."

"That's perfectly understandable," Benjo said. "I could tell my call was a surprise just from your tone on the phone."

"I was surprised," Darcy admitted, "but I was also very happy to hear that someone was investigating what happened to Sarah." Her eyes suddenly teared up a little. "She was my best friend. I loved her more than I love my own sister. There's no way Sarah attacked anyone. That woman is a liar. I tried to tell that detective for the sheriff's department that, but he wouldn't listen. Asshole." She blushed suddenly. "Sorry for that. I shouldn't say stuff like that."

"I used to work for the sheriff's department and I know the detective who handled the case," Benjo said. "I think that's a pretty accurate and fair assessment of him. I've used a lot worse words than asshole to describe him." He removed his notepad from his pocket. "Do you mind if I take a few notes?"

"Not at all," Darcy said. "I'll be glad to help in any way I can. Sarah deserves it."

"I understand you and Sarah were friends since high school?" Benjo asked.

"We became friends in our freshman year of high school," Darcy affirmed. "We had a lot of common interests and we just hit it off. We had a lot of classes together as well. We were more like sisters than friends."

"And that friendship continued all the way through college?" Benjo asked.

"Yes," Darcy said. "One of the things we had in common was that we both were interested in the medical field. We both wanted to be doctors when we were freshman in high school. That changed as we got older and realized what it would take to get through medical school educationally and financially. We both ended up wanting to be nurses. Fortunately, the local branch of our state college system here has a highly-ranked nursing program that we both managed to get into, so we were able to stay local. We went to a lot of the same classes and graduated the same day. We were actually roommates in college, as well. Once we graduated and got our nursing licenses, we decided to be roommates as well."

"It seems easy to say that you and Sarah were a big part of each other's lives for several years at least?" Benjo asked.

"That's right," Darcy said. "Ever since freshman year of high school. Sarah and her family were like a second family to me. All of them, her brother, her mom, and her dad. They were good people."

"Darcy, there's no way I can ask this without it coming across as weird or creepy," Benjo said, "but I have to ask. Please don't take offense. Were you and Sarah ever more than friends?"

Darcy wrinkled her nose and shook her head. "Absolutely not," she said fiercely. "We both like men. Like I said earlier, we were more like sisters. That's just gross."

"I'm sorry," Benjo said sincerely. "Sometimes the hardest part of this job is having to ask questions like that. In all of the time that you knew Sarah, did she ever act in a way that made you wonder if she was having any mental or emotional health issues?"

Darcy fixed him with a look. "Do you mean did I ever wonder if Sarah had a screw loose?" she asked. She rolled her eyes. "That detective asked me a bunch of similar questions about Sarah. It was pretty obvious that he though my best friend was some sort of lunatic that fixated on Monica Cole because she was pretty and locally famous. I'll tell you what I told him: Sarah was normal to the point of being a little boring. Never, in the entire time I knew her, did I ever see Sarah act in a way or do anything that made me think she wasn't all there. And trust me, I would be one to notice."

"What do you mean by that?" Benjo asked curiously.

"Well, she was my best friend and we lived with each other for about four years total," Darcy said. "Also, during my last two years of the nursing program in college, we had to do practical, hands-on training in different nursing specialties. One of my favorites was psychiatric nursing, where you work with nurses in mental health related fields.

It really interested me and for a while I was considering making it my field, so I took more training in that field. I worked in mental health centers during my practical rotations."

"Really?" Benjo asked. "So, you had specialized training in recognizing and helping treat mental health issues?"

Darcy nodded vigorously. "I explained all of that to Detective Marsh," she said bitterly. "I told him that Sarah had never shown any signs of any mental health issues, but his reply was- and I will NEVER forget this- was 'you're just a nurse, not a doctor.' It infuriated me, even more than when he tried to imply that I had faked the burglary to hide evidence."

"Wait, come again?" Benjo asked.

"You know our apartment got broken into literally the day Sarah was killed?" Darcy asked. Benjo nodded. "I was staying with my boyfriend because I couldn't stand the thought of staying in the apartment afterwards. I went back the next day and found some stuff missing, so I called the police. The city officers had barely been gone thirty minutes when Detective Marsh showed up with a search warrant to go through Sarah's things. When I told him about her missing laptop and showed him a copy of the report the city officer had left, he accused me of staging it to hide evidence that she was stalking Monica Cole."

"Marsh is a piece of work," Benjo replied. "Getting back on track, you say that you never saw anything from Sarah that made you believe she might be having mental health issues? Do you think your prior training as a nurse in mental health issues would have helped you spot it if there were any signs?"

"You're damned right," Darcy said firmly. "Sarah was not crazy and she was not fixated on Monica Cole. You will never make me believe otherwise. It infuriates me that the police and the prosecutor's office made that claim without anything to back it up. Sarah will always be remembered now as the crazy lady who tried to stab the preacher's wife."

"I'm going to be honest with you, Darcy," Benjo said as he leaned back in his chair. "Learning your background as a psychiatric nurse and hearing you say that you never saw Sarah do or say anything that made you wonder about her mental state actually gives me a sense of relief. No one I've spoken with who knew Sarah believes that she was delusional and fixated on Monica Cole. None of those people had training in the field like you do, so to speak, and none of them lived with her. Hearing it from you eases my mind. According to the Coles and the police, that was Sarah's motive for attacking Monica Cole."

"They're liars," Darcy retorted.

"I agree," Benjo answered. "Now I have to figure out why Sarah was at the church that day. I really believe that once I know that, everything else will fall into place."

Darcy nodded. "I've tried to figure that out myself," she said. "Chase, Mr. Whiteside, and the police asked me the same question: what did Sarah have to do with Monica Cole? God, I wish I knew the answer to that question. Not for them, but for my own peace of mind."

"I'm going to be frank with you, Darcy. I think Sarah was murdered," Benjo said. "It was not self-defense; I think the Coles or their director of security lured Sarah there. I don't know if they planned to murder her and the church secretary coming in earlier than was planned interrupted them and self-defense was an excuse to get away with murder or if something escalated to the point where Sarah was trying to defend herself and the Coles twisted it around once they were discovered."

"I think the same thing!" Darcy said as she jumped up out of her chair. "I've said that from the minute I found out what happened. Sarah was a fighter, Benjo. I was there when she got into a couple of fights in high school with girls that tried to bully her. She didn't like to fight, but she could fight like a tiger when she had to. Sarah could throw a punch like a brawler when she had to. She always said her dad, Rick, was an amateur boxer when he was younger and he'd taught her and her brother to defend themselves early on."

"Darcy, do you have any idea what might have brought Sarah into contact with Monica Cole?" Benjo asked. "Any theory at all, no matter how crazy it seems?"

Darcy leaned against the kitchen counter and thought about it for several moments. "No," she finally said in frustration. "I have analyzed every interaction we had in the weeks leading up to Sarah's death and I'm still just confused."

"Is there any chance Sarah could have had secret life you didn't know about?" Benjo asked. "Could she have been flirting with someone online? Could she have been having an affair with someone?"

"No way," Darcy said. "I used to tease Sarah by saying she was a sixty-year-old woman trapped in a twenty-five-year-old's body. The girl would be in the bed by nine PM at night if she wasn't working."

"That just confirms what others have said," Benjo said. "Someone else I interviewed told me about Sarah taking care of her mother when she was in hospice. Do you recall that?"

Darcy sank back down into her chair. "Oh yes," she said. "When Sarah wasn't working, she would go take care of Reena. When Reena was put in hospice, Sarah was constantly by her side. All the way up until Reena passed away."

"Following Reena's death, did Sarah act differently?" Benjo asked. "I've been told that Sarah was possibly upset by something Reena might have told her on her deathbed."

"The day her mother died, Sarah came home and slept for about fifteen hours," Darcy said. "She was wiped out physically and emotionally. She was very quiet and distracted, but I assumed it was grief over her mom's death. During the funeral service, she just sat there staring off into space. As I said, I assumed it was just grief."

"In the days following her mother's death, did Sarah do anything odd?" Benjo pressed. "Did she go anywhere out of the ordinary? Did she start spending time with people she normally didn't? Stay on the computer or telephone?"

Darcy sat there and thought for a few moments. Benjo sat and waited. The refrigerator kicked on, filling the kitchen with a soft humming sound. "The only thing I can think of is her trip to the county health department," she finally said. "About three days after Reena's funeral, Sarah dropped her car off at the dealership to get some work done on it. It happened to be a day off for both of us, so I picked her up there and we went to lunch. After lunch, she asked me to run her by the county health department. She said she had to go by the state Division of Vital Records office in the same building to pick up something. I assumed it was copies of her mother's death certificate. However, when she came out, she didn't have anything in her hands. She didn't say much for the rest of the day."

"You sure she went there for her mother's death certificate?" Benjo asked. "It usually takes several days if not a couple of weeks to get death certificates following a death. I doubt they would have them that soon after a funeral."

Darcy shrugged. "I assumed that's what it was," she said. "Sarah didn't really say what she needed."

Benjo felt the first, faint inklings of a theory stir in the back of his brain. "Later that day, did Sarah spend any time on her laptop, by chance?"

"Yes," Darcy said immediately. "I dropped her off to pick up her car. She beat me back to the apartment because I had a couple of other errands. When I got home she was sitting at the kitchen table working on her laptop. I didn't really pay attention to what she was working on."

"Within say a week or so after the trip to the health department, did Sarah get any packages or anything in the mail?" Benjo asked. "I assume you both picked up the mail?"

"I don't remember," Darcy replied with a troubled expression on her face. "I worked nights, so I sleep during the day. Most of the time Sarah would grab our mail out of the apartment mailbox when she came home from work."

"Okay, Darcy, anything else at all you can think of?" Benjo asked. "Anything Sarah ever said or did that was out of character for her? Any strange visitors or the like?"

"No," Darcy said. "I'm sorry. I don't think I was much help at all."

Benjo smiled reassuringly. "Actually, Darcy, I think you were more help than you realize," he said. "I think you gave me a few more pieces for this big puzzle I'm working on. I just have to figure out how they fit. Once I do, I can figure out the big picture." He closed his notepad and slipped it into his pocket. "I appreciate you taking the time to chat with me. I'll let you get on with your day."

Darcy walked with him from the kitchen to the front door. "Do you really think they murdered Sarah?" she asked quietly as she opened the door for him.

"I do," Benjo said.

"Why would two preachers murder someone?" Darcy asked.

"I'll let you know," Benjo said.

15

The state Division of Vital Records office was located on the second floor of the county health department building on Spring Street. Benjo walked into the office to find a small lobby area with a few chairs in front of a large counter. Two women, both older, heavyset white women who could have passed for sisters, were working behind the counter at individual desks. They looked up when he entered. Neither of them looked thrilled to see him. Signs in the lobby listed the types of documentation available, such as birth and death certificates and marriage licenses, as well as the cost for copies of each one of those items. Another sign listed the documents needed in order to get a US passport. Benjo walked up to the counter and stood patiently. After nearly two full minutes of the women glaring at each other as if willing the other to go help him, one of the women got up and waddled over to the counter where Benjo stood. A plastic name badge hanging on a lanyard around her neck identified her as Roberta.

"Can I help you?" Roberta asked in a voice that made it sound like she would rather be set afire than actually help him. Standing up, Roberta was about five feet tall and about the same in diameter. She was badly in need of a visit to the hair salon and perhaps a makeup tutorial from someone who didn't have a side gig as a circus clown.

"Yes ma'am," Benjo said politely. "My name is Benjo Lane. I am a private investigator investigating a homicide," He retrieved his credentials from his pocket and presented them to Roberta. "I need to see someone's birth certificate. What do I need in order to do that?"

"Do you need to see the long form birth certificate or the short card?" Roberta asked.

Benjo was familiar with both types. The short card was exactly the way it was described: it was a small card about the size of a standard driver's license issued by the state that listed the person's name, date of birth, and the county in which they were born. It was an officially recognized form of state identification and the one that Benjo and most of the people he knew used when a birth certificate was needed. It was also the standard form that people were given when they requested a copy of their birth certificate. The long form birth certificate was a single page document about the size of a standard piece of white copy paper. The long form listed the person's birth name, date and time of birth, and location of the birth just like the short card. Unlike the short card, however, the long form listed the newborn child's mother and father as well. Benjo was willing to bet that most residents of the state didn't even know the long form version existed. "I would like to see the long form, if I may," he said.

"It's not your birth certificate?" Roberta asked with a scowl.

"No," Benjo replied. "It's the birth certificate of the victim in the case I'm investigating."

"You will need a copy of that person's death certificate before I can let you see their birth certificate," Roberta said firmly. "Do you have that?"

"No," Benjo replied patiently. "Fortunately, I see that I can also get copies of death certificates here. What do I need to get a copy of a death certificate?"

Roberta scowled so hard that Benjo was afraid that the bottom of her face was about to fall off. "Is the person deceased?"

"Yes ma'am. Being the victim in a homicide usually means you're deceased," Benjo said calmly.

Roberta obviously wasn't a fan of sarcasm judging from the glare she directed at Benjo. "Are you a family member?" she asked grouchily.

"No, but there are no restrictions on death certificates. They are public record," Benjo said. He leaned forward and rested his elbows on the counter. "I'm not trying to be difficult, but I think you are. You can look in your computer and see that a person has both a birth and death certificate on file. Instead of being difficult, why don't you be a decent human being and actually help me? It's not my fault that you're apparently having a bad day."

Roberta stiffened. "I am not having a bad day, sir. I am trying to follow the rules."

"And I am trying to solve a murder case," Benjo retorted. "To do that, I really need to see the victim's birth certificate. If my hunch is right, I think doing that might help me go a long way towards doing that. So, why can't we be friends and you let me see the long form birth certificate without being difficult? The person whose birth certificate I need to see is dead. Their death certificate is on file. Look it up, please."

Roberta looked at him as if he'd spat in her face, but she shuffled her way over to a computer resting on the counter. "What was the person's name?"

"Sarah Anne Fleming," Benjo said. "She was a white female and her date of birth was April 20th, 1997."

Roberta typed on her keyboard. "The computer is slow," she said tersely.

"Then it fits right in here," Benjo replied.

Roberta ignored him and continued to peruse the computer screen. "There is no birth certificate for Sarah Anne Fleming," she said. "Sorry," she added without an ounce of actual pity in her voice.

Benjo stood there for a few seconds as his mind reeled. *How could Sarah not have a birth certificate?* he wondered. A sudden thought struck him. "Could you check under Sarah Anne McAllister?" he asked.

Roberta glared at him but turned back to her computer. Nearly a full minute ticked by before something popped up on the screen. She hit a button and a printer beneath the counter whirred. She retrieved the form from the printer tray. She held it up. "That will be seventeen dollars, sir," she said maliciously.

Benjo smiled. "Go ahead and get me a copy of her death certificate too," he said politely. "It will be under Sarah Anne Fleming." He took his wallet out of his pocket and removed his credit card. "I'm feeling flush today."

Roberta scowled even harder, if that were possible, and the scowl was only magnified when the second woman seated at her desk behind her snickered. Roberta clicked a few more things on the computer keyboard and the printer whirred again. She took Benjo's card and vanished into a back room. She returned a couple of minutes later with the receipt for him to sign. Lastly, she gave him the copies of the birth and death certificates.

Benjo took them from her and examined the birth certificate first. Sarah's birth name was Sarah Anne McAllister. Reena had used her maiden name as the child's last name. The reason for that was halfway down the page. On Sarah's long form birth certificate, the section for biological father was blank. The mother's section was filled out with Reena's maiden name, Reena McAllister. The place of birth was recorded as the local hospital. The time of birth was nine seventeen PM on April 20th, 1997. At the bottom of the form was a woman's signature. The woman's name was Sharon Collins. She was the representative for the county health department who had confirmed the birth.

Benjo felt his heart start to pound as he examined the birth certificate. "Excuse me, ma'am," he said politely to Roberta. He laid the birth certificate down on the counter in front of her and pointed to the blank spot for the father's information. "What exactly does this being blank mean?"

"It means the father of this girl was not identified," Roberta said. "It could have been that the mother did not want to name him because of some conflict or it could mean that she didn't know who the father was. Sometimes the mother isn't really sure who the father is, so they will leave it blank. It's much easier to leave it blank and later add someone than it is to list the possible father and then discover that the named father isn't biologically the child's father."

Benjo digested this for a few seconds. *If Reena was already involved with Rick and Sarah was an unplanned pregnancy, why wouldn't she name him as the biological father, especially if their plan was to marry eventually?* he thought. *At the very least she would have given the child her father's last name, I would think.*

"Is that all you needed, sir?" Roberta snarled.

"Just one more thing if you don't mind," Benjo said. He pointed to the woman's name on the bottom of the birth certificate. "Who would this person be? Does she work for the state or the hospital or what?"

Roberta leaned forward and examined the signature at the bottom. "She would have been an employee of the county health department at the time," she said. "When a child is born in a hospital, the hospital staff records the birth in their records. The staff fills out a form for the state listing the details of the live birth. That form is picked up by a person at the county health department. That person verifies everything, signs off on it, and the form is forwarded to us, the Division of Vital Records. We issue a birth certificate and it is sent to the address of record for the parents." She squinted at the name. "Sharon Collins would have been the person working for the county health department at the time who performed that duty."

"Okay," Benjo said nicely. "So is there one person who covers a certain hospital or does one person cover a whole county or district or what?"

Roberta sighed as if Benjo had asked her the true meaning of life. "Each county had one person who covered all of the hospitals," she said wearily. "At least that's how they used to do it. Now everything is digital."

"Well, that's very helpful," Benjo said sincerely. He smiled beatifically. "Now, was that really that hard?" That remark once again drew a muffled chuckle from Roberta's sidekick seated at her desk behind the counter.

"Are we done, sir?" Roberta asked. "I have something I really need to be doing right now."

"As much as I hate to trouble you and keep from whatever task is at hand, I'm afraid I'm going to have to get two more death certificates,"

Benjo said. He opened his notepad and read off the names of Sarah's mother and father. With a scowl that would have probably turned a lesser man to ashes on the spot, Roberta sighed and went over to her computer.

Once he left the state Division of Vital Records office and Roberta's stimulating presence, Benjo drove a couple of blocks to the county courthouse. He parked in the attached parking garage and went into the courthouse. He knew exactly where he was heading in the courthouse from prior experience as a sheriff's detective. After a quick trip though the metal detectors at the entrance and a few friendly words with some of the staff he recognized from his sheriff's department days, Benjo made his way to the third floor of the building to the Family Court Records Office. The young lady working in the office was younger, prettier, and way nicer than Roberta was. The girl looked to be in her late twenties and actually seemed eager to help someone. Considering that her and Benjo were the only two people in the office at the time, Benjo imagined that she must be bored. An identification badge affixed to a holder on her belt identified her as Courtney.

"Can I help you, sir?" Courtney asked as she stood up from her desk and hurried to the waist-high counter that separated her work area from the small waiting area where Benjo was.

"Yes," Benjo said. "At least I hope you can, Courtney. I need to find some information on an adoption. I have the names and a time frame on when the adoption probably occurred."

Courtney stopped at the counter and leaned against it. "Okay," she said cautiously. "Are you the person who was adopted or did you adopt someone or what? I need a little more information so I can determine if you would have access to the records in question. Adoption records are sealed for a certain period of time following the date of the adoption hearing, so I might not be allowed to give you access to them."

Over the years, Benjo had learned that honesty was usually the best policy. He presented his private investigator's credentials. "I am investigating a case for a client. During my investigation, I have found evidence that leads me to think that the victim might actually have been adopted by the man she thought was her biological father. In other words, the man she thought was her biological father actually was not. If I'm right, I think it might help me actually solve the case," he said.

Courtney examined his credentials, then examined him. "You are kind of an odd-looking private investigator," she said. "I imagine you've heard that before," she added when she saw the grin pop up on Benjo's face.

"I have," Benjo replied. "I don't know why. I think it's the hair."

"I guess people expect private investigators to look like Magnum P.I.," Courtney replied with a grin of her own.

"You know, I said the exact same thing to a young lady I spoke with a couple of hours ago," Benjo said triumphantly. "You look like you might be in your mid- to late- twenties, so she was a couple of years younger than you. She had no idea who that was. It made me feel like somebody's grandfather."

Courtney giggled. "Don't get to feeling too good about it," she said. "I only knew about it because my mom used to watch reruns of it on cable in the afternoons after I got home from school. She loved her some Tom Selleck. To be fair, he was a fine- looking man when he was younger."

"From triumph back to old, just like that," Benjo retorted. "Thanks, Courtney."

She smiled and shrugged. "Sorry," she said. "When did the adoption you need info on happen?"

"The adoption in question probably happened around 1999 or thereabouts," Benjo said. "All of the persons involved are deceased, by the way. I don't know if that will get us around any privacy issues. I have their death certificates here if you need them." He held up the papers he'd brought with him.

"With the adoption being that old, it won't be an issue," Courtney said as she took the papers. "Having the death certificates helps though." She studied the names and other information on the death certificates. "I take it that Sarah Fleming was the adoptee."

"Yes," Benjo replied.

"I'll have a look," Courtney said. She took the death certificates and walked back to her desk. She sat down and immediately started typing away on her keyboard. Benjo stood there and leaned on the counter while he waited. While he waited, he ran through different scenarios in his mind that might explain how Sarah crossed paths with the Coles. There were several possible scenarios, but some of them were pretty farfetched. Even as he pondered on them, he still felt like he was missing something that ought to be obvious. It was a maddening feeling, almost like that feeling when you went to the refrigerator to get something, open the refrigerator door, and then have no idea what you were after.

Courtney must have found something because she got up from her desk and walked to another door in the back of the office. As she opened the door, Benjo looked into the room where she was headed. He saw racks and racks of paper files. Courtney went inside the room and the door closed behind her. Benjo continued to lean casually on the counter, but inside he was anything but relaxed. There had to be something or there would be no need for Courtney to go into a file storage room.

It seemed to take forever, but in reality, Courtney returned in slightly under four minutes according to Benjo's watch. She held a file folder with a court docket number and the name Fleming on the tab. She laid the folder on the counter in front of Benjo and opened it. She scanned over it and then looked at Benjo. "According to this record, Richard Fleming legally adopted Sarah Anne McAllister when she was twenty-six months old," Courtney read. "He married Reena McAllister who already had a baby girl named Sarah. Richard Fleming legally adopted the girl and gave her his name."

Benjo managed to keep a poker face, but it was tough. "Courtney, I need to ask you something," he said. "I'm sure I know the answer, but I just need someone familiar with adoptions and the court process to confirm I'm right."

"Fire away," Courtney said. "If I don't know the answer, I can call one of the judges. I don't think any of them are tied up in court right now."

"Is there ever a situation in which the biological father of a child would need to go through the adoption process?" Benjo asked.

Courtney looked at him like he'd just jumped up on the counter and started dancing a jig. "Why would any man need to adopt his own child?" she asked in confusion. "If you are the biological father of a child and you have proof of that, you are legally recognized as that child's parent."

"What if, for some reason, the biological mother didn't put you on the birth certificate as the father?" Benjo asked. "Suppose she left the father portion of the birth certificate blank? Say she was mad at the father for example and did it out of spite?"

"That's completely irrelevant," Courtney said, shaking her head. "All the biological father would need to gain their full parental rights is present evidence to the court that he was indeed the biological father. A DNA test from a certified lab would be sufficient to have any judge in the state grant him visitation, barring something else that might endanger the child. Putting his name on the birth certificate takes one form and about five minutes of time."

"That makes sense," Benjo said. He smiled apologetically. "I'm sorry for bothering you with stupid questions. You've been very nice and patient and I appreciate it."

Courtney smiled. "It's okay," she said. "I've had to answer some pretty strange questions during the time I've worked here. People wanting to see adoption records isn't that unusual anymore, especially since all of those companies that research your ancestry became so popular. You know, the ones on the internet where you can submit a DNA sample and find out who your ancestors were and ethnicity and everything else? People do those things and sometimes they learn things they never knew about themselves. I've had people in here who found out via those tests that the people who they thought were their parents had actually adopted them. They were never told the truth."

Courtney's words caused the light to come on in Benjo's brain. All of a sudden, many of the disjointed puzzle pieces in his mind clicked together. "There's no freaking way," he muttered as he realized what was bugging him so bad.

"Beg pardon?" Courtney asked as she stared at Benjo.

Benjo realized that he'd just spoken out loud. "That's amazing," he said. "Courtney, can you print me a copy of the court declaration that finalized the adoption for Sarah?"

"No problem," Courtney said. "There's a ten-dollar charge, though."

Considering Benjo was so excited he could have kissed the girl squarely on the lips, ten dollars was a small price to pay. "Print away, Courtney," he said with a grin.

The moment he got back to his truck in the parking garage, Benjo grabbed his cell phone from his pocket and called Chase Fleming's cell phone. Chase answered on the second ring. "Chase, it's Benjo. I'm following up on a lead I uncovered today. Did your mom have any family or close friends that were around when you were little?"

"My mom had no family in the area. She had an uncle that lives in Florida, but that's all I ever knew about. Our grandparents and aunts and uncles were all on my dad's side. Why?"

"Did your mom have any close friends or neighbors?" Benjo asked. "This would have been when you were little. Did someone babysit you regularly?"

There was silence for a few moments while Chase thought about it. "We had a neighbor next door to our first house. Her name was Patricia Blackwell. Mom paid her to babysit us when Sarah and I were little. She did that until I started pre-school. We moved when I was about seven to the house Mom owned when she died. I remember Miss Pat, as we called her, because Mom stayed in touch with her for years afterward. She came to Mom's funeral."

"What's her address?" Benjo asked.

"I don't know her exact address, but she was next door to our old home address," Chase replied. He rattled off the address of their house when he was a kid. "It was a brick house to the left of the house we lived in if you were looking at the front door."

"Okay," Benjo said. "Thanks, Chase."

"What have you found, Benjo?" Chase asked.

There was no way for Benjo to answer that question without blowing Chase's mind. He would have to tell Chase and David Whiteside what he'd found, but on the telephone was not the way to do that. "Nothing worth mentioning on the phone," he answered. "I'll meet with you and David in person soon."

With that, he ended the call, started his truck and headed for the address Chase had given him.

16

The address Chase gave him took Benjo back to Highway Ten and past the same wooded area that Sarah had marked on the printed map he found in her apartment. Highway Ten changed names about a mile past that plot of woods and became Millhouse Road. It was a rural area and houses were few and far between. Fortunately, the GPS on his cell phone took him right to the address. It was a neat, brick ranch-style house with green shutters and an asphalt driveway. The brick house was maybe twenty yards away from another smaller house with beige vinyl siding and a covered front porch. A wooden split-rail fence separated the two houses. Based on what he'd learned in his investigation, the house with the vinyl siding was where Reena McAllister had lived before she married Rick Fleming. It was also where the young family lived until Chase was seven years old. That would have made Sarah close to ten years old at the time.

There was a slender, older woman with short, curly hair stooped over pulling weeds from a flower bed in front of the brick house. She turned and looked as Benjo turned into the asphalt driveway and stopped. She continued to watch him as he turned off the truck's engine and hopped out of the vehicle. He moved slowly and tried not to look threatening as he got out. The old woman wore jeans and a faded yellow, long-sleeved shirt. She looked to be in her early sixties. She scowled when she saw Benjo. "If you're selling something, I'm not interested," she said. "And I already belong to a church and I'm not interested in changing my religion."

"Patricia Blackwell?" Benjo asked as he approached her.

The older woman narrowed her eyes as she studied his face. "That's me," she said firmly. "I have no idea who you are, though."

"My name is Benjo Lane and I am a private investigator," Benjo said as he stopped in front of her. "I was wondering if I could bother you for a few minutes. I think you might be able to help me."

"Private investigator?" Patricia said. "Why in the world would a private investigator need to talk to me?"

"I'm investigating a case involving Sarah Fleming," Benjo answered. "She used to live next door to you. I think you used to babysit her when she was little. Rick and Reena Fleming used to live in that house over there, if I'm not mistaken."

Patricia's look changed from confusion to sadness. "I know who you're talking about," she said. "They lived in that house until about sixteen years ago. My husband and I used to own that house and use it as a rental property. We rented it to Reena when she was a young thing. Her and her husband lived there for a few years after they married. I used to babysit Sarah and her brother when they were little ones."

"Mrs. Blackwell, I'm investigating Sarah's death," Benjo explained. "She was killed about two months ago."

The old woman nodded. "Call me Pat, young man," she said. "I know what happened to Sarah. Preacher Cole's wife shot her. I heard Sarah went crazy and tried to stab her or something."

"The only family Sarah had left is her brother, Chase," Benjo said. "He's trying to figure out what happened that made Sarah end up getting shot. The lawyer Reena worked for hired me to see what I could find out."

The old woman pointed to a couple of metal deck chairs arranged around a matching table that sat on the opposite side of the driveway under a towering oak tree. "Let's go have a seat while we talk, young man. I've been weeding these flowerbeds for the last hour and I need to sit down."

"By all means, Patricia," Benjo said. He followed the woman over to the outdoor table and chairs. Patricia pulled one of the chairs out from beneath the table, wiped the seat out with her gloved hand, and sank down wearily. Benjo pulled out the other chair and sat down in it. Even though the day was warm, it was pleasant in the shade of the oak's limbs.

Patricia wriggled around and got comfortable. "What exactly are you trying to find out?" she asked once she was settled.

"Sarah's family and friends want me to figure out why Sarah went to the church and confronted Mrs. Cole the way she did," Benjo said. "They really don't believe that Sarah was suffering from some sort of mental health issue. I've been talking to Sarah's friends and others familiar with the situation. During my investigation, I've found some things that made me wonder about Sarah's birth and childhood. Chase gave me your name. He said you took care of them when they were little. He has fond memories of you."

Patricia smiled. "He always was a sweet kid," she said fondly. "Sarah was too, for that matter."

"Patricia, how old was Reena when she started renting that house over there?" Benjo asked.

"She was barely eighteen," Patricia said. "She was a pretty thing, just out of high school and with her first real job at the hospital. She had been working at the hospital for a couple of months when she called us about renting the house after we put an ad in the newspaper. At first, me and Earl, my husband, were reluctant to rent to a single young woman because we didn't want a bunch of drama or parties there, but Reena impressed us, so we took a chance on her."

"So, Reena was a good tenant?" Benjo asked. "Did she have any friends over? Did she have a boyfriend?"

"Not for the first year or so," Pat said. "She was single and struggling to survive by herself. Rick, the guy she ended up marrying, showed up a about a year and a half after she started renting. We liked him too. He seemed like a good man and really treated her well."

"When did little Sarah come into the picture?" Benjo asked directly.

Pat's eyes shifted and she looked down to fidget with a button her shirt. "Reena had started dating Rick and the baby was born several months later. I'm not really sure on the timing."

Benjo knew that the older woman was lying as soon as she spoke. He could also tell from her body language that she was uncomfortable with lying to anyone. "Pat, I've seen Sarah's birth certificate," he said gently. "I've also done the math on when Sarah was born and when Rick Fleming entered the picture. I know he was not Sarah's biological father."

Pat turned and looked at a squirrel that happened to be scurrying by at the moment. "I have no idea what you're talking about," she said.

Benjo leaned forward and made Pat look him directly in the eyes. "Pat, I respect what you are trying to do," he said sincerely. "I know that you swore to keep a secret for Reena, someone you liked and cared about, years ago. Unfortunately, Reena is dead now. Rick and Sarah are too. All of the people who could be hurt by that secret are all gone now. I've spoken to Chase, the last surviving family member, and I believe he can handle the truth, whatever it may be. I'm trying to find out why Sarah ended up dead and I think you can help me by telling me the truth. Please help me. Sarah deserves it."

Pat looked away from his gaze. She was quiet for a couple of minutes before she spoke again. "What do you know, Mr. Lane?"

"I know Sarah was born out of wedlock," Benjo said. "I don't know who her father was, but it was not Rick Fleming. Reena already had Sarah and Rick officially adopted her and gave her his last name when she was barely over two years old. Reena didn't list any father on Sarah's birth certificate. I've also seen the adoption records."

Pat fidgeted with the button again for a few seconds before she looked at Benjo. "The baby girl Reena named Sarah showed up about four months after Reena moved into the house," she said reluctantly. "Reena brought her home. It was quite a shock, to say the least."

"Why was it a shock?" Benjo asked. "Did she keep the pregnancy a secret? Was she able to conceal the fact that she was pregnant from you whenever you were around her?"

"Yes," Pat replied. "Reena didn't tell anyone she was pregnant. I never saw anything that indicated she was pregnant. She gained a little bit of weight after she moved into the house, but only a few pounds. She never said anything at all about being pregnant."

"Could she have concealed it from you because she was worried that you might make her move?" Benjo asked.

"I don't think she would have because of something like that," Pat replied. "Me and Reena hit it off. I really liked her. Earl and I had three sons. They were all grown and moved out by the time Reena moved into that house. Having her was like having a daughter almost."

"Yet, four months after moving in, she has a baby," Benjo said. "How did you react to that?"

Pat looked back at Benjo, her face unreadable. "I was shocked and a little mad, to be honest," she said. "I thought we were friends and I was treating her like family, only to have her pop up with a newborn baby girl. Once she explained it all to me, though, I got over being mad about it and I fell in love with that little baby girl." She smiled. "We had three grandkids by then. All boys yet again. Me and my offspring seemed to be cursed for a while with just having boys. My youngest boy and his wife finally broke the curse a few years ago with twin daughters."

Benjo smiled. "How did Reena explain it when she showed up with a baby girl, to use your words?"

"Reena swore to me that she never knew she was pregnant," Pat said. "She told me that she never felt anything strange that would let her know she was with child. She told me that her monthly cycle had always been weird, that she might go two or three months and never have one. She swore that she'd even had a period a month before she delivered the child. She never knew she was pregnant until she started having cramps at work and then her water broke. Coming from a woman who had three kids, there's no denying what's going on once your water breaks."

"Did you believe her?" Benjo asked frankly. "Granted, I'm speaking as a man, but it seems like it would be nearly impossible to carry a child to term without realizing that you were pregnant."

"Trust me, it's possible," Pat replied. "I was six months pregnant with my first boy before I found out we were having a kid. I didn't have any symptoms at all; no morning sickness, nothing. Everything was as normal as it could be. The only reason I knew I was pregnant was because I had to go to the lady doctor for a routine checkup and she discovered it. I still remember the medical term she used to describe what I had. It was called a cryptic pregnancy. It's rare but it does happen. With my second and third boys, there was no denying it. I was sick and miserable with both of them."

"I guess there's just some things that men never think about," Benjo said. "I guess if you're not trying to get pregnant, you're not watching for it." He shook his head ruefully. "That sounds weird."

"Women are taught that the main thing to watch for that means you're pregnant is no monthly period," Pat replied. "That's not always the case, though. Everyone's body is different. Reena told me she never knew she was pregnant. I believed her, not just because she told me that, but because, as a woman who'd had kids, I saw other things that convinced me she was telling the truth."

"Such as?" Benjo asked.

"I hadn't seen Reena in about two days," Pat said. "She called me and asked me to come over to the house. She sounded really strange. I thought the poor thing might be sick, so I walked over. When she let me in, she showed me this newborn baby. Aside from some diapers, a few cans of formula. and some baby things from those kits the hospital gives to new mothers, Reena didn't have nothing for a baby. She didn't have a bassinet, a crib, or anything else, not even a real baby blanket. Sarah was wrapped up in a towel."

"What did you do?" Benjo asked.

"My mother hen instincts kicked in," Pat said. "I could tell poor Reena was tired and overwhelmed. How would you feel if you think you have a stomach ache only to pop out a brand-new human being you have to care for from now on? I helped her get the baby settled in. I had some baby stuff stored in the attic for any future grandkids that might be coming down the pike, so I grabbed some of that stuff. I sent poor Earl to town with a list of stuff for the baby and Reena."

"I can only imagine how overwhelming that must have felt," Benjo conceded. "To suddenly have a baby in the house that you had no idea was coming. I don't have kids, but I know my wife went to baby showers for her friends and coworkers regularly it seemed."

"It happened at a bad time for her too," Pat said. "She was living on her own and struggling, with no one to help her. She was renting our place, but the only furniture she had was the stuff we already had in there when she rented it. She had this old piece of junk car that had a problem with overheating. She used to have to pull over to let the thing cool off before she blew the motor. Her life was tough. Me and Earl felt so sorry for her."

"It must have sucked to have all of that going on and a baby all of a sudden," Benjo replied. Especially one you are completely unprepared for."

Pat nodded. "It ain't like bringing a puppy home, that's for damned sure," she said. "Speaking of puppies, I used to pick at Reena about popping up with a baby no one knew was coming. Reena used to joke that she really didn't have the baby, a dog had dragged her out of a bush and she had found her." She chuckled at the memory. "She always did have a funny side."

"Was Reena a good mom?" Benjo asked.

"When you're a new mother, there's a time when you first bring that baby home from the hospital where you nearly freak out," Pat said. "You realize that you have to take care of this helpless newborn and now you don't have nurses helping. If you're lucky, you've got a good husband to help out. Reena didn't have that. She was a little freaked at first, but she got the hang of it right quick. She loved that little girl more than life itself."

"I imagine she struggled as a single mom," Benjo said. "That had to be tough."

"That was one thing the poor girl was freaked out over," Pat said. "When she showed me the baby, it was on a Friday. She had to be back at work on Monday. She couldn't even take time off because it was just her. I offered to babysit little Sarah. I was at home anyway and it gave me something to do. I took care of her during the day while Reena worked. I did that for her and for Chase all the way up until they started kindergarten." She smiled. "I loved those two kids like my own."

"Pat, did Reena ever tell you who Sarah's father was?" Benjo asked.

"She refused to," Pat said. "When she was struggling financially, I told her that she ought to go after Sarah's father for child support. She told me that it wasn't worth it, that he was a no-account piece of trash who wouldn't pay it anyway."

"Apparently, he was good enough to have sex with at least once," Benjo said.

That remark drew a glare from Pat. "Spoken like a true man," she said. "Women can make mistakes just like a man can. The only difference is that you men will brag about yours to your friends. A woman won't say a word and will take her shame to the grave."

Benjo was quiet for several seconds. "You know, you're right," he said, chastened. "I was out of line with that comment. I apologize. Did Reena ever say anything at all about who the father was? A name? Initials? Did you ever see her with a boyfriend?"

"No," Pat replied. "That's why you could have knocked me over with a feather when I walked over to her house and she showed me a baby."

Benjo took his cell phone from his pocket and pulled up a picture. It was a picture of August Cole when he was a young man around the age of eighteen. He had found the picture on the church's website along with Cole's biography. It was one of several posted online of August through the years. He zoomed in on August's face. "Pat, did you ever see this young man around these parts? Did you ever see him around Reena?" He held out his telephone so Pat could see the picture closely.

Pat leaned forward and studied the picture. Her brow furrowed as she studied it. "That's August Cole," she said in surprise. She looked at Benjo. "You think August Cole was Sarah's father?"

"You know August Cole?" Benjo asked in surprise.

"Just from television," Pat answered. "I've watched some of his sermons on television before. He's easy to remember."

"I'm trying to figure out what caused Sarah to go after the Coles," Benjo answered. "Why Sarah originally made contact with Monica Cole has been the puzzle in all of this." Benjo didn't dare tell her that he suspected the Coles had murdered Sarah.

"The police said Sarah was having some sort of mental health issue," Pat said. "At least that's what the news said."

"Nothing I've found and no one I talked to who knew Sarah well has made me believe that's accurate," Benjo answered. "When I found that Rick wasn't Sarah's father and that he'd adopted her when she was two, it made me start looking at other theories, no matter how farfetched. August Cole being Sarah's father was one."

Pat shook her head. "Nope, I never saw him around her. I know that he was in this area though. He worked a little while at the Pearson's dairy farm down the road."

Benjo remembered the nice old man who'd stopped when he was looking at the wooded area back down the road, the area Sarah had a printed map of with it circled. "Really?" he asked. "How do you know that?"

"I remember Maggie Pearson, Tom's wife, talking about it one time," Pat replied. "It was just when August Cole was starting to get known as a preacher around here."

"I didn't know that," Benjo said. "I think I might need to talk to Mr. Pearson. I think we've met before."

"The Pearsons are good folks," Pat said. "I'm sure they'll talk to you about it."

"Pat, is there anything else you think might help me figure this all out?" Benjo asked. "Anything might be helpful."

Pat thought about it for a few seconds. "I hate what happened to Sarah," she said sincerely. "I guess there's a chance, if young August Cole was in the area, that he could have hooked up with Reena. She was a pretty young woman and he was -still is- a fine-looking man. I remember what it was like to be young and have all of them hormones running crazy."

"Reena confessing to Sarah that August was her father would make her want to meet him," Benjo said. "It would explain a lot."

Pat nodded sagely. "That might not be what happened though," she opined.

"Yes ma'am," Benjo said as he stood up to take his leave. "There's always that."

Pearson's Dairy Farm was just a mile back down the way Benjo had come. There was a sign with that name on it beside a gravel driveway that took him to a large farmhouse with painted wooden siding and a couple of huge barns right behind the house. As luck would have it, Tom Pearson, the cheerful old man in the baseball cat who'd stopped to offer Benjo help the day he was exploring the land on Sarah's map, was outside when Benjo drove up the driveway to the house. The old man was leaning against the open tailgate of the same pickup truck he was driving the first time they met and talking on a cell phone. He put the phone away as Benjo drove up and parked his truck behind the old man's pickup. Benjo rolled down the window and waved as the old man walked toward him. "Good afternoon, Mr. Pearson."

A look of recognition appeared on the old man's face. "I thought that truck looked a little familiar," Pearson said. "You're the feller who was checking out my land the other day."

"That's me," Benjo said with a friendly smile. "Mr. Pearson, I didn't introduce myself the other day when we met beside the shoulder of the road there. My name is Benjo Lane. I'm a private investigator."

The old man stopped at Benjo's truck door and looked confused. "A private detective?" he asked.

"Yes sir," Benjo answered. "Tommy, I wasn't fully truthful with you that day. I was looking at your land because someone had it circled on a map, but it wasn't a friend of mine. The person with the map was the victim in a case I'm investigating. She was a young woman who was killed. I apologize for not telling you the whole story."

The old man took his baseball cap off and scratched his head. "Well," he said. He seemed to be at a loss for words.

"Tommy, you and your family have done nothing wrong in what I'm investigating," Benjo explained. "No one is in trouble and nothing is coming back on you or yours, I give you my word. Some information I have uncovered has brought me back to you with a couple of questions. I would love to be able to explain it all to you, but at this stage in my case I can't."

Tommy put his cap back on. "I'll help you if I can," he said. "I don't have a clue what in the world this could be about."

"Tommy, back around 1997, did a young man named August Cole work here at the farm with you?" Benjo asked.

Tommy nodded immediately. "He did," he said. "I went to church where his daddy preached at the time. The church is about five miles from here. I knew August from the church. He came through needing some money after him and his daddy fell out and his daddy run him off. I gave him some work and let him live in an old camper trailer I had at the time. He worked for me for just a couple of months before I run him off. The drugs had him bad back then. He stole some stuff."

"Okay," Benjo answered. "Did you ever see him have a girlfriend?" Any female visitors?

"The girl who's now his wife would come around ever now and then," Tommy replied. "I caught her staying the night a few times. My wife didn't like that at all. Her coming around and some tools and stuff going missing was what led to me running him off."

"I've been given to understand they weren't good people back in their younger days," Benjo said.

"Yeah," Tommy said. "That'd be true. It's amazing what the Lord can do when He starts working on your heart. Both of them changed and look what they turned into."

Possible murderers? Benjo thought, but he didn't say it out loud. "Yes sir," Benjo said. "It really is something."

"Can I ask why you wanted to know about August Cole being here almost twenty-five years ago?" Tommy asked. "I feel like you owe me that at least."

"It's a paternity case," Benjo answered. "The case I'm working on involves someone who thinks August Cole might be their daddy from way back then when he was running around buck wild like that."

Tommy shook his head. "Them damn drugs has led many a man astray," he said. "It seems like one of them new DNA tests you hear about on television would answer that question once and for all."

"I suspect that might be the way to an answer," Benjo said. "That's all I needed, Tommy. Thanks again."

"Glad to help," Tommy said. "Good luck, young man."

Benjo thanked him, started his truck, and drove back down the driveway to the road. He turned onto the highway and headed back to the city. Tommy watched as he drove away. Once his truck was out of sight, the old man dialed a number on his cell phone. "Hope Springs Church," a crisp female voice answered.

"Hey there," Tommy said pleasantly. "I need to speak with Pastor Cole," he said. "Tell him it's Deacon Tommy Pearson."

17

Following his talk with the old farmer, Benjo drove back to his cabin at a speed that would have made any state trooper looking to write a ticket a happy man. Once he reached the cabin, he hurried in through the side door and went straight to the kitchen where his laptop computer and the files from the case were. He sat down at the table, opened the one containing Sarah's checking account records, and found the page he was looking for. It was the page with the two unusual charges on it for something listed as WIA. The charges were almost three hundred dollars total. Benjo grabbed the legal pad he had laying on the table and noted the dates. With that done, he started poring over the case file, his notes, and everything else he had on the case, listing all of the dates that were relevant from the date Reena Fleming died to the first telephone call to the church and then on to Sarah's death. He filled up three legal pad pages with dates and notes. He laid out the three pages on the table with the dates listed chronologically. With it laid out like that, he started comparing everything he had.

With everything written out before him, Benjo immediately spotted something interesting. The first charge to Sarah's bank account for WIA was three days after Reena's funeral. The second charge was the day after Sarah went to the church and allegedly assaulted Monica Cole. The first telephone call was seven days after the first WIA charge. The second call was six days after the second WIA charge. Two days later the third call from Sarah's cell phone to the church. That was the one where Monica had spoken to her for over twenty minutes. After that date was when the burner phone calls to Sarah's cell phone had started.

199

Benjo grabbed his laptop and inserted the thumb drive of the video from the church's lobby camera that showed Sarah's alleged assault on Monica Cole. In the color footage, Sarah approached Monica and August as they stood in the lobby near the sanctuary doors and spoke to people leaving the day's service. Sarah approached Monica from the side and appeared to touch Monica's right shoulder. Monica turned and reacted visibly as if startled. Sarah patted her on the shoulder, spoke, and then walked away. Monica reached up and flipped her long hair away from her shoulder with her right hand and then went back to speaking with the people in front of her. Benjo re-watched the clip several times, zooming in as much as he could on his laptop by enlarging the screen a little more each time. The more he watched the video play out on his screen, the more he realized exactly what he was seeing. "I'll be damned," he said softly.

Benjo closed out the video and pulled up the internet. He searched WIA. Several results popped up, ranging from that being the stock market listing for a company out of Utah that made truck parts to a charity that worked with orphans in Asia. There was nothing that seemed like it would remotely tie into Sarah's case. He tried other ways of looking up the letters, but it all seemed to be a dead end. He was about to give up when another thought struck him. He tried another search, this time under 'companies that do genetic testing'. Dozens of results popped up, most of them ads detailing the services each company offered.

Benjo was on the second page of the search results when he found what he was looking for. He clicked on the link and went to the company's website. The company listed a number of services that they offered to clients, promising quick results from their state-of-the art testing labs after clients submitted a sample for testing. Kits to obtain a sample were sent discreetly. The website actually had a picture of the cardboard boxes used to ship the collection kits. Benjo immediately recognized the picture, it was the cardboard box with the stylized W he'd seen in Sarah's bedroom. and results were sent via email or by certified mail at the client's request. Most test results took less than a week. Benjo looked at the dates he had scribbled on his timeline. The cloudy picture suddenly started getting way clearer.

The company's website listed a telephone number for customer service. Benjo dialed the number from his cell phone and within minutes was speaking to a very helpful young man who spoke English. Benjo pretended that he was a potential client and asked the young man several questions regarding what the company could do with a sample if he sent it in. The young man, whose name was Dennis, carefully explained everything the company was capable of, depending on the type of sample. When Benjo explained the type of sample he would be sending in, Dennis patiently explained the things they could do and the things they couldn't do with that type of sample. Benjo was struck by what the company could supposedly deliver. After nearly thirty minutes on the telephone, Benjo told them exactly what he needed from their company. Dennis quoted him a price for what he needed. Benjo used his credit card to complete the order and paid extra for express shipping and service. Dennis said his package should arrive in two days maximum. Benjo thanked him and ended the call.

Benjo laid his cell phone down on the table and stared off into space. For the first time since he'd been drawn into the case, he had an idea of what had really happened. Interviewing Patricia and then the old farmer had been extremely helpful in opening his eyes to a possibility that he'd never even considered because it was too implausible. However, given what he'd learned in the last hour or so, that theory, no matter how incredible, now seemed very possible. If his theory was correct, it would explain why the Coles had decided they needed to kill Sarah Fleming. There was no way he would be able to prove part of his theory- it would always be an educated guess- but he could build an extremely good circumstantial evidence case.

Benjo was reaching for his cell phone to make another call when it rang. He picked it up and saw that the call was from David Whiteside. "David," Benjo said when he answered the call.

"I just got a very interesting call from the attorney for the Coles," David said without preamble.

"They want to sue us?" Benjo asked as he settled back in his chair.

"No," David said. "He gave me this long spiel about how August and Monica Cole were devastated about what happened with Sarah."

"Not nearly as devastated as Sarah," Benjo interjected.

David made a noise, but Benjo couldn't tell if it was a sigh or exasperation. "Anyway, per their attorney, they want to reach out to Sarah's family to try to, as he put it, 'ease their suffering in this dark time'. They are willing to pay fifty thousand dollars to Sarah's remaining family. That's Chase, as you know."

Benjo grinned. "In exchange for what, David?"

"In exchange for the money, I have to drop my investigation into what happened with Sarah," David answered. "Their lawyer told me that there's no sense in continuing to dig into this tragic event. The police and prosecutor's office have already closed the matter and to continue to press the Coles regarding it only serves to make them relive a tragedy that they would prefer to put behind them. Also, continuing to have you running around interviewing people and making allegations is borderline harassment, according to their attorney. I have to end the investigation, pay you off, and stay as far away from the Coles and their church as possible."

"Is that all?" Benjo asked.

"No," David said. "Aside from the fifty thousand to Chase, the attorney also offered ten thousand to you for your fee and expenses. They also plan to donate twenty-five thousand dollars in Sarah's name to a mental health program of our choosing."

"So, about eighty-five thousand dollars for us to go away," Benjo said. "That's very generous of them. What do you say, David?"

David was quiet for several seconds. "I think you've scared them to death," he finally said. "They obviously don't want you sniffing around them. I guess when the two goons they sent didn't get the job done, they figured they would try paying you to go away. You must be close to finding out something they want to keep a secret." He was quiet for a few moments. "Are you?" he finally asked.

"Yes," Benjo answered. "Today has been an eye-opener for me, to say the least. I think I'm pretty close to being able to tell you and Chase why the Coles wanted Sarah dead. I think they killed her in order to keep a secret that would threaten the church empire they're building."

"Would you care to share what that secret is?" David asked.

"Not right now," Benjo said. "My theory is kind of out there. Someone once said that incredible claims require incredible proof. Before I say anything and get anyone worked up, I want to be able to prove what I'm saying."

"That's reasonable," David said. "What do you think about the money they're offering?"

"You can take it if you want to," Benjo answered. "I'm still not stopping, David."

"I'm not taking the money," David said flatly. "Actually, I've already told their attorney that we weren't interested in their money. The fact that they offered it proves to me that they did something wrong. Stay after them, Benjo."

"I will," Benjo said. "And as soon as I'm able to substantiate my theory, I will brief you and Chase face to face. If things go like I hope they will, it won't be too much longer."

"I can hardly wait, and I mean that sincerely," David said. "Happy hunting."

Benjo ended the call, but he didn't put his phone down. Instead, he glanced at his notes, found the cell phone number he needed, and called it. Marsha West, the former church secretary for Hope Springs Church that he'd interviewed a couple of days earlier, answered. Benjo identified himself. Marsha sounded excited to hear from him. "Marsha, do you still stay in touch with any of the people you used to work with at the church?"

"Yes," Marsha answered. "I'm still friendly with most of them."

"I need to get in touch with one specific person," Benjo explained. He explained to her the person he needed to speak with. As luck would have it, the person he needed and Marsha were still friends and Marsha had a cell phone number for her saved in her phone. The person in question was a woman named Dakota Taylor and she still worked at the church a couple of times a week. "Marsha, can you help me get in touch with Dakota? I need to as soon as possible."

"I suspect Dakota's probably at the church right now," Marsha replied. "The Coles should be filming their television show right now. She would be there for that."

"Please reach out to her, give her my number, and have her call me. The sooner, the better," Benjo asked. "It doesn't matter what time it is."

"I'll call her now," Marsha promised.

Benjo thanked her and ended the call. He glanced at his watch and realized that it was getting close to six PM. That was normally dinner time for him and Harley. As if summoned by telepathy, Harley strolled into the kitchen, sat down on the rug in front of the refrigerator, and looked up at him expectantly. "Let me guess, you're hungry," Benjo said as he walked to the pantry and removed a can of cat food from the pantry shelf stacked with cans of cat food. He opened it and poured the whole can into Harley's bowl. The cat pounced upon the food eagerly.

With the cat taken care of, Benjo prepared his own food. He was an excellent cook, even before his wife's death, so he knew his way around the kitchen. Still, it had been a long day and he was waiting for the telephone to ring, so he settled for a sandwich and a baked potato cooked in the microwave. He had finished the sandwich and was halfway through the potato when his cell phone rang. An unfamiliar number popped up on the screen. He laid his fork down and answered the call. "This is Benjo Lane," he said.

"Mr Lane, my name is Dakota Taylor," a strong female voice said. "Marsha West asked me to give you a call."

"Yes ma'am, thank you for calling me," Benjo said. "Miss Taylor, I understand that you work at Hope Springs Church for August and Monica Cole. Is that correct?"

"I work for them part time," the woman replied. "I have my own business, but I work for them a couple of times a week, mainly before they film their show or do stuff for social media. I'm actually at the church now, but I'm not busy at the moment. The Coles are here in the studio taping their show."

"Dakota, if I may call you by your first name, I need some help with something. You are about the only one who can help me with it," Benjo said. "Let me tell you what I need. It's a little odd, to say the least. You can tell me if you can help me or not. If you help me, I will make it worth your while. Are you interested?"

There was no hesitation at all. "It depends on what it is and what you're offering," Dakota answered. "If it's something weird or gross, it's going to be no." Benjo told her what he needed from her. "That's it?" she asked.

"Yes," Benjo answered. "Just those two things. How's a hundred bucks apiece sound?"

The line was silent. "I'll do it," Dakota finally answered. "I need to be careful, though, because I don't want anything coming back on me."

"They will never know," Benjo promised sincerely. *And if this goes the way I think it will, if they do find out it will already be too late,* he thought.

"I'll be done here around nine PM," Dakota answered. "There's a bar named Hank's a couple of miles from the church on the main highway. I pass it on my way home. Do you know it?"

Benjo was familiar with the bar. It was a local watering hole that catered to the country music/ wannabe cowboy crowd, complete with line dancing and a mechanical bull. "I do," he said.

"Meet me there in the parking lot at nine thirty," Dakota said. "I'll park on the far edge of the lot away from the highway so there's less chance to be seen. I drive a burgundy Toyota Four Runner."

"I'll be there," Benjo replied. He described his truck to her. "See you at nine thirty sharp."

Benjo ended the call and laid his phone down. He still had over two hours before he needed to go meet Dakota. He finished his dinner, cleaned up his mess, and sat back down at the table. He re-organized the files and made a few notes on what he'd learned that day. An hour had passed by the time he was done. He carried his notes and files upstairs and locked them in his gun safe upstairs. He came back downstairs and went back to his pantry. He grabbed three gallon-sized plastic storage bags from a box in the pantry, left the cabin, and locked up behind himself.

Harley was sitting outside on the top step when he reached the steps. The huge cat looked up at him and meowed loudly. "It's dark," Benjo said to the cat. "Shouldn't you be inside?" Harley's answer was to turn and stare off into the darkness. "I worry about you coming outside and roaming around," he said as he reached down to scratch the cat's head. "There are coyotes out here." Harley simply looked at him, stood up, and padded away across the porch to vanish in the shadows. "God help the coyotes," Benjo said as he descended the steps to his truck.

18

The parking lot of Hank's was about half full when Benjo arrived at a few minutes before nine thirty. The parking lot wrapped completely around the building and the building and parking lot were surrounded by trees on three sides. Pulling around the building into the rear parking area would hide someone from the highway, making it an excellent spot to meet secretly. Benjo drove through slowly, looking for Dakota's burgundy Toyota Four Runner. He spotted it immediately. It was parked in the far corner of the parking lot at the rear of the building away from the streetlights in the shadows. The driver had backed it into a parking space so that the vehicle was facing outwards. The headlights of his truck revealed a single figure sitting in the driver's seat as he drove toward it. Benjo switched off his headlights as he drove toward the empty parking space beside it. He drove in straight into the parking space so that his driver's side window was beside the driver's side window of the other vehicle. He lowered his window and switched off the truck's engine. The driver of the Toyota lowered her window. With the darkness and shadows, all Benjo could see of the driver was the faint outline of her face and hair.

"Dakota?" Benjo asked.

"That's me," she replied. "Benjo Lane?"

"Yes," Benjo replied. "Thanks for meeting with me tonight. Were you able to get what I asked for?"

"I was," Dakota answered. "It was pretty easy. I have them with me now."

Benjo smiled. He produced two of the gallon-sized plastic storage bags he'd grabbed from his pantry. The storage bags were the kind with a colored space on the plastic where you could write in order to label the bag's contents. "Put each one in a separate bag," he said as he handed them to the girl through the open windows. If you can, write who each one belonged to on the bag so I will know. I have a marker if you need it."

Dakota switched on the interior light in her vehicle so she could see what she was doing. The light revealed her to be a pretty brunette in her early-thirties with features that hinted at Native American ancestry. She had a small tattoo on the left side of her neck that appeared to be a feather. She fumbled around for a couple of minutes as she sealed the objects she'd brought with her into the two bags. Once she was done with that, she asked Benjo for the felt-tip marker he'd brought with him. She wrote a name on each bag, then handed him the marker back. "Did you bring the money?" she asked.

Benjo held up two hundred-dollar bills. "I did," he said. He handed her the bills through their open windows. She took the money and handed him the two plastic bags. He looked at each one to make sure the bags had a name on them. "Thank you."

"I've heard about you," Dakota said. She reached up and switched off the interior light, making her just a dark silhouette again. "The Coles sent all of the people who work for them an email a couple of days ago warning us not to talk to you. They said you were hired by a lawyer trying to get money out of them over shooting that crazy girl in their office a couple of months ago."

The characterization of Sarah as 'that crazy girl' irritated Benjo, but he didn't let it show. "That's the Cole's version," he said calmly. "In reality, the girl's family hired me to look into the circumstances of her death because there are some things about the whole deal that don't make sense."

"The police didn't seem to have an issue with it," Dakota said.

"I'm not the police," Benjo answered. "I look at things differently."

"Why do you need those?" Dakota asked as she pointed to one of the bags he still held in his hand.

Benjo turned and put the bag down on the seat beside him. "I need to test a theory," he said. He didn't want to elaborate because the woman might be playing both sides of the fence with him and the Coles. "I'm curious," he said. "Why are you helping me out?"

"Oh, I hate the Coles," Dakota answered easily. "Anything I can do to screw with them is a good thing."

"But you work for them," Benjo said. "Why do you work for someone you hate that bad?"

"The money," Dakota replied simply. "I just opened my business. Working for the Coles part-time helps me make ends meet while my business is growing. Also, it gets me some free advertising from their television show and social media. People want to know who keeps them looking good, and that brings them to me."

"Why do you hate them?" Benjo asked. "I've found out enough in the last few days to make me dislike them, but why do you?"

"They treat everyone who works for them like they are their servants," Dakota said softly. "They are bullies. Both of them. And Paul, their security guy, is an even bigger asshole than they are. I'm part Navajo; my father was a full-blooded Navajo from Utah. You want to guess how many stupid remarks that's earned me from Paul and the Coles? Too many! Watching them squirm over the last few days because of you has made me very happy."

"Are they squirming?" Benjo asked curiously.

"Tucker and Mr. Cole were even more obnoxious than usual," Dakota said. "Mr. Cole was really snapping at everyone today during filming." She shook her head. "It amazes me how he treats everyone normally versus how he acts when the cameras are on. He's a world-class hypocrite. Monica has been a basket case for well over a month now. She hasn't been on the show or at the church services. The last time I saw her at the church, she was obviously stoned out of her mind."

"Do you think what happened with the girl in her office bothers her?" Benjo asked.

"Something is eating at her, for sure," Dakota said. "She looks like she's about to go over the edge."

"That's good to know," Benjo said. "Once again, thank you for helping me."

"No problem," Dakota's silhouette said from the dark interior of her truck. "Keep my name out of it if you can."

"I will," Benjo promised.

Dakota nodded in the darkness. With that, she started her truck and drove slowly away. Benjo gave her a couple of minutes' head start, then he started his truck and drove out of the parking lot to his next stop.

Benjo's next stop was Sarah's apartment complex. He parked in front of Sarah's old apartment, grabbed the keys Chase had given him the first time he came to the apartment, and walked up the stairs to her apartment. He unlocked the apartment door, reached inside to switch on the light, and went inside. He headed straight back to the bathroom. Everything was exactly like it was the last time he was there. He grabbed the item he needed and placed it in one of the plastic bags. He sealed the bag and then headed into the bedroom. In the bedroom he walked over to the bedside table and picked up the family photo that sat there. He'd noticed the photo on the last trip. He took the photo and, with it and the bag in hand, walked back to the front door. He switched off the lights, locked the door behind him, and headed back down to his truck.

With his tasks for the evening completed, Benjo drove home. As he drove, he was smiling broadly. For the first time since he'd started on the case, he felt like he was getting somewhere. He just needed to do a little more online research before he called it a night and got some sleep. He hoped to find one more person to talk to. If this person told him what he expected she would, it would all come together.

While Benjo was driving back to his cabin, August Cole and Paul Tucker were in August's office at the church. August had finished filming his television show a couple of hours ago. The church building was now empty, save for the two men, and the building was securely locked. August sat at his desk with a glass full of expensive bourbon.

Tucker also had a glass, but his was empty. He'd already drained the drink August has poured him earlier. August had drained his first drink as well; the liquor in his glass was currently his second round. August went to take another sip of the bourbon, but he spilled a little as he brought the glass up to his mouth, thanks to his visibly shaking hands. He steadied the glass with both hands and drained half of the liquid in the glass.

"Thanks to Deacon Pearson's call today, we know that Lane is close to finding out the truth," August said as he lowered the glass. "Also, as you know, the church attorney called this afternoon. He made our offer to Mr. Whiteside, the attorney for the girl's remaining family and the man who hired Benjo Lane. He declined the offer."

"I'm aware," Tucker answered as he gazed into his now empty glass. "I fully expected the lawyer to turn down the first offer, simply because all lawyers are greedy pricks and he's hoping we offer more. I am surprised that Lane has made it as far as he did. I figured he would hit a few dead- end streets and give up."

"Apparently, he's resourceful enough to be able to turn dead-end streets into freeways," August said miserably. "He might not have figured the whole thing out yet, but it looks like he will. I would not bet against him."

Tucker nodded. "Yep, the whole thing has gotten out of hand." He glared at August. "You should have just lied to the girl," he said bitterly. "You could have told her that Monica gave her up for adoption or something."

August glared back, the color in his face rising. "There were no adoption papers," he answered. "It's hard to claim it was an adoption when there's no papers to prove it. You know someone would have looked once the story got out. Hell, the girl obviously was pretty smart. She might have been the one to dig into it and realize it was a lie."

"Her mother was dead, you moron," Tucker spat back. "It was literally Monica's word against a dead woman. Monica could have claimed she and the girl's mama were teenaged best friends and that she gave the girl to her mother as some sort of under-the-radar favor to a friend."

"That girl's mother told her the truth before she died," August replied angrily.

"You mean the old woman dying of cancer, the one drugged out of her mind on pain medication?" Tucker retorted sarcastically. "The one who was dead and couldn't refute any lie you told? That one? Jesus Christ, August, you could have claimed that her mother had kidnapped her or something and she couldn't prove or disprove it. It was all just allegations."

"If she had gone to the media, it might have been enough to bring this church down," August argued back. "People are weird about scandals like that, Paul. It might have cost us a few members or it might have cost us all of them. What would happen if we dropped from two thousand people at a service to fifty? I'll tell you. There's no way we could explain the amount of money we're moving through this place, so we would have to cut it by ninety-nine percent or stop doing it completely. Thanks to your Mexican friends, doing that is not an option. You want a visit from your buddy, Xavier, and his friends with power tools?"

Tucker didn't reply because he knew that his friend was right. "Okay," he finally said. "We both agree that this thing got way out of hand. Hindsight is always twenty-twenty, as they say. Maybe there were better ways we could have handled the girl, but we were flying by the seat of our pants."

"Thank you for your wonderful insight," August replied sarcastically. "I know that what's done is done. The question now is how do we fix this without someone going to jail or the cartel murdering all of us?"

Tucker sat there, staring off into space and thinking. "We need to go scorched earth on this," he finally said. "Lane is obviously smarter than we gave him credit for. That was a mistake on our part and we need to fix it. If Lane uncovers the whole truth about Sarah, the police will reopen the investigation into her death. That scandal by itself will ruin this church, probably faster than the truth about her would. I think there's enough reasonable doubt to keep us out of jail, but there would be a trial for her shooting."

"A trial is definitely out of the question," August said instantly. "I'm not going to jail."

"Then there's the lawyer, Whiteside," Paul continued. "Offering the lawyer more money is only going to convince them that they are onto something major. No lawyer is going to settle for a few thousand dollars when they could potentially win a lawsuit and seize millions of dollars in assets. If Lane uncovers the real story about Sarah, that's motive for her shooting. We might come out okay if we get charged criminally, but the burden of proof for a civil suit is much lower. We would lose."

"So, what do we do?" August asked desperately. "What do you mean by scorched earth?"

"The private detective has got to go," Tucker said with grim finality. "We get ahold of him and his case files. We find out what he knows exactly, then kill him and destroy the files."

"If Lane gets killed, the cops will be all over us," August replied. "Whiteside will tell them what he was working on and the cops will be all over us. No way."

Tucker shrugged his shoulders. "Okay then," he said acidly. "What's your plan then?"

"Don't get bitchy, Paul," August answered. "I'm just trying to keep this from blowing up in our faces."

Tucker stood up and leaned on the desk so that his face was inches from the seated August's face. "News flash, Reverend. This has already blown up in our faces," he said angrily. "Lane is probably very close to figuring it all out. When he does, you're either going to jail or your church is finished. If you go to jail, our friends from south of the border will get nervous. They'll assume that you will try to save yourself by ratting them out. They'll make sure that doesn't happen by taking you out as fast as possible. Monica and me too, for that matter. Even if you get lucky and no criminal charges are filed against you, this church is done. Nobody will come to hear a preacher who did what you did, even if it was twenty-five years ago. If the church shuts down, that affects our Mexican friends' money. They will not be happy that you let your personal drama screw up their revenue streams. That will not go unpunished. "

August stood up so that his face was level with Tucker's. "All I'm saying is that if Lane dies, we will be the cops' number one suspects," he said angrily. "It will be all over the news. We'll be finished either way."

"We can make Lane disappear," Tucker replied. "We can make it look like a suicide. I've been digging around and doing some research on Lane. Did you know he was considered the number one suspect in the murder of a man named Jacob Clement a year or so ago? Supposedly, this Clement dude hired some hitmen to kill Lane but they killed the man's wife instead. A couple of days later, the state police found Clement dead. He'd been shot four or five times. Lane was the main suspect, but they couldn't pin it on him." He shook his head. "I knew he was a killer. He had the look. Anyway, we kill Lane and get rid of the body. There's a place I know close to where he lives where there's a back road with a high bridge over a river. We dump his truck there to make the police think he jumped off the bridge. The river there is all rocks, submerged trees, and fast water. If his body was never found, it wouldn't be unusual."

Tucker could see he had his friend's interest, so he continued. "If the police think it's a suicide, it's over. If we get our hands on any files Lane has, all of his records are gone. Also, with Lane gone, the lawyer will take some money and run. Even if he doesn't, we have Lane' files, so we'll know who Lane talked with to get as close to the truth as he did. We can clean up those loose ends with a little creativity. You know, an accident here, some cash in the right hands there. I still think we can contain this, Gus, and avoid pissing off the cartel and getting snagged by the cops."

"You thought sending your two biker buddies would get the job done," August said. "They are in the hospital right now."

"I underestimated the man," Tucker conceded. "I won't make that mistake again. I'll take care of everything personally, including dumping the truck and making it look like a suicide."

"The police still might look at us," August said.

"It will look like Lane had a breakdown from the pressure of being a murder suspect and offed himself," Tucker argued. "That or the grief over his wife got to him. If things go right, we'll have an ironclad alibi if they look our way."

"What do you mean?" August asked. The anger in his voice had lessened. He sounded genuinely curious now.

"I'll do it tomorrow," Tucker said. "I'll go to the man's house. I already know where he lives because the two guys he put in the hospital were watching him before they jumped him the other day. He lives alone way out in the middle of nowhere. I'll kill him, clean up any evidence, and get rid of the body. I've got a place where I can guarantee the body will never be found. Then, I'll take the truck to the spot where I'll leave it. I figure four to five hours max. Tomorrow night is Wednesday, so you'll be on stage doing the Wednesday night service. If I'm done in time, I'll be right there with you in front of all those nice people. If I can't take care of it before then, I'll be there prior and be seen by a few people before I slip out and do what I need to do."

August sat back down in his office chair. He sat there silently, pondering Tucker's plan. "That might work," he said with a trace of hope in his voice.

"It's the best plan we've got," Tucker replied. "If it doesn't work, we're probably screwed. If the cops don't get us, the cartel will."

"Do it," August said. He looked at his watch. "You've got slightly less than twenty-four hours to work out any kinks in your plan. Go over it until it's perfect. No more mistakes or we all end up in jail or dead."

"I've got this," Tucker said confidently. "If I take care of Lane, that leaves one more thing I'm worried about and that's Monica. How's her state of mind?"

"She's okay for now," August replied. "Sometimes I think she's turned the corner and will be okay, but then she loses it again."

"That worries me," Tucker said. "After tomorrow, take her somewhere out of the country. We can't take a chance on her, not in her condition. There's no telling what she might say if the police question her."

"I'll handle my wife," August promised. "You worry about Lane."

Tucker smiled. "After tomorrow night, nobody will have to worry about Lane."

19

The medical records office at the hospital where Reena McAllister had worked back in 1997 was located on the first floor of the main hospital building, an older five-story building of brick that was the oldest building on the sprawling medical campus that surrounded it. Every other building for two solid blocks was newer, made of glass and steel, and had something to do with healthcare, be it a doctor's office, a cancer treatment facility, or outpatient surgery center. The medical records office opened at precisely eight A.M. every weekday. At ten minutes past eight, Benjo walked into the medical records office and explained to the lady behind the counter what exactly he needed. She made him sit down and wait to speak to her supervisor. The supervisor, an older man with a fringe of hair, glasses, and a mustache, arrived precisely fourteen minutes later. He invited Benjo into his office, which was located down a short hallway off the main lobby where Benjo had waited. The office was small, with a desk with a chair behind it, one other chair in front of the desk, and a couple of filing cabinets. A sign on the desk bore the supervisor's name, Ron Gentry.

"How can I help you today, Mr. Lane?" Ron asked as he settled back into his office chair behind the desk.

"I am a private detective investigating a case. I need to know if a child was born here at your hospital on a certain day," Benjo replied as he settled into the only other chair. "I need to know if you have the medical records pertaining to the actual birth."

"We would have the records if the birth happened here in our hospital or in any of our satellite facilities," Ron said as he studied

Benjo across the desk between them. "What exactly do you need from the records?"

"I just need to prove that the child was actually born here at your hospital," Benjo said patiently. He opened the folder he'd brought with him and slid Sarah Fleming's long form birth certificate across the desk to Gentry.

Gentry took the birth certificate and studied it for a moment. He looked confused. "Mr. Lane, it's right here on the certificate, sir," he said as he turned the birth certificate to face him and pointed with his finger where the place of birth was listed. "This person was born here."

"I saw that, Mr. Gentry," Benjo said. "I know what it says, but I need to verify that the child's mother, Reena McAllister, actually gave birth to a female child here at your hospital on the date and time listed there on the birth certificate."

The look on Ron's face transformed from slightly confused to completely befuddled. "But, she did," he insisted. "It says so right here." He tapped the birth certificate once again.

Benjo nodded and smiled. "May I call you Ron?" he asked. The supervisor nodded. "Great, then call me by my first name as well. It's Benjo. Once again, Ron, I know what that birth certificate says. However, I think some of the information on that birth certificate might be faked. All I need to know is if the child's mother, Reena McAllister, actually had a child at your hospital back in 1997. That's all."

Ron studied the birth certificate carefully, even going so far as to hold it up to the lights in the ceiling above. "The birth certificate is not fake, Mr. Lane," he said. "It's an official state-issued birth certificate, complete with a watermark and everything else."

Benjo suppressed the urge to reach across the desk and slap the man until he understood. At the rate it was going, that would take a lot of slapping. "Allow me to clarify this, Ron," he said as patiently as possible. "I believe that the actual birth certificate is real, okay? During the process of investigating the case I'm on, I have found information that leads me to believe that the birth documented on that legitimate birth certificate did not really happen. I think that someone spotted a loophole in the system at the time. I think that person, who worked in a position where they could take advantage of the loophole, did exactly that and procured a birth certificate naming them as the parent for a child they actually did not physically birth. You with me so far?"

"Yes," Ron answered. "I'm following you."

"In order to prove or disprove my theory, I need someone in this office to look at either the mother's medical records or on a listing where the hospital tracked births on the date and time in question to see if the child on the birth certificate was actually physically born when that certificate says," Benjo explained.

Ron put the birth certificate down on his desk and stared at it. Benjo could almost hear his brain processing what he'd just heard. Benjo hoped Ron was finally comprehending what he was explaining because the next step on the road to explaining it was crayons or a sock puppet. "How could they fake that?" Ron finally muttered. "That would be nearly impossible to pull off today. It's all computers now. The technology they have now tracks newborn babies like they are made of pure gold. They can tell you everything about the child and the birth mother from the second the child is born up until it goes home."

"This happened in 1997, Ron," Benjo answered. "That was a quarter of a century ago. I don't know how it is now because I'm not in the medical field, but I would be willing to bet that, when it came to how information was compiled and tracked, a lot more things were done by human beings than computers in 1997. Anywhere there's a human being involved, there's a chance for a mistake or something under-handed. There has never been a system invented that someone smart didn't find a way to beat. That's humanity's real genius."

Ron was silent for a bit longer. "I've been working in this field for twenty years," he finally said. "The technology has definitely improved and made everything faster and easier to keep track of just in that time. Even now, we still have cases where people mess up. Most of the time it was a genuine human error and not something intentional or malicious. Anything is possible, I guess."

"The mother listed on that birth certificate worked on the maternity unit as what they called a ward secretary back in 1997," Benjo said. "She was involved in handling the paperwork for newborn babies at the time. Common sense says that would put her in a position to know what was involved in getting a birth certificate. Knowing that would also help her to know ways she could exploit the system if she needed a birth certificate for a child."

Ron seemed to have gone from puzzled to intrigued. "I would imagine so," he said. "But, why would she put herself as the mother for a child that she didn't really deliver?"

"I have a couple of theories," Benjo said, lowering his voice. "I suspect she might have kidnapped the baby or that it might have been sold to her. That's what I'm trying to find out."

Ron considered this. "Are you related to either of these people?" he asked as he tapped the birth certificate. "If not, do you have a signed medical records release?"

"Both of them are dead," Benjo answered. "I have their death certificates here if you need them."

"I still can't legally give you their medical records," Ron replied. "Federal privacy laws say that I can't release their records to anyone but the person or a representative with a signed release."

Benjo sat there and wondered if he had somehow entered the Twilight Zone. "The people I am interested in are dead," he said slowly. "How can they possibly sign a release? Furthermore, who is going to complain if both of them are dead?" He leaned forward. "Also, I'm not asking you for anything specific about either person's health or treatment. All I'm asking you to do is look and see if one woman gave birth here on a specific date more than twenty-five years ago. I know what the federal medical privacy law says, Ron, and I'm sure you can give me that basic information."

Ron sat there for several seconds and thought about it. "I guess that's kind of a gray area," he said.

"All I need to know is if the woman listed on the birth certificate there on your desk gave birth to a female baby on that date at that time," Benjo said reasonably. "Nothing more specific than that."

Ron sighed. "Okay," he said. "I think I can do that for you."

"Thank you, Ron," Benjo answered as Ron turned to his keyboard. Ron spent the next five minutes typing on his computer and then clicking on the mouse. "I'll need to go to the records storage room to pull these because they are so old. Everything from the last fifteen years has been digitized, but the older stuff is this weird mix of paper and digital. Basically, the computer tells me that there is a record and where it is, but I have to find it physically."

"Do I wait here or out in your lobby area?" Benjo asked.

"Grab a seat in the lobby area," Ron said as he scribbled down some information on a piece of paper on his desk. "This might take a few minutes." He handed Benjo the birth certificate back.

Benjo took the certificate, put in back in the folder, stood up and walked out into the small waiting area. He sat down in a hard, plastic chair and pulled out his phone. He pulled up his email account and checked it while he waited. Last night, he'd done some research online looking for a woman named Sharon Collins. Sharon Collins was the woman who, as part of her job with the state health department, had signed off on the newborn Sarah McAllister's birth. After a couple of hours of online research through social media, he'd found the Sharon Collins that he thought might be THAT Sharon Collins. The social media site he'd found her on allowed him to send her an email, so he'd sent one explaining who he was and asking if she was the woman he was looking for. He was pleased to see that he had a reply to that email. He opened the email and read it. She was indeed the woman in question and she would meet with him. The bad news was that she now lived three hours away in a small town in a neighboring state. The worse news was that she would only be available today because she was leaving for a cruise the next day.

Benjo closed the email and pondered his options. Depending on what he learned in the next few minutes, he might need to interview

Sharon Collins. It would be a lot easier to call her and ask her a few questions on the telephone. However, Benjo preferred to question people in person, especially if there was a chance the person he was talking to might not be honest with him regarding the subject matter. Lying to someone on the telephone was much easier than lying to them in person. Questioning someone in person gave him access to the person's whole body, allowing him to watch their body language and facial expressions. Those two things could be a seasoned interrogator's best friends when questioning someone. Questioning a voice on the phone took those options away.

Benjo sat there quietly for another twenty minutes before Ron appeared behind the counter. "We need to step back into my office," he said quietly. Benjo nodded and walked back down the hallway to Ron's office as Ron came from behind the counter to follow him. Once the two of them were in the office, Ron closed the door behind them. "I found what I was looking for," he said nervously.

"Let me guess," Benjo said. "Reena McAllister did not give birth in your hospital on April 20th, 1997."

"Or any other hospital in our system," Ron answered. "That birth certificate is wrong."

"That's what I figured," Benjo replied. "Things are making a lot more sense now."

"So, what happens now that you know this?" Ron asked.

"I get to make a three-hour drive to talk to the woman who is at least partly responsible," Benjo answered. "I expect it's going to be fun."

"Well, good luck, Mr. Lane," Ron said. "I think I might need to call my boss about this."

Benjo simply shrugged, turned around, and left.

While Benjo was walking to his truck in the hospital parking garage, Paul Tucker was slipping through the forest that surrounded Benjo's cabin. Tucker had ridden his motorcycle to where Benjo's driveway met the main highway, then stashed his bike in the woods nearby. Once his bike was concealed, he'd started making his way through the forest, staying parallel to the driveway. He moved slowly and carefully, keeping his eyes open for any type of security cameras or other alarms and making sure he was as quiet as possible in case Lane was outside his home. Tucker wore camouflage clothing and carried a small backpack with him.

It took him several minutes to make his way to the clearing where Benjo's cabin was. Once he had the cabin in view, he moved to the crest of a small hill overlooking the driveway and the side of the cabin. He lay flat on the ground on his stomach and removed a pair of powerful binoculars from the backpack he wore. Using the binoculars, he began to carefully examine the outside of the cabin and surrounding area. The man's driveway was empty and the cabin looked unoccupied, leading him to believe that Lane had already left for the day to go somewhere. He was happy about that because it gave him time to check out the area. So far, he was very happy with what he'd found. The cabin was nearly a half mile off the roadway and completely surrounded by thick forest in an area where the nearest neighbor was nearly a mile away. The end of the driveway and the side area of the house where people would park had several avenues of approach that would allow him to get as close to Lane as he needed to when he made his move. In short, it was perfect killing field with nearly zero chances of an eyewitness and numerous ways to ambush his victim.

Tucker spent the next couple of hours surveying the outside of the cabin. He paid careful attention to the areas on the exterior of the cabin and nearby garage building where people normally placed security cameras, looking for any indication that Lane had cameras watching over his property. He took his time and moved from his position to other areas in the tree line several times in order to see everything from different angles. He did not see anything obvious, meaning either that there were no cameras or that the cameras Lane had were well-concealed. Tucker was willing to bet that there were no cameras. He also didn't see any of the telltale stickers from an alarm company on the doors or windows indicating that company had installed an alarm at the house.

Tucker was still eye-balling the cabin when he heard the sound of a vehicle coming up the driveway. He cursed silently as soon as he heard the approaching vehicle. If it was Lane returning, Tucker was not yet ready to make his move. His plan called for him to catch Lane outside, subdue him at gunpoint, find out where his files were, and then take him elsewhere to kill him. Given Tucker's current location, he would have to take Lane out with a shot from over fifty yards away or try to rush closer as Lane was getting out of his truck. He couldn't take a chance on either because the distance was too great for the pistol he planned to use and the distance he had to cover running to get closer gave Lane ample opportunity to spot him. If he shot and missed or Lane saw him, it would give Lane the chance to defend himself if he was armed or to make it into the cabin. The last thing Tucker wanted was a shootout or for Lane to make it inside to safety and a weapon. Tucker's plan required complete surprise if it was to succeed.

The vehicle coming up the driveway drove into view and Tucker breathed a sigh of relief. It was the familiar brown delivery truck for a major delivery service. Tucker remained concealed and watched as the delivery driver stopped, put the truck in park, and then vanished into the freight area of the truck. A few seconds later, the driver emerged carrying a small package that he scanned with a device in his hand and then placed on the side porch of the house. With that done, the driver returned to his truck, turned around skillfully, and drove back down the driveway out of sight.

The sight of the package sitting there on the side porch gave Tucker an idea. He made his way through the forest along the perimeter of Benjo's yard until he was close to the end of the driveway and the side porch. Once he was settled in position, he whistled loudly twice and then trained his binoculars on the house. He watched and listened to see if he would get any kind of response from either someone in the house or a dog. Earlier, he'd noticed the large dog door mounted in the side door at the top of the steps. The dog door puzzled him because there were no other signs of a dog, no water bowls, no dog toys scattered in the yard, not even a chewed tennis ball lying around. He'd been very cautious during his surveillance of the house, expecting any moment for a large dog to either emerge from the house unexpectedly or to come wandering up through the woods, but so far there had been nothing. Surely, if there was a dog, the delivery truck would have caused it to bark or something, but not a sound. Tucker's loud whistles was the last test to see if a dog came running from anywhere.

Tucker waited several minutes while he scanned the area and listened. Nothing happened, confirming his belief that if Benjo had once had a dog, he did not anymore or that the previous owners of the house prior to Benjo had owned a dog and Benjo had just left the door there. Now satisfied that there was no monster dog to come bounding out to attack him, Tucker used the bandanna around his neck to cover his face, pulled the hat he wore low, and stepped from the forest with his pistol, a nine- millimeter semi-automatic he'd bought from a man the motorcycle club used for all of their untraceable weapons. With the gun in his hand and at the ready, he moved across the yard toward the house.

He reached the side porch without anything happening. Once he was there at the side of the house, he made a careful search for any outside cameras or alarms. He found nothing at all, confirming his earlier belief that Lane did not have any type of security cameras or system. He went up onto the porch and peered through all of the cabin's windows that he could. He saw no signs of anyone in the house. He was surprised by how neat and orderly the place appeared to be. With Lane being a widower, he'd expected the place to look like a typical bachelor's pad with dirty clothes and pizza boxes everywhere. Instead, the place looked spotless. One thing that did surprise him was the number of books in what he assumed was a living room or study. There were books piled everywhere in neat stacks. Apparently, Benjo Lane was quite the reader.

Now thoroughly convinced that Benjo wasn't home, Tucker made his way back to the side porch and the package there. He picked up the package and studied it. It was a small, flat cardboard box, similar to one a book or similar small object would be shipped in. There was nothing on the box but an address label with Benjo's name and the cabin's address on it. There was nothing on the label that indicated who the package was from. The only other thing on the package was a stylized "W" on the side of the box. For a moment Tucker was tempted to open the box just to out of curiosity, but he didn't. He needed the box unopened for now. After Lane was dead, he would open it.

Tucker took the box and walked off the side porch. He placed the box squarely in the middle of the paved area where people coming to the house parked. Anyone coming up the driveway would see the package there, stop their vehicle, and get out to remove it. They would assume that the person who delivered it was just lazy and left it there. Once they were out of the vehicle and distracted by the package, Tucker would make his move from the tree line. At this point, the trees he would be hiding in were less than twenty feet away. Tucker could close that distance quickly and quietly and subdue Lane at gunpoint. He'd brought a pair of handcuffs with him he'd use to bind Lane. Once Lane was under control, he would get the location of the files out of him. He would then put Lane in his truck and drive him to an abandoned farm owned by the family of one of the men in his biker gang. The old farm bordered a river and a swampy area. He would kill Lane there, weight his body down with some stuff he had already had there, and sink it in the swampy water. In about five days there wouldn't be anything left for the cops to find even if they knew where to look. He would then drive Lane' truck to the bridge on the back road that was about two miles from where he now stood. He would dump the truck there with the driver's door open and the keys still in the ignition. Someone would see it and call the cops. The police would assume suicide. An even better scenario would be if someone actually found the vehicle and stole it. Eventually someone would report Lane missing. The police would search for the truck and eventually find it. Whoever happened to be in the truck at the time would be the prime suspect in Lane' death.

His trap set, Tucker walked back into the trees to set up his position. All he had to do now was wait for his quarry to return and take the bait. Tucker glanced at the sky as he walked back into the forest. It was clouding up and the weather report was calling for a chance of rain later in the afternoon. That didn't bother Tucker at all. Rain would increase the element of surprise when Lane did show up and it would wash away any potential evidence he might accidentally leave behind. If everything went the way he planned, the rain would just be an added insurance policy.

20

CHAPTER 20

Sharon Collins lived in a neat townhouse with a brick façade in a retirement community located on the edge of a small town in the mountains. The retirement community bordered a golf course and hosted a nice view of the nearby mountains. Sharon had a nice view of one of the greens through the large windows of the sunroom where she led Benjo once he arrived. It was later in the afternoon and cloudy, but several golf carts were making their way across the green. All of the men driving the golf carts were old and all were dressed in particularly loud outfits. Benjo wondered what it was about playing golf that required the people who played it to dress like someone from the mid-seventies with color blindness. According to Sharon, one of the old men was her husband of forty-five years, Jack.

"Do you play?" Benjo asked politely as he sat down in the white wicker chair Sharon directed him to. Sharon sat down in a similar white wicker chair across from him.

"Absolutely not," Sharon answered with a slight smile. Sharon was a short, slender woman with short black hair streaked with gray, green eyes, and features that made Benjo think of a cute little bird. "I think it was Mark Twain who said that 'Golf is a good walk spoiled'. I could not agree more. It's a horrible game invented by someone solely to make men spend outrageous amounts of money on clothes a self-respecting gay man wouldn't wear and clubs that would be better used knocking some sense into each other."

Benjo chuckled. "I've never heard it summed up like that, but I have to admit it fits," he said. "I don't play either."

"You don't look like the type of man that plays golf," Sharon replied. She looked Benjo up and down in a way that made him feel like a side of beef. "You look like a man's man. I'll bet women love you."

The way she said that made Benjo want to open the sunroom's sliding door and yell for Sharon's husband, Jack, to come in and join the two of them. "I've never really thought about it," he replied.

"A good-looking, rugged man who's a private detective to boot," Sharon said. "That's so intriguing in so many ways. So, what brings you my way, Mr. Lane?"

"Call me Benjo," Benjo said. "Sharon, I need to ask you about something that happened in 1997 as part of your job with the county health department."

"My goodness, twenty-five years ago?" Sharon said. "What could I have possibly got into that long ago that would bring a private detective to my door now?"

"It was a routine part of your duties with the county health department," Benjo explained. "It was something so routine you might not even remember it clearly, but I needed to follow up on it as part of this case I'm on."

Sharon held up a hand. "County health department is actually incorrect," she said. "All of the county health departments are actually just offices for the state Department of Health and Environmental Control. The Department of Health and Environmental Control is the state agency that's responsible for a number of different programs pertaining to health and environmental standards in the state. DHEC, as we called it, handled everything from inspecting restaurants to public health programs to making sure your drinking water was pure. DHEC also had a division that handled environmental things like making sure big companies were not polluting and meeting different environmental standards."

"So, you actually worked for the state?" Benjo asked. "You just had an office in the county?"

"When I first started my career, I got lucky," Sharon said. "There happened to be an opening in the office in the county where I lived and was raised, so I didn't have to move."

"And what did you do there?" Benjo asked.

"I began my career as a public health nurse," Sharon explained. "I was fresh out of nursing school with a Bachelor's of Science in Nursing and my registered nurse's license. Halfway through my hospital rotations as a nursing student, I realized that I didn't want to work in a hospital or a doctor's office, for that matter. I know it sounds weird, but I liked the science and the medical field, but I really hated my fellow nurses and doctors. They were all obnoxious, terrible people, with very few exceptions. They were nice to the patients, but they treated each other and their coworkers like crap when the patients weren't around." She looked embarrassed. "I know how it sounds, but please don't judge me too harshly."

Benjo smiled. "You don't need to explain, Susan. I worked in law enforcement for sixteen years before I quit and became a private investigator. For every good cop I knew and liked, there were ten I hated because, as you said, they were not good people. What did you do as a public health nurse?"

"I started working for the agency in 1995," Sharon continued. "I did everything from vaccinations for kids to sex education and sexual health programs for poor communities. I also did programs for the elderly as well. It was tough and discouraging sometimes, but I really felt like I was doing something good."

"I'm sure you did a lot of good," Benjo said. "You seem like the type of person who puts their heart into things."

"Uh oh," Sharon said. "You're laying on the flattery pretty early. That could be a bad sign, especially when a P.I. wants to question you about something from way back then."

"That was not just flattery, Susan," Benjo answered. "Doing this job and my prior career in law enforcement has made me an excellent judge of people. I don't think I'm wrong when I say that you strike me as a someone who's very diligent and particular about things."

Sharon considered this. "I will take that as a compliment," she said. "What exactly do you need from me, Benjo?"

Benjo opened the folder he'd brought with him and removed Sarah Fleming's long form birth certificate. He handed it to Susan, who took it from his hand and looked it over. "As you can see, Susan, your name is at the bottom of the page," he said. "You signed off on this birth."

Sharon examined the paper and then nodded slowly. "Yes," she said. "That was another one of my duties in public health. I had a couple of hospitals assigned to me that I was required to go to, collect the state birth forms, and then turn them in to my office head. She sent them on to the state Division of Vital Records where they issued birth certificates and mailed them to the new parents."

"Explain that process to me, Susan," Benjo pressed. "What was a state birth form?"

"Well, when a new baby was born in a hospital, the physician who delivered the child filled out a standardized form that had the baby's date and time of birth, sex, race, and other statistics," Sharon explained. "Every couple of days I would make my rounds and pick up the forms. I would review the forms there at the hospital, make sure everything was filled out correctly and was verified, and then bring them back to our office. I would turn them in to our director and she forwarded them to the Division of Vital Records. They are the ones who mailed out the birth certificates to the new parents."

"Did you pick up the birth forms directly from the doctors or was there a central spot they left the forms for you to pick up?" Benjo asked. "I'm asking about back in 1997, by the way."

"The maternity wards had administrative staff that kept up with the forms and things like that," Sharon answered. "Those folks are really the unsung heroes of any hospital, if you think about it. Someone has to keep up with all of those medical records, doctor's orders, and other forms. Even now, when most things are done by computer, there's still mountains of paperwork. Most people would be amazed by how much paperwork a routine surgery and a short stay in a hospital can generate."

"I'm sure," Benjo said. "The reason I wanted to meet with you today was because of that particular birth, the birth of Sarah Anne McAllister, a girl, to Reena McAllister."

Sharon grimaced. "Benjo, I don't know what exactly you're looking for in this case you're investigating, but one thing I can promise you is that, if you want me to remember specific details about this one particular birth, you're going to be out of luck. This was twenty-five years ago. In the five or so years I was responsible for picking up and reviewing the birth forms, I'll bet you I've signed dozens, if not a few hundred, of these."

"I completely understand that," Benjo said agreeably. "The problem with that birth is that it never really happened."

Sharon frowned and looked puzzled. "You mean this birth certificate is fake?" she asked. She held it up. "It looks very authentic."

"No, the birth certificate is real," Benjo answered. "The birth it records never happened. Reena McAllister never gave birth to a female child she named Sarah Anne McAlliister on that date at that hospital."

"Wait, what?" Sharon asked. "I have to confess I'm a little confused."

"The birth form that was filled out, picked up by you, signed by you, and then turned in so a birth certificate could be issued showing this woman was the mother of a little girl was fake," Benjo said. "The mother, Reena McAllister, pulled a fast one on everyone. She came up with a way to get a legal birth certificate making her the mother for a child she did not actually birth."

Sharon looked at Benjo like he'd just stepped off a UFO. "Why would she do that?" she asked.

"I think the mother, Reena, ended up with a child that was not hers biologically," Benjo said. "I'm still not one hundred percent sure of the circumstances as to how she ended up with this child, at least not yet. I wanted to talk to you to see if it was even possible for her to pull this off."

"Did you check with the hospital about this?" Sharon asked.

"Just this morning," Benjo replied. "This woman never had this child at the hospital listed there on the birth certificate."

"That would make it nearly impossible to get a birth certificate then," Sharon said defensively. "There's no way I would have signed off on a form that I knew was fake. That's a felony. Plus, the mother would have had to be someone who had access to the proper forms and who knew exactly what to do to not arouse suspicion."

"The mother, Reena McAllister, worked at the hospital during this time on the maternity ward as a ward secretary," Benjo said. "She filled out the birth forms and other paperwork pertaining to new births. Would that make it possible?"

Sharon was quiet for several seconds. "Probably," she said. "She would know the forms. However, there is no way I would knowingly have signed off on the birth if I knew it never happened."

"I don't doubt that," Benjo said. "No one is questioning your integrity, Susan. I don't think you would knowingly sign off on a false birth form. Is it possible, however, that you might sign off on a form without doing the due diligence you were supposed to?"

"You're asking me if I screwed up on my job?" Sharon asked defensively. "I don't like what you're insinuating, Mr. Lane."

"I understand that, Sharon," Benjo replied. "But, I'm not judging you, by any means. How many of those forms did you pick up when you stopped at a hospital? I'm sure it ranged from just a couple a few times to possibly several at a time. I figure you reached a point where you knew which ward secretaries did the paperwork right and which ones you had to follow up on. Did you ever just grab the papers, sign them, and turn them in? Did you verify everything you needed to verify each time? Common sense says that you might have just pencil-whipped it a few times."

Sharon stood up. "How dare you accuse me of not doing my job," she said angrily.

Benjo held up his hands soothingly. "Sharon, you are already retired, so they can't fire you," he said. "They can't stop your state retirement checks either. The two women on that birth certificate are both dead. This is not going to come back on you in a negative way. Lastly, I'm not asking you to admit to anything. All I'm asking is was it possible, way back then, for a ward secretary to slip in some paperwork that you might have signed off on without verifying certain things?"

"I could open myself up to all sorts of civil liability if I admitted something like that," Sharon said. "That's not going to happen. No matter how charming you are, Mr. Lane."

"Sharon, I'm working on a murder case," Benjo replied. "A twenty-five-year-old woman was murdered. The motive was really stumping me, but now I think I've got it figured out. You're my last stop. I just need to know for my own sake if it was possible for someone who didn't give birth to take advantage of the system and get one for the child they ended up with. Look at it as I'm asking you as a consultant with years of knowledge about the matter. I'm asking you about a hypothetical situation."

Sharon was silent for a couple of minutes. "I'll just say that it's possible for the forms to be slipped in and signed off on without some of the proper vetting," she finally said. "Picking up the forms from the hospital was one of the last things someone in my position did during my workday a couple of times a week. If a person was in a hurry or just wanted to get home on time, theoretically they might skip a few steps if they knew the people at the hospital were up on their game."

"I assumed as much," Benjo said. "Just for the record, I have no interest in making you look bad. I intend to keep your name out of this if at all possible. Everything I asked you here was a possible expert witness for a hypothetical case."

"Thank you," Sharon said. "But, like you said, they can't fire me anymore, so I'm not too worried about it."

Benjo stood up. "I've got everything I needed. Thank you for your help." He glanced out the window at the golf course and distant mountains. "Enjoy your day."

21

Halfway though Benjo's trip back home, it started drizzling rain. By the time he reached his driveway, it was raining steadily and thundering with dark, heavy clouds. It was raining so heavily by the time Benjo drove up to his cabin that he almost didn't see the cardboard box sitting squarely in the middle of his driveway. He saw it at the last moment and swerved around it to avoid hitting it. "What the hell?" he muttered as he drove past it. He had no idea why the package would be sitting out in the middle of his driveway like that; usually the delivery drivers would put things on the side porch. *Maybe a gust of wind blew it off the porch,* he thought as he parked his truck in its normal spot, killed the engine, and got out.

The rain pounded him as he walked over to the package. Even though the cardboard was wet, he recognized the package as the one he was expecting. He was bending over to pick up the package when he sensed movement to his left. He turned his head just in time to see a figure emerging from the trees about twenty feet away. He realized instantly that the figure was a man wearing soaking-wet camouflaged clothing with a something concealing his face. The man had a pistol in his hand that he was bringing up to aim as he ran toward him. It seemed to happen in slow motion as the man charged toward him and brought the gun to bear.

Benjo reacted instantly by doing what most people would do in that situation: he ran. He left the package where it was, straightened up, and took off in a dead run toward the front corner of the cabin. His intent was to get around that corner and out of the would-be assassin's line of fire so he could escape or defend himself. It was a good, tactical plan but, unfortunately, it did not work. He was almost to the corner when something punched into his back right below his left kidney. His brain was still registering the sharp crack of the gunshot as the breath was knocked out of him and his legs crumpled beneath him. He collapsed onto the soaked grass on his side and lay there, gasping.

Benjo lay there helpless as the figure approached him. He expected another bullet, but instead the figure approached him and used a booted foot to push him over onto his back on the grass. The steady rain poured down, drenching his face and running into his eyes. Benjo lay on his back with his left hand twisted beneath him, breathing raggedly, and in terrible pain. *I guess this is it,* he thought. *I guess the Southern Devils weren't willing to overlook what I did to their two prospects.*

Paul grinned as he walked over to Benjo and used his foot to shove him over onto his back. Benjo had seen him coming and reacted way faster than Paul expected, forcing Paul to shoot at him as he was running away. Luckily, his shot had hit Benjo in the back, dropping him to the ground with what was probably a mortal wound. Paul looked down at Benjo and watched as he gasped for breath. He pulled the bandanna covering the lower half of his face down so Benjo could see who he was. "You're fast, but you ain't faster than a bullet," he said triumphantly. "Where did you think you were gonna go?"

"Somewhere the bullet wasn't," Benjo croaked. He groaned in pain. "Finish it."

Paul grinned down at him. "Na, I want you to suffer a little bit more," he said. "You deserve it for what you did to my two boys."

"Is that what this is for?" Benjo said weakly.

Paul shook his head, causing water to spray from the bill of the cap he had pulled low on his head. "Hell no," he replied. "They weren't even full members. Now, we don't even want them because they ain't tough enough. You ain't got a mark on you and they are in the hospital. It was two against one, so that says something about them."

"The Coles sent you?" Benjo whispered.

Paul nodded. "We can't let you ruin everything because some of their personal drama showed up out of nowhere twenty-five years after they thought they got rid of it," he said. "They thought that girl was dead and gone, only for her to call them out of the blue one day. The two of them hit the panic button, so I had to handle it."

"You killed Sarah," Benjo said. It was a statement, not a question.

"I did," Tucker answered. "The stupid bitch admitted that no one else knew her secret, so we decided the best plan was to kidnap her and make her disappear, but she put up a fight, so I did it there in the church. The damned secretary showed up before we could ditch the body. The self defense story was made up on the spot."

"Figured," Benjo said. He was no longer gasping and wheezing, but Tucker hadn't noticed.

Tucker aimed his gun at the center of Benjo's chest. "Where's your files on the case?" he asked. "Tell me where it is and I will finish you fast. If you don't, I'll put the next one in your knee. Ain't no need to suffer. It's over."

Benjo raised his right hand, the one that wasn't under his body, and used it to give Tucker the middle finger. "You'll never get your hands on them," he said. "They're locked up tight."

"You're dying, but it can be fast," Tucker said coldly. "You've got to the count of three to tell me where they are. If you do, I'll put one straight through your heart and end this."

"No head shot?" Benjo whispered. "Pussy."

"Too much mess to try to get rid of," Tucker snarled. "The rain will take care of the blood on your grass, but I can't have the police finding brain and bone fragments, if they even bother to look."

"Get on with it," Benjo replied. "I'm not telling you a thing."

"Okay, tough guy," Tucker said with a grin. "I'll bet you that attitude changes quick." He aimed his pistol at Benjo's knee and his finger tightened on the trigger as he prepared to fire.

A split second before the gun was about to fire, a snarling, spitting ball of fury hit Tucker in the chest, causing him to jerk to the right and fire the bullet into the ground near Benjo's leg. Fire blazed across

Tucker's face and he jerked backwards in shock. He shoved the thing that hit him in the chest away reflexively. It landed on the ground, hissing and spitting. Tucker spun to face his attacker as it landed on the ground. It looked like some kind of demon straight from Hell at first, but then he realized it was some kind of huge cat with soaking wet fur plastered to its body and blazing eyes full of fury. It had blood dripping from its mouth. Tucker felt something hot dripping off his chin and then he realized why his face was burning. The cat had sunk its fangs into his cheek. He reached up and felt that he was missing a chunk of flesh. He recoiled in horror. The cat shrieked again and crouched to lunge.

Tucker screamed in fear and rage and fired a couple of shots at the beast. He was so panicked that he missed both shots as the cat came toward him. The cat lunged up and sunk its teeth into Tucker's thigh. It felt like someone had jabbed him with a red-hot needle. He kicked the cat away and it slid across the wet grass. He aimed the pistol at it and fired two more shots, but the soaked monster out of a nightmare tore off across the wet grass and vanished in the downpour. "What the fuck was that?" he said aloud as he pressed one hand to his bloody cheek and watched fearfully for it to return with its teeth and claws.

"That was Harley," Benjo said loudly from behind him.

Tucker had forgotten all about his intended victim during the cat's attack. He spun around expecting to find the mortally wounded private detective bleeding out onto the soaking grass. To his complete shock, the spot where the wounded man had been laying seconds ago was nothing but a patch of matted grass. He looked up and realized that Benjo was on his feet about ten feet away. Benjo had a pistol in his left hand, the one that had been twisted under him when he was down on the ground. Tucker cried out and tried to aim his pistol at Benjo. Without a moment's hesitation, Benjo shot him twice in the abdomen.

To Tucker, it felt like someone had stabbed him in the stomach with a red-hot knife. He crumpled forward with a scream and the pistol in his hand fell from his grasp to the ground nearby. He sank to his knees first, then toppled face forward onto the grass. Water and the smell and taste of wet earth filled his mouth for a few seconds before he was able to roll over onto his back. Mercifully, the pain in his stomach eased when he rolled onto his back. He pressed a hand to his stomach and then held it up to look at it. Blood and rainwater glistened on his skin.

Benjo staggered forward and kicked Tucker's dropped pistol out of the wounded man's reach. Each move he made and every time he breathed was a jolt of pain in his back. He kept his pistol, a compact nine- millimeter Glock he'd kept in a concealed holster underneath his shirt at the small of his back, trained on Tucker as he approached him gingerly. Tucker lay on his back with his hands pressed to his abdomen. His eyes were wild and panicked and his head thrashed from side to side. The front of his shirt and hands were soaked with blood. He stopped moving his head as soon as he saw Benjo approaching him. "You shot me," he hissed through clenched teeth.

"You started it," Benjo answered. He reached up with his free hand and pulled up the front of the shirt he wore. Underneath his shirt he wore a black bullet-resistant vest. The vest was the latest model, designed to be concealed under clothing with minimal signs it was there and guaranteed to stop anything short of the most powerful rifle bullets. Benjo had bought it two years ago to wear under the plain clothes he wore as a detective with the sheriff's department because the department-issued vest was too uncomfortable. He'd paid a pretty penny for it, but it was worth it. He'd started wearing the vest after he'd stomped the two motorcycle club members in David's parking lot because he assumed that there was a better than average chance there would be some sort of retaliation. He'd stared carrying the gun for the same reason. "At least I was dressed for the dance."

"Call me an ambulance," Tucker begged, "Please, for the love of God, call me an ambulance."

"I'll tell you what," Benjo said. "I'll call you an ambulance if you tell me why the Coles had you kill Sarah."

Tucker took a deep, shuddering breath and told Benjo why he'd shot the girl in the church's office. Hearing it from Tucker made a whole lot of the different pieces in the puzzle click. Benjo was pleased to see that he'd been about ninety percent right and was well on his way to making it to one hundred percent. "The Coles didn't have the balls to pull the trigger, so I did," Tucker said. "The girl could have brought down the entire operation."

"You mean the money-laundering operation?" Benjo asked as he looked down at Tucker.

Tucker nodded. "Now, please call me an ambulance," he croaked.

"No," Benjo said flatly as rain poured down his face. "You murdered an innocent girl and then would have murdered me if not for this vest and my cat. You're bleeding out anyway and it would take the ambulance at least fifteen minutes to get here since we're so far out. I suggest you use the little bit of time you still have to get right with God."

Tucker laid his head back on the grass. His face was ghostly pale and his breathing was getting ragged. "I knew you were a killer," he mumbled.

Benjo looked down on him without pity. "Oh, I am that, sir," he said. "You're the fourth man I've put in the ground. The first three were for my wife. You are for Sarah Fleming, a young lady who never got to live because of you and two crooked preachers."

Tucker breath was now a series of sharp, shallow pants. "God will judge you," he whispered weakly.

Benjo nodded. "You first," he said as he slid the pistol he held back into the holster at the small of his back. The move caused a sharp wave of pain in his back that was so intense it made him dizzy. He took a couple of deep breaths and composed himself. When he looked back, Tucker was dead, his sightless, open eyes fixed on Benjo.

Benjo's legs shook slightly as he made his way back to his driveway. He squatted down gingerly and picked up the soaked cardboard box. He carried it to the side porch and sat down on the steps. He took a couple of deep, slow breaths. The breaths caused pain, but it was not as bad as it was a few minutes ago. He might have a cracked ribs and some internal brusing, but he would survive. "Harley," he called. "Here, kitty, kitty!" The soaked cat emerged from around the corner of the cabin and ran to him. Benjo reached out and stroked the big cat's head and back. "Good girl," he said shakily. "You saved my ass. That's my big girl." The cat rubbed against his leg a couple of times, then scampered up the steps. There was a loud beep and the pet door slid up. The cat vanished inside.

Benjo watched the cat go inside. The rain was starting to lessen. He pulled his cell phone out and dialed nine one one. "I need the police and an ambulance," he said when the operator answered. He gave his address. "A man attacked me in my driveway. I shot him and I think he's dead."

Benjo was still sitting on his steps when the first police vehicle drove down his driveway eleven minutes later. He raised his empty hands up in the air as the deputy stopped the marked SUV and got out.

22

Five Days Later

Deke Jeter was waiting in the lobby of the sheriff's department when Benjo walked in through the double glass doors. "You made it," Deke said as soon as Benjo entered. "How are you feeling?"

"I'm still moving slow," Benjo replied. "The vest did its job, but the bullet bruised my kidney and cracked one of my ribs. The doctor told me to take it easy and I should be fine."

"Thank God for that," Deke said sincerely. "Did you talk to your lawyer, Billy Cleveland, yet?"

"Nope," Benjo replied. "Should I? I know he was supposed to meet with the state police today since you guys turned my case over to them because I'm a former employee."

"I guess I should let him tell you, but I was in the meeting and I figure you want to know," Deke said. "Unofficially, you're in the clear. It was an open-and-shut case of self-defense. The prosecutor's office is supposed to announce that tomorrow morning in a press conference."

"Good," Benjo said. "That makes one legitimate case of self-defense they've handled this year." He pointed to the door that separated the lobby from the rest of the building where the uniformed deputies and others worked. "Are they here?"

Deke nodded somberly. "August and Monica Cole are currently in one of the interview rooms. They brought their lawyer with them. They think we are interviewing them as to why their church's security director tried to murder you in an ambush."

"That's partly true," Benjo replied. "You are going to ask them about that." He held up the manila folder he'd brought in with him. "I have the answer for you, though."

"I've already read your statement from the Tucker shooting," Deke said. "I know you say he confessed to shooting Sarah Fleming at the Cole's orders before he died."

"I now know why the Coles wanted Sarah and me dead," Benjo said. "I just needed one more thing to tie it all together. I got that yesterday." He held up the folder. "Their motive is in here. That's why I called you and asked if you could arrange this meeting."

"I'm going out on a limb with this, Benjo," Deke said. "Sheriff Crowe was not happy at all about me including you in this. The only reason he relented was because Kathy Miller from Channel Seven has him on the hot seat over Marsh being involved with the original investigation."

"Oh?" Benjo asked. "I figured Tucker admitting to me that he murdered Sarah Fleming might be a factor in my participation."

"I can tell you right now that the Cole's lawyer will fight that tooth and nail for a multitutde of reasons," Deke said. "It's your word against a dead man's word for one. The guy was shot and bleeding out, so anything he said was under extreme duress. Also, you were investigating the Coles, so it could be argued that you would say anything to further your case. Not to mention, you still haven't come up with a motive as to why the Coles would want Sarah Fleming dead."

"All fair points," Benjo conceded, "except for the last one." He handed the folder to Deke. "Here's your motive."

Deke took the folder and opened it. It contained three printed pages. He skimmed over the three pages quickly. His eyes widened and there was a sharp intake of breath. "Holy crap," he said sincerely. He looked up at Benio with his eyes full of questions. "How did…..?"

Benjo held up his hand. "Save it for when we speak with the Coles," he said. "You might want to record this."

There were two different kinds of interview rooms used in the sheriff's department. The first kind were the ones they used to interrogate people they suspected were guilty of whatever crime they were accused or people who were already under arrest for an offense. These rooms were bare-bones affairs with heavy steel tables with eyebolts to secure handcuffs if needed, a couple of metal chairs, and doors that locked from the outside. The other kind were more like conference rooms you would find in any business office, complete with nice, wooden tables to sit at, comfortable chairs, and windows with views of the outside. These rooms were reserved for meeting with cooperating witnesses, victims, or people who were merely suspected of a crime. Both types of rooms, however, were outfitted with cameras and microphones to record what was happening inside them. August and Monica Cole were waiting in one of the nicer interview rooms along with their attorney.

Deke paused to make sure the audio and video system for the room was switched on and recording before he entered the room. Benjo followed him. The Coles and their attorney, a fat, older man with curly hair, heavy jowls, a perpetual scowl, and a very expensive suit sat on one side of the table. All three of them looked up as the two men entered. August Cole and his lawyer looked angry and impatient while Monica looked dazed and out of it. Deke and Benjo sat down beside each other on the opposite side of the conference table.

"Good morning, Mr. and Mrs. Cole, I am Deacon Jeter," Deke said after he was seated. "I am a detective with the sheriff's department. I asked you to come in today so I could ask you a few questions about Paul Tucker, your church's head of security and a friend of yours. This is an informal interview at this point." He briefly explained the Coles' legal rights and informed them that the interview was being recorded. "This other gentleman is Benjo Lane. He is currently a private investigator, but he used to be a detective for the sheriff's department as well. He was retained by Sarah Fleming's family to look into what happened with her at your church."

"I am Patrick Lattimer Morgan of the Morgan and Associates Law Firm," the Cole's attorney said loudly in a booming voice better suited for courtroom theatrics than the small interview room they were in.

He sat there for a few seconds as if he expected Deke and Benjo to be blown out of their seats by the awesomeness of that announcement. They weren't. "I'm representing the Coles in this matter. I want to state immediately that I have an issue with this civilian being included in this meeting." He made the word 'civilian' sound like a slur. "My clients came here voluntarily to try to help find answers in this unfortunate matter after a request from you, Detective Jeter. They were not expecting to have to face a private detective whose sole purpose seems to be finding something that can be used to shake down my clients."

"Mr. Lane is investigating your clients," Deke said matter-of-factly. "He's also the man Paul Tucker, your clients' personal friend and director of security, tried to murder in his front yard."

"An act my clients' had absolutely nothing to do with," the attorney answered fiercely. "Mr. Tucker was a grown man capable of making his own choices. Only he can explain why he targeted Mr. Lane."

"He did," Benjo said with a slight smile. "While he was laying there after I shot him, we had an interesting conversation." He locked eyes with August Cole. "Tucker told me why he killed Sarah Fleming and why he came after me."

"So you say," Morgan, the attorney, replied. "That's easy for you to say without him here to dispute it. He could have said that, anything else, or nothing at all." He looked at Deke. "If you try to bring a case against my clients for Mr. Tucker's actions against Mr. Lane or over what happened with Miss Fleming based solely on that, I will rip you to shreds in court. It won't even get past the preliminary hearing stage."

"You are correct, sir," Benjo answered. "If the case was based solely on what a dead man allegedly said, any criminal case would go nowhere. Fortunately, I have other evidence." He smiled at August Cole. "Your clients and Tucker murdered Sarah Fleming after luring her to their church."

Morgan bristled. "The unfortunate incident with the Fleming girl was ruled a justifiable shooting in self-defense. The sheriff's department and the prosecutor's office have already cleared Mr and Mrs. Cole. Miss

Fleming stalked and harassed my clients, attacked Mrs. Cole and tried to murder her, and was shot as a result of that attack. It's a tragedy, but that's all it is."

"That's how it looks," Benjo answered. "The problem was that no one who knew Sarah thought she had any mental health issues that would make her stalk and attack anyone. All of the people who knew Sarah refused to believe that she did what the Coles claim she did, so they asked me to try to figure out why she ended up dead in their office. I was able to do that."

"Really?" Morgan asked skeptically. "You found something that the thorough police investigation and review by the prosecutor's office missed. You must be one hell of a great investigator, Mr. Lane." He smirked at his own wit. "What did you find that everyone else missed?"

"August and Monica Cole's reason for wanting Sarah Fleming dead," Benjo answered. He looked directly at Monica as he spoke. She tried to hold his gaze, but then averted her eyes. She stared at the table in front of her.

"Then, by all means, enlighten us," Morgan answered.

"Gladly," Benjo retorted. "To do that, I need to go back to April of 1997. Somehow, during that last few days of April, Reena McAllister, a single woman who worked in the maternity ward at the local hospital, ended up with an infant girl. Reena, who was just eighteen at the time and living on her own with no boyfriend, called her next- door neighbor and asked her to come over to the house she rented next door. When the neighbor, Reena's landlord and friend, arrived, she found Reena with a baby girl and practically nothing else a baby would need, save for a few basic items like diapers and some formula. No crib, no car seat, no cute onesies, nothing. Reena claimed that she had given birth to the child forty-eight hours earlier and that she had no idea that she was pregnant until she got sick at work with what she thought was a stomach issue. The neighbor, Patricia Blackwell, helped her get situated that night. Patricia ultimately ended up helping care for the child, Sarah, and for her younger brother, Chase, who would come nearly three years later.

"Two years after Sarah appeared, Reena met and married a man named Rick Fleming," Benjo continued. "Rick raised Sarah as his own and then fathered Chase. Sarah never knew Rick was not her biological father and Chase was actually her half-brother. Rick quietly adopted Sarah when she was a toddler and Rick and Reena never told Sarah the truth. Reena kept Sarah's long-form birth certificate from Sarah her whole life, because that form revealed that Sarah did not have a biological father listed at the time of her supposed birth at the hospital. Instead, Sarah was given the short birth certificate that doesn't list the parents on it. Sarah used that birth certificate her whole life to register for school, get jobs, and everything else you need a birth certificate for.

"Everything was all well and good," Benjo continued. "Life went on. Sarah and her brother grew up and became adults. In 2016, Rick Fleming died. Reena McAllister Fleming died four months ago after a bout with ovarian cancer that had spread everywhere else. Sarah, at that point a registered nurse, took care of her mother while Reena was in hospice dying. At some point right before she passed away, Reena, either wantng to clear her conscience or out of it on pain meds, told Sarah the truth about how she came to be her mother. That truth was that Reena had not actually given birth to Sarah, but had come in possession of the child another way. Based on my interview with Patricia Blackwell, I think Reena ending up with a newborn happened very unexpectedly, simply because the young woman was woefully unprepared for a child. I believe Reena actually told Sarah exactly how she ended up with a baby."

"This is a waste of our time," August said tersely. "The young woman's questionable ancestry has nothing at all to do with myself and my wife."

Benjo held up a hand. "Hold on, Auggie, I'm getting there," he said pleasantly. The nickname caused August's face to redden. "Sarah learned that Reena was not her biological mother and Rick had adopted her. Reena's funeral and the aftermath of her death prevented Sarah from following up on her mother's claim for a few days. When she finally got a chance, she went to the health department and looked at her long-form birth certificate. She realized that it was all true. That then led her to the next logical step: finding out who her real parents were. What's the best way to do that nowadays? She contacted a company called Who I Am, or WIA, and submitted a DNA sample. WIA compared her DNA to a database of submitted DNA samples. What a lot of people don't realize is that anytime you submit a DNA sample to any company for testing, it gets saved and registered in an accessible database. That's how all of these companies promising to find your ancestors based on a DNA sample work."

Monica Cole made a choking sound, causing the lawyer and her husband to look over at her. "Mrs. Cole, are you okay?" Morgan asked. Monica nodded and kept her eyes fixed on the table in front of her.

"Now, imagine Sarah's surprise when WIA notified her that they have found a match on the maternal side," Benjo said as he fixed his eyes on Monica Cole. All he could see was the top of her head. "Also, imagine her surprise to find that the woman in question was not only a local, but someone relatively well-known, Monica Cole."

Morgan, the attorney, looked like he had just walked into a surprise party. "Now, hold on just a minute," he said.

"Sarah was stunned by this," Benjo continued without pause. "She wanted to be sure about it before she approached anyone. How could she do that without approaching the woman in question and telling her the test results? Well, Sarah was pretty smart, so she figured out a way. She came to your church, attended a service, and waited until you were out in the lobby speaking with the folks who were leaving. She approached from the side and plucked one of your hairs. That moment was caught on camera. You claimed it was an assault in order to bolster your self-defense claim. Sarah took that hair home, ordered another kit from WIA, and when it came, she submiited one of her hairs and your hair for testing. It was a match and confirmed that you, Monica Cole, were Sarah's biological mother."

Monica's head began to move slightly and her hands came up to her face. A muffled sob emerged. "We're taking a break," Morgan said softly.

"No, we're not," Deke answered firmly. "Proceed, Benjo."

"Sarah reached out to you, Monica," Benjo said. "I was puzzled at first as to why Sarah, an alleged crazed stalker, reached out to you. August is the leading man and you're the backup. It seems like she would have been more likely to be fixated on him than you. In reality, she called to tell you the whole story. The first call was about five minutes. She broke the news. I imagine you hung up on her. A few days later, she called back but you hung up on her in just a few seconds. Your mind was still reeling and you were trying to process how the daughter you thought you had gotten rid of had reappeared. I assume you spoke to your husband and broke the news to him. Sarah's third call was about twenty minutes long. You were asking her questions and feeling her out about how she was going to handle the revelation. From that point on, you started using a burner cell phone to call her in order to avoid leaving a trail. I think you started doing that because you were already trying to figure out how to fix this situation. You knew what her appearance in your life might mean for you, your church, and more importantly, for the money-laundering operation you two and Paul Tucker were running out of the church."

Morgan bolted to his feet. "This meeting is over," he said angrily. "My clients and I are not going to sit here and listen to these insane allegations. Giving up her child? Money-laundering for a drug cartel? Enough is enough!"

"You talked Sarah Fleming into coming to your office," Benjo said calmly as he stared directly at August. "She brought the DNA test results with her. Those were the papers in her hand, the ones that vanished because you got rid of them. The three of you had planned to get rid of Sarah. You couldn't take a chance on her blackmailing you or letting the word get out. The plan was to kidnap her, take her somewhere, kill her, and dispose of the body. That's why you had her come in through the door she did; there was less chance of someone seeing her arrive on that side of the building. Unfortunately, your secretary, Marsha West, came back way too early, so you adjusted the plan on the fly. It became Sarah was a crazed stalker and Monica shot her in self-defense. It had to be Monica because August and Tucker were convicted felons and couldn't legally have a gun. Tucker is actually the one who shot Sarah. Well, actually, he shot her once. They made you, Monica, fire one shot as well in case the police did a gunshot residue test on your hands. Luckily, they did not. I know that's how it went because Tucker told me that as he was dying."

"Mr and Mrs Cole, we're leaving," Morgan said. He glared at Benio and Deke. "We're leaving. Everything this man has said is rumor and hearsay. Since he killed Mr. Tucker, he cannot refute his allegations, and therefore they are useless in court. Stay away from my clients until you have enough to arrest them on these insane allegations."

Benjo tapped the folder he'd laid on the table. "I already have enough evidence," Benjo said. "Once I learned about Sarah's mysterious birth, I started wondering if August might be Sarah's biological father. He was in the area at the time she could have been concieved. At first, I thought Reena and August here might have hooked up. August, you were young, wild, and living in the area on the Pearson farm at the time. That theory got blown to bits when I discovered that Reena had never given birth. That made me think that maybe Monica had ended up pregnant with August's baby. You both were around seventeen or eighteen, a couple, and, by your own admission, running around doing crazy stuff. That theory was much more plausible than August and Reena. Needless to say, I was very happy when I was able to confirm that was indeed the case." He looked directly at August. "Sarah Fleming was your daughter, August." He then glanced at Monica. "You, Monica, were her mother. You two are the confirmed biological parents of Sarah Fleming."

At that moment, Monica began to sob loudly. The attorney, Morgan, suddenly lost all of his bluster. He blinked a couple of times and then slowly sank back down into his chair. "You're lying," he said. "How could you confirm that withour DNA from my clients?"

"I got DNA from your clients," Benjo answered simply. "The company Sarah used, Who I Am, specializes in cutting edge technology that harvests DNA from human hair. That's why Sarah approached Monica in the church and plucked a hair from her head several days before she first made contact with Monica. Sarah had submitted hair for analysis. WIA harvested a DNA sample and ran it through their database. At some point, Monica has sent in a DNA sample before. They kicked back a match. Sarah couldn't believe it, so she got a hair from Monica the only way she could think of."

"It was a church thing," Monica said, her voice barely above a whisper and choked with tears. "Some of the women in our adult senior fellowship group had done it and were talking about the things they'd discovered. I got curious."

"Mrs. Cole, do not say another word," Morgan said. He glared at Benjo. "Tell me, Mr. Lane, how did you get my clients' DNA? No one here has been served with a search warrant regarding such a thing."

Benjo looked at the attorney like he was an idiot. "Sir, I am a private detective," he said. "I have no way of getting search warrants. Only the police can do that. I got their DNA by getting my hands on some of their hair. I submitted it, along with some hair from Sarah's hairbrush she'd left in her apartment, and sent them in to Who I Am. I received a submission kit the day Paul Tucker tried to murder me at my home."

"How did you get samples of their hair?" Morgan demanded.

Benjo remembered his promise to keep Dakota Taylor's name a secret. Dakota was the Coles' personal stylist who worked for them part-time as part of their backstage staff. He'd paid for a hairbrush from each of the Coles. The hair he'd harvested from each used hairbrush was the samples he'd sent to Who I Am. "I refuse to name my source at this time," he said. "I will give the name to law enforcement if compelled to as a part of an official investigation."

"This could all be fake," Morgan said triumphantly. "You're bluffing!"

Benjo slid the folder across the table. "Here's the reports, freshly e-mailed from Who I Am's lab yesterday afternoon, for your reading pleasure," he said. "Have at it."

Morgan ignored the folder. "I want this man arrested for violating my clients' privacy," he said to Deke Jeter. "If he had a sample of their hair for these so-called tests, then he stole it."

"Actually, I didn't," Benjo said. "Mr. Morgan, I think you have bigger fish to fry than badgering the police to arrest me. I haven't even told the best part, the part about how young Reena McAllister ended up with August and Monica Cole's newborn daughter. It's also the motive as to why they killed Sarah and claimed it was self-defense."

"Enough of this!" Morgan exclaimed dramatically. "Let's go," he said as he tapped August on the shoulder. "Mrs. Cole, you too."

"No!" Monica shrieked so loudly that the attorney and her husband literally jumped. "We deserve this! I knew this was coming!" She pointed at Benjo. "The truth comes out. God is not mocked. Say what you have to say!"

Benjo looked at Monica. "You and August were running around, using drugs and committing crimes," he said softly. "You ended up pregnant. You had the baby, but neither of you wanted her. You had no idea of what to do with her, so you did the unthinkable. You threw your child away. From his work there on the Pearson's Dairy Farm, August knew a patch of woods close by where there was no chance the baby would be found. You took your newborn baby there to those woods and you left her there for God knows what to happen. You didn't care, you just wanted to be rid of her."

"He made me get rid of her!" Monica screamed as she turned to glare at August. Her eyes were mad with anger and pain. "I had her in the back seat of the car we had at the time. I wanted to keep her, but he refused. He told me if I couldn't do it, he would. I wrapped her in a towel and we put her in the woods there. We drove off and left her to die!"

August reached out and tried to grab his wife. "Monica, shut up!" he said loudly. "She's on powerful medication for mental health issues. She has no idea what she's saying right now."

"Young Reena McAllister found the baby a few hours after you dumped her in the woods," Benjo said. "How that came about, I can only speculate. Reena had a car at the time that would overheat. She frequently had to pull over to let the engine cool off or risk blowing the motor. Maybe she pulled over in that particular spot and heard the child crying. She once joked with Patricia that a dog had dragged Sarah up. People have a tendency to hide hard truths in jokes or offhand comments. It's a psychological thing to make such things more palatable. It's possible that as Reena was driving home, she came upon a stray dog dragging a wrapped bundle out into the road. That wrapped bundle turned out to be a human baby. Regardless, Reena found the baby."

"There's no way you can prove that did or didn't happen," Morgan said lamely. The lawyer looked like he'd been kicked in the groin repeatedly.

"I found a printed map in Sarah's apartment with that plot of woods on Highway Ten a couple of miles from where Reena was living at the time circled," Benjo said. "I would wager that Reena told Sarah that's where she found her that day. It makes sense."

"This interview is officially over," Morgan said firmly. "This whole meeting has been nothing but a chance for this man to spin his wild theories. Mrs. Cole is obviously not well mentally and emotionally. Anything she has said in here is just her medication talking. Detective Jeter, if you are going to charge my clients with anything, do so now. If not, we're leaving."

"But, if you leave, you're going to miss the motive part," Benjo said. "The Coles are using their church to launder money for a drug cartel. Sarah shows up. What would happen to a church if the head pastors were revealed to have tried to murder their own newborn baby? I don't care how charismatic or good-looking you are, pretty much all of the people who come to your church and watch you on television would never do it again. You would be finished, not to mention the possible criminal charges if Sarah went to the police. Even scarier is what the cartel would do since you ruined their money-laundering operation. In your mind, it was you or Sarah and Sarah lost."

Monica opened her mouth to say something, but August literally put his hand over her mouth. "No, Monica, let's go!" he said forcefully. He pulled Monica to her feet by the shoulder. Morgan ran to open the door.

"I have one last thing to say," Benjo said. "I found out all of this without any of the resources an average law enforcement agency has. No access to judges who can sign search warrants, no computer systems connected to law enforcement databases, just my little old self. Can you even begin to imagine what Detective Jeter here is going to find once he starts looking?"

"And I will," Deke said instantly. "Mr. Morgan, I am putting you on notice that the investigation into the shooting of Sarah Fleming will be reopened, given recent developments. I'll be in touch."

Morgan hastily guided his two clients out into the hallway. "I will fight this tooth and nail with every resource at my disposal," he said firmly. He turned and followed the Coles away down the hall.

Deke stood up and walked over to close the door. "Well, that was…different," he said.

"Considering she just admitted it," Benjo said. "I take it this was all recorded?"

Deke nodded. "I need to go talk to Captain Mason and the sheriff," he said. "The next few days are going to be bad ones for the Coles. I promise you that, my friend."

Benjo smiled. "It's already a bad day for them," he said. "I called Kathy Miller from Channel Seven before I drove over here this morning. She's waiting in the parking lot with a camera crew. I suspect they will be tonight's big story.

Deke shook his head in admiration. "You're an evil genius, Benjo Lane," he said.

"Thank you," Benjo replied. "Do you want me to send you my report?"

"Please," Deke said. "Sheriff Crowe is going to lose his freaking mind over this one."

"Good luck," Benjo said. "I've got to go see David Whiteside and Chase Fleming and explain all of this to them. Chase is about to learn that a sizable chunk of everything he thought he knew about the people he loves was a lie. I'd rather tangle with the sheriff all day long than go tell the kid that."

"I don't envy you," Deke said sympathetically. "I do have to give you credit, though. You're a damned genius for figuring this out. You seem to have knack for this stuff. You ought to make it a career."

"I've thought about it," Benjo said. "It feels good to be back in the saddle, so to speak. It took my mind off Presley and what happened for a little while."

Deke clasped his friend's shoulder. "Dude, maybe it's time to come out of the shadows and start living again. Presley would want that."

Benjo nodded. "I suspect she would."

23

Later in the evening that day, Benjo was in his garage loading his truck with camping gear when he heard someone coming down his driveway. He retrieved his pistol from the workbench and walked outside to see who it was. His previous encounter with Paul Tucker had made him a little edgier than usual. He wasn't expecting any more trouble, but he wasn't going to let his guard down anytime soon. The Southern Devils Motorcycle Club might be willing to let bygones be bygones or they might not at this early stage. He'd found it better to be prepared for the worst and to hope for the best than vice versa.

He stood concealed behind the edge of the garage door opening and waited as the vehicle in his driveway came into view. It was a blue unmarked Chevrolet Tahoe police vehicle. He recognized it immediately as the one Deke Jeter drove. Once it got closer, he could see Deke behind the wheel. He laid the pistol back on the workbench and walked outside as Deke pulled to a stop. Deke stayed in the Tahoe and rolled down the window when he saw Benjo emerge from the garage. "Evening," Deke said amicably as Benjo strolled over to the Tahoe's driver's side door to talk.

"Deke," Benjo said with a nod. "What brings you all the way out here this late in the evening?"

"I just wanted to see how the rest of your day went," Deke said. "I know you were going to meet with David Whiteside and Sarah's brother after you left our office. How'd that go?"

Benjo grimaced. "Chase took it pretty hard," he said. "I can't say I blame him at all, really. He found out that his beloved sister was actually not related to him at all and that their mother and father had lied to both of them for all of those years. His whole world got rattled. Finding out that the investigation into Sarah's death was being reopened thanks to what I'd found helped ease the pain a little."

Deke rested his arm on the edge of the door and stroked his chin. "There was something I wanted to ask you about Reena. Why do you think she didn't call the police when she found the baby under whatever circumstances she found it?" he asked. "It seems like it would have been a lot easier for her to just call the police. Social Services could have taken the child and found her a home. Outside of maybe testifying about how she found the kid if the police found the real parents, she would have been done. No stress of raising a kid, no tricks to get a birth certificate, and no lying."

"I've pondered that one myself," Benjo said. "Reena was raised in foster care from the age of about seven until she aged out of the system. I know that she was probably abused physically at a few foster care facilities and possibly sexually abused as well. I honestly think she couldn't bear the thought of putting another human being into the system that had been so hard on her. I think she was a good person who wanted to spare a child from that, even if it meant being a single mom and living a lie for twenty-five plus years."

Deke was quiet for a few moments. "That makes sense, I guess," he finally said. "There's another reason I drove all the way out here to saber-toothed tiger country." He stuck his head out and looked around. "Where's that monster?"

"That monster saved my life," Benjo said. "If Harley hadn't shown up when she did, I would be dead and Tucker and the Coles would still be laundering money and gloating about how they got away with murder."

"I saw Tucker's autopsy report," Deke said. "I saw the injuries inflicted by that cat. That's why I'm keeping my black ass in this vehicle."

Benjo rolled his eyes. "She's very protective of the human that puts food in her bowl twice a day, you drama queen," he said. "You know that wee kitten loves you to death."

"Yes, I know that," Deke said. "However, now she's had human flesh. She might be like big cats in the wild who learn to love the taste. I could be her next victim."

"Wussy," Benjo said succinctly.

"There's one other reason I'm here. I've got a couple of pieces of news I felt like I should deliver in person," Deke said, suddenly serious. "One piece is definite good news for you. The other could go either way, depending on how you see it."

"Start with the potential bad news first," Benjo said.

"About an hour ago, we got a call to Hope Springs Church," Deke said. "One of the janitors went in to August Cole's office to clean up after business hours." He looked at his watch. "This was about ninety minutes ago. He thought everyone else was gone for the day. He was surprised to find August Cole lying in the floor behind his desk. He'd been shot three times, two in the chest and once in the face. The janitor ran out and called nine one one. The first-arriving officers searched the building. They found Monica back in the studio part of the church. She had hung herself there. She left a note. She killed August and then herself. She blamed him for what happened with Sarah all the way back to when they dumped her in the woods as a newborn. She said she couldn't go on."

The news shocked Benjo so bad that he actually rocked back on his feet like he'd been punched. "Wow," he said.

"The note admitted the whole money-laundering thing as well," Deke continued. "According to her note, there's allegedly two million dollars of the cartel's cash stashed at a horse farm they just bought in the mountains. The department is busy getting a search warrant as we speak."

"Why aren't you out there?" Benjo asked.

"The sheriff said I was involved in the Fleming homicide case and he didn't want the two to overlap," Deke said. "I understand that, I guess. Bixley and Davenport are leads on it."

"They're good guys," Benjo said. "I'm sure you will end up working with them to tie everything together and close both cases."

"I can tell you who's not involved," Deke said. "That's the good news. Detective Marsh is suspended indefinitely, pending an internal affairs review of his work in the Fleming case. Kathy Miller's investigation forced the sheriff to do the right thing. The sheriff has to go before County Council next Tuesday night to explain himself. I suspect it's not going to be pretty. After Kathy's report on the local news, County Council was swamped with angry calls."

"Finally," Benjo said.

"I suspect Sheriff Crowe's political dreams are over," Deke said. "People have long memories around here."

"He made his choices," Benjo said.

"I figured you would want to know the latest," Deke said. He looked past Benjo into the open garage door. "What are you doing to your truck?"

"I'm loading it with my camping gear," Benjo replied. "I'm thinking about taking a long road trip. I plan to end up in South Dakota. I need to scatter Presley's ashes in the Black Hills. It's time, I think."

"I think you're ready. It's time to stop being a recluse and to start doing what you're great at again," Deke said. "What about Harley?"

"She's going with me," Benjo said. "She likes road trips, plus she keeps me out of trouble."

"You and that monster-sized cat on the road in your truck," Deke said with a shake of his head. "I think I'll end up seeing you two on the national news before it's over with." He smiled. "You've got my number if you need me. Good luck, my friend."

"I appreciate everything you did, Deke," Benjo said sincerely. Deke simply nodded, started the SUV, turned it around, and left. Benjo watched as Deke drove away down his driveway. He watched until his friend was out of sight, then walked back into his garage to finish packing.